*PRAISE FOR*

# UNPAVED

"Anthony Horton paints the 'extraordinary seasons' of family through unexpected milestones with magical words, painting his canvas with nature's affirming light. Horton frames memory in Pat Conroyesque prose, along with a page-turning corporate plot."

—Tim Conroy, Author of *Theologies of Terrain* and *No True Route*

"A compelling story told in a way that holds the reader's interest. The many twists and turns in this saga beckon one to not stop but to continue reading to learn what will happen next. Anthony Horton's work deserves to be made into a movie."

—Charles E. Watson, Author of *Frontline Management Excellence*

"*Unpaved* is a compelling emotional interplay between the heartbreak of loss and the mind-bending tumult of corporate life, set against the soothing balm of nature. From the opening chapter, Horton engages readers through his use of vivid characterization and setting, ultimately carrying them full circle, where they are left to consider the jarring necessity of change in propelling one's life forward. *Unpaved* is an intriguing story that leaves readers longing for the serenity of the north woods."

—Brenda K. Massman, Author of *Yet, Here We Are*

"This highly charged, emotional story takes you to some of the world's largest cities, including New York, Boston, London, Mumbai, and more. But it finds it beginnings during a young boy's brief stay in the Canadian wilderness. The author takes you from there to the high-stakes corporate governance and politics of a large technology company. The surprising twists, tragedies, and betrayals will shock you to the core and leave you wanting more."

—Michael A. Sisti, Author, 2023 Firebird Book Award Winner for *On the Brink*

"There is so much of real human life in this rich, complex story. It explores life's exhilarations as well as its brutal tragedies; life rearranges reality, and individuals rearrange their lives. Mr. Horton's sophisticated and intriguing writing style interweaves poetry and prose into an elegant, beautiful tapestry of words and images. He uses the complete writer's palette of artistically arranged word-images, which draw you in like a magnet and transport you to landscapes you never could have imagined."

—Joseph Seechack, Author of *A Love to Die For*

"*Unpaved* is the kind of book that gets you reflecting. It's deep, thoughtfully written, and engaging. Anthony Horton artfully transports you through Russell's harrowing journey."

—James "The Iron Cowboy" Lawrence, Author, Guiness World Record Breaker, and Family Man

"When I read Anthony Horton's novel *Unpaved,* I was floored by the author's ability to evoke such depth of relationships and landscapes. Gorgeous detail, compelling characters, and a juicy look-see into the world of tech."

—Kimberly Kafka, Author of *True North* and *Miranda's Vines*

*Unpaved*
by Anthony Horton

© Copyright 2024 Anthony Horton

ISBN 979-8-88824-304-6

All rights reserved. No part of this publication may be reproduced, stored in a retrieval system, or transmitted in any form or by any means—electronic, mechanical, photocopy, recording, or any other—except for brief quotations in printed reviews, without the prior written permission of the author.

This is a work of fiction. All the characters in this book are fictitious, and any resemblance to actual persons, living or dead, is purely coincidental. The names, incidents, dialogue, and opinions expressed are products of the author's imagination and are not to be construed as real.

Published by

**köehlerbooks™**

3705 Shore Drive
Virginia Beach, VA 23455
800-435-4811
www.koehlerbooks.com

# UNPAVED

ANTHONY HORTON

VIRGINIA BEACH
CAPE CHARLES

Dedicated to the strong, exceptional women in my life.
The Future is Female!

# 1

Memory is often an uninvited guest. It spends its time spinning the fine silk of recollection in the anterooms and cellars of the mind. Bleak or painful memories remain there in waiting, biding their time until they scratch and claw and plead to be let out. When they arrive, we find ourselves wishing instead that they would remain buried or slip hastily through the fingers of the here and now.

Memories flow through Russell Nowak-McCreary as he rides clouds high above the earth, heading north to Canada for the first time in years. And the same spill of memories stops only when the plane encounters turbulence. Then his thoughts are jarred into more immediate considerations.

The woman seated next to him, a middle-aged corporate type and ostensibly a seasoned air traveler, glances over at him. "Are you doing, okay?"

It's unclear if she is being patronizing or demonstrating genuine concern. He is a nervous flyer. During a lifetime, we all gather our own assortment of unconquerable fears. Russell's discomfort with flying tops the list as the one he knows he will never overcome. His trepidation, a fount of disconnectedness, is stranded in limbo as he glides the slipstreams between heaven and earth.

Still, it's been impossible for him to avoid commercial air travel, given the trans-Atlantic reality of his life and the frequency with which his career demands it.

"Just the turbulence," he responds. "When it's this rough, it always makes me jump a bit. Believe it or not, I fly quite often."

"It always works to remind myself that these things practically fly themselves these days," she says. "Technology has made flying the safest form of transportation."

Russell ascertains that she is being neither patronizing nor particularly concerned. She's simply looking for conversation.

"When I think about the number of cheap electronics I've purchased over the years, only to have them malfunction within months, I have to say my confidence in machines is guarded at best," he says, imagining a minuscule circuit deep in the entangled viscera of the jet shorting and sending the entire contraption into a death spiral. "Especially up here where we are tickling the bottom of the ozone layer."

Russell thinks technology is second only to Mother Nature in its proprietorship over disaster.

Russell turns his head slightly toward the woman. "To tell you the truth, I thought I had perfected the art of hiding my little tense-ups when a bad patch of air pressure hits."

"I'm a clinical psychologist," she blurts. "I like to think of my observational skills as first-class. They should be. I've been practicing for two decades."

"Maybe I can still fool the non-psychologists into believing I'm a confident passenger, then."

She trains her eyes to the armrest between them and shoots him an insightful smile. "It was your knuckles that gave it away."

He is squeezing the armrest.

"Ha, well that is pretty obvious I guess, isn't it?" He returns the smile.

This seems to satisfy her need for discourse. She faces the entertainment monitor on the seat back in front of her and digs in her laptop bag for a set of earphones.

Were she to ask his destination or reasons for subjecting himself to this self-imposed torture, Russell would probably respond with a casual "just a quick visit with friends." He's not generally one for superfluous conversation. Someone once suggested to him that his reticent nature grew from having been an only child. He smiles quietly to himself at the thought while enduring another bump of the aircraft and thinks that maybe it would be more fitting to classify himself as an orphan if the term could be applied to someone in their forties.

Russell's mother, the only parent he had ever known, passed away almost four years ago, and after many months of procrastination, he is traveling to Toronto to finalize her will and put her so-called *affairs* in order. The consistent urging of her estate lawyers and his career turning into complete chaos over the past year made it seem suddenly worth it. It is the only reason he has strapped himself into the window seat of this Airbus 333, fingers drumming on the empty plastic meal tray as the turbulence endures.

He checks the time on his iPhone, as he habitually does every couple of minutes. According to his calculations, the plane should land in Toronto in about an hour. After a delay at Logan, he's now eager to be reunited with the dependable ground and visit the city of Toronto for the first time in years. By the time he reaches his downtown hotel, his nerves will have settled enough to allow for a decent sleep before meeting with his mother's attorney in the morning.

"I'll never become a full-fledged Brit," his mother would often proclaim. "I must hold on to my Canadian roots."

He would usually appease her with, "Completely understandable, Mom."

She had been lured to London by the prestige and financial benefits available to her early in her career before she became one of the world's leading cardiac surgeons. Although London eventually became her much beloved home, she insisted on maintaining her Canadian citizenship, resolutely refusing to apply for anything more than permanent residence in the UK. Of course, his mother, Dr. Judith M. Nowak-McCreary, was strong-willed and steadfast about anything that caused her emotions to surface, which they rarely did.

Were it not for his mother's inimitable qualities, it is highly improbable that he would be on this plane, piercing the clouds somewhere over upstate New York. The same Toronto law firm, Haplich, Hauz, and Zubnig, still handled all her Canadian legal concerns.

Dr. Judith had once revealed her logic. "The original partners of that law firm are now probably resting in some quiet cemetery or sinking an endless stream of double-bogies in Arizona retirement villages. But their institution has earned my trust, and that's worth my enduring loyalty."

This was just one of the many personal edicts by which she had managed to simplify her complex existence. In the end, Russell had to admit that he was glad that she was so dependable in her resolve. On many occasions, he has thought about making this journey north to Canada. Now, with his mother's Canadian will sitting in a file fifty-four floors above the pavement of Toronto's Bay Street, he has a compelling reason to take it.

He hasn't been back to Canada for almost two decades. The last visit occurred under the auspices of another melancholy event, when his resilient grandmother, his mother's mother, died of heart failure at the incredible age of ninety-four. Russell was in his mid-twenties when it happened. He recalls skipping a week of university classes to accompany his bereaved mother on the unfortunate trip back "home," as she was fond of calling her country of origin.

That trip holds some pleasant memories for him; flying over the cold north Atlantic from Heathrow to Montreal and then, taking the VIA train across a snow-whitened world to Toronto, followed by another train ride north to the tiny town of Collingwood. It was one of the rare instances in his adult life when a feeling of implicit, unspoken intimacy existed between himself and his mother.

"I miss the winters sometimes, don't you?" she had asked him during that train ride. "Out here in the countryside, the snow is so pristine."

"I wouldn't say I've missed the cold too much," Russell avowed.

"It gets cold enough in London at times."

"Yeah, but not for five straight months. Maybe neither are ideal options," he had suggested in response. "Give up warmth or give up sunlight for almost half the year."

"You're being dramatic, Russell."

And, with that, the discussion concluded. He knew her conversational patterns intimately and when an exchange of information or ideas was over for Dr. Judith, it came with unspoken yet very perceptible clarity.

This is not to suggest that she was cold or indifferent. Her career and how she treated all aspects of her life with unwavering pragmatism kept her sometimes expressively remote. Her affections manifested to him more through respect and obvious devotion than outward sentiment.

Her life had not been an easy one.

His mother had raised him single-handedly while putting herself through medical school and excelling at her demanding career. A survivor like his mother does not achieve that character by being soft and malleable, but rather through sheer toughness and unyielding tenacity.

On that memorable journey back to the place of her upbringing, to nurse her own mother in her final days, her aloof exterior had peeled away and revealed layers of tenderness that Russell had not often experienced before.

In fact, when they arrived at the hospital, she had taken his hand as they walked from the snow-covered parking lot into the building. They walked down the corridors of the Sunny View Home and Hospice hand-in-hand, like young friends who gain some form of needed reassurance by displaying their unity to anyone who happens to notice.

"This is not going to be easy," she had stated as they navigated the hallways of Sunny View. "I've sort of put off facing this day, even though it was always there, floating right in front of me in some imminent state."

"I know, Mom." Russell had stated, at first taken aback by the introspective and candid admission. "It's been a long time you've been watching over her. I know how sad and challenging it has been for you."

"Not as hard as it is going to be. I honestly believe that." His mother continued. "I've known ever since she came to Sunny View that it was her final home, that she would ultimately die here. I just pushed it out of mind but probably would have been less of a blow if I had admitted it more directly and *pre-bereaved* a little in preparation."

"It's definitely not sudden, but that doesn't mean the grief is any less," he offered.

"We all find ways to construct these mental barricades when it comes to our most unpleasant worries," she replied. "I've done it with your grandmother. I'm a physician but I am also a daughter whose maintained a self-erected obstacle of denial."

He remembers the distinct contrast between Sunny View and the familiar, weathered interior of St. Bartholomew's Hospital, not far from the Thames and St. Paul's Underground station where, as a child, he had wandered the hallways unnoticed on countless afterschool incursions while waiting for his mother to finish her shift. While St. Bart's was an ancient, perpetually frantic, and hurried place by nature, Sunny View was modern, placid, and composed. Nurses did not race down decades-old hallways; patients could not be heard bellowing from their rooms, and no intercom system buzzed every thirty seconds to summon doctors by codes in a lexicon that only they could comprehend.

Sunny View was a sterile, private hospital, a place where wealthy patients in their fragile years came to quietly accept that their money would ultimately fail to save them from their own mortality. The antiseptic, polished decor was not enough to eradicate or even camouflage the many ghosts that drifted down those disinfected hallways. Underneath the soft waves of soulless shopping mall music, you could almost hear the hollow voices of many lives' energies gathering in one consolidated final gasp. The attempt to disguise this as anything other than a place of finality seemed useless.

"Will there be any relief in her passing?" he had asked his mother. "She's been nearly comatose for the past several months from what you've told me."

"There is some relief. Yes. Absolutely. Lamentable relief is what I would call it," Dr. Judith admitted. "Before the coma, she was in the last stages of dementia, which was terrible to witness."

"I'm glad you had a chance to visit her often just before she was too incoherent and stopped recognizing you," Russell had offered, hoping to reassure her. "You made all the trips over to help her get settled here and take care of her."

"Thank you for that, Russell. Over the years our relationship would sometimes be close and sometimes more distant. But the realization of her proximity to death served as a catalyst in cultivating a deeper fondness between us."

When they stepped into Ella Nowak's warm hospital room, his mother had exhibited the assured countenance of a seasoned physician while Russell entered more tentatively. This was the first time he had been acquainted with death at its most profound level; his father died in a car accident before his mother had even detected her pregnancy, and his long-deceased grandfather, who unknowingly became one of the central archetypes of the man he has become, was buried in his absence after a sudden stroke ended his life.

He did not have the opportunity to attend his grandfather's funeral, even though he had played a brief yet unequivocal role in Russell's development. After he passed away, Russell's mother insisted on his absence. She had encouraged him to center his reflections away from the end of his life, saying, "Instead, I think it would be better for you to concentrate on all the memories you have of him during the amazing summer you shared."

With the phenomenon of human departure so common in her professional life, she felt the need to shield her only child from life's most sorrowful virtue with which she was so familiar. Having since experienced losses that caused fault lines in the deepest layers of his soul, Russell now believes that her need to protect him from tragedy probably left him somewhat unprepared. He doesn't blame her for this though; his mother parented out of pure love for him and her unique outlooks on life.

At first, in that hospital room at Sunny View, he had been shocked at the pathetic sight of his grandmother's emaciated body in a fetal curl on the bed, a thick plastic hose protruding crudely from a slit in the front of her gown.

"It's a feeding tube," his mother had explained upon witnessing his reaction. He could see that there was no spirit housed in her dormant body any longer and, to Russell's mind, that tube served as an insult to the life that had once resided there. His grandmother had long since abandoned her sickly body whose persistent heart was now beating by the mere force of inertia, like the engine of a car sputtering long after the driver had left.

He finds it difficult to stifle a smile whenever he recalls how his mother, forever the physician, had immediately assumed control, as though her afflicted parent were simply another one of her patients, checking her pulse, rolling her on her side, and propping up the pillows behind her, monitoring the IV drip, and dabbing a tissue to dry the beads of perspiration on her wrinkled brow.

Then, Dr. Judith had solemnly conferred with the demure physician who was assigned to care for her ailing mother, receiving silent nods of approval. Soon afterward, a nurse unobtrusively removed the feeding tube from under the gown as Russell and his mother sat on cushioned, polypropylene chairs at the bedside.

It took only one day for his grandmother's ancient body to come to a standstill. Ella Nowak was buried within two days, and in another two, Russell and his mother were back on the train to Montreal for their flight back to London, still enjoying the same obscure yet mutually acknowledged sense of closeness that had remained with them throughout the trip.

When it came to her own death, Judith's final hours were quite different. On a bed much like the ones in the hospital where she'd spent most of her life treating others, she sat pin-straight and alert. Although the essence of life had left his grandmother long before her final moment, it remained fully intact within his mother's cancer-ridden frame. At sixty-three, the desire to continue living needed no prompting, but the sickness that feasted on her would not permit it.

She first told him about the metastasizing disease deep within her organs, in a typical matter of fact fashion. Russell had handled it with confusion and disbelief. For some reason, the idea of a doctor getting cancer seemed inexplicably illogical to him.

"I have some disturbing news to give you," was how she had begun the conversation over the phone. It was a Saturday morning. "I've been having some difficulty digesting. I asked Dr. Dhillon to run some tests. I'm in worse shape than I had hoped, I'm afraid."

"Oh, God," he said and immediately asked, "what's wrong?"

"I have pancreatic cancer. It's a very difficult one to detect and can often be at an advanced stage before you even know it."

Russell was silent as the surreal slap of shock hit him.

She added, "It's stage three, which means it's already spread."

"So, what can we do? What's the treatment plan?" he asked, still not fully absorbing the news. "I mean, you know the best doctors in every field, there must be medicine, surgeries . . . something!"

"The prognosis isn't good," she said. "I'll do chemo and there are some drugs that will help slow it down temporarily. I know the markers and progression though. As I said, the prognosis isn't good."

The full weight of her words had swirled and then settled in his mind. He had a difficult time breaking free from the suspended state of disbelief. Eventually, after twenty minutes of asking more questions, there was nothing left to say.

His mother had delivered the news with little emotion, giving him all the information as well as her calculated analysis. Where she seemed calm and clinical, Russell's chest cavity was left shaking.

Judith Nowak-McCreary had manufactured her strength of character from her father, a man of extraordinary fortitude, and she clung to this, her most laudable trait, until the very closure of her being. Russell remained at her bedside, and she had befittingly assumed this same demeanor that had enabled her to approach life's ups and downs without fear.

On the final morning, after sleeping on a cot brought to him by a sympathetic nurse, his dry distended eyes met hers, dark and sunken with fatigue, a moment of unblemished understanding passed between them. They bridged the impalpable distance between one who is destined to continue living and another facing her own impending end.

Only then had he recognized a certain quality of defeat in her eyes. The sea wall of strength she had erected over a lifetime crumbled as disease consumed her. At her request, when her lungs failed her for the last time, the medical staff did not employ the respirator waiting in the corner of the room, and instead allowed her to depart from the world as Russell sobbed at her side.

The pilot has just announced their descent to Pearson International Airport in Toronto. Outside Russell's window, the sun has set. It is the exact moment of twilight when an undefined gray foretells the onset of the evening's shadows, holding them back for a final moment as an immaculate silver beam shimmers through the clouds. Far below, the patchwork quilt of countryside farm fields gives way to the jigsaw grids of metropolitan lines. Russell squirms in his seat, which elicits a deep sigh from his icy neighbor.

"You know, most air disasters occur during either takeoff or landing," he wants to tell the woman next to him. Instead, he turns to her and remarks, "Finally. I am not sure my knuckles can take many more of these jolts."

She looks again at his hand, still grasping the end of the armrest and smiles. "I think you get a pass on this one. I'll admit, it was a jarring ride overall."

"Tell me about it," he mutters.

"I do this same flight every week, and even I had a few tummy-flips."

"I can't tell you how much better that makes me feel," he exclaims.

Russell turns his attention to the front of the plane, where a woman is making her way down the center aisle with a child in tow. The woman is young, he guesses late twenties, and handsome in a smart tweed jacket with patches on the elbows above a long, dark skirt, her hair pulled into a loose ponytail. The child, a girl of no more than four or five, has a million freckles and short red hair and, by the devilish expression on her wide-eyed face, is taking delight in the realization that her restroom excursion has grabbed the passengers' collective attention.

"Isn't she adorable?" his neighbor poses.

"Hmmm," Russell nods in agreement.

For a moment, he allows himself to be reminded of Anna, who became so detached in the last months of their marriage that she was no more familiar to Russell than this woman on the plane. He studies the duo until he is once again acutely aware of Anna's distance, physically hundreds of miles away, light-years in the heart. But he can't gather the necessary nerve to look at the child again. He is still haunted by too many apparitions, too many sorrowful memories resurfacing in a painful crush.

For a fleeting instant, they are Anna and his son Joshua, skipping down the cabin of the plane to greet him, smiling once he is spotted. And then, just as quickly, they are taken from him again and this unknown woman and child are restored to their true selves.

It is moments such as this one that cause him the greatest difficulty, when he comes to the distressing realization that his sadness has no schedule. An intruder arrives when he lacks focus on any single conscious thought, a force deceiving him into thinking that the departed members of his past are waiting around the corner or preparing to walk through a door and back into his world as if they'd never left. He has found himself incapable of conquering the loss or accepting the unacceptable. He has merely done his best to adapt, like an amputee who still manages to walk but needs only to examine his own reflection to become achingly aware that a part of him will always be missing.

It's curious that, at a time when so many men seem resolved to the voluntary deconstruction of their families amid mid-life woes, Russell's was ravaged and left devastated by a force over which he had no control or recourse to plead for clemency.

# 2

"Life is absurd." This was one of Dr. Judith Nowak-McCreary's simple, homespun phrases that seemed always to emerge from an inexhaustible catalog of witticisms she kept ready to deploy.

In recent years, life hadn't seemed absurd. It was relatively ordinary, in fact. After a mostly solitary adolescence, Russell had paved a conventional turnpike into adulthood. After he had completed lower secondary and sixth form in London, he returned to North America to study accounting, lured from England by a scholarship from Boston University and earning a respectable GPA by the end of his first semester.

He had always excelled at number-crunching, having inherited his mother's knack for math and sciences. However, what he possessed in proclivity he sometimes lacked in affinity. Russell had been drawn to a variety of creative pursuits over the course of his life and was certain that his father must have passed to him an artistic or musical aptitude.

The field of accounting did not naturally provide an outlet for this craving. Nonetheless, he kept accounting as his major after toying with a creative writing class as one of his required English electives. He wrote a short story about a troubled kid who finds direction in helping his old neighbor fix a dilapidated '57 Chevy. It was an awkward and predictable first step into the world of prose, but he had been proud of it. The professor gave him only a C-plus.

"*Needs character development. Rambles too much in parts and should be more succinct.*" Somewhat stinging comments, handwritten on the title page.

Considering this a failure, Russell abandoned writing and instead tried to embrace the philistine, objective marking schemes of his accounting instructors. Over the following four years he completed his degree with honors.

In his last year at BU, a friend lured him into the world of computers where he found an application for the creativity snuffed out by his stern English professor. After taking a few off-campus computer science courses, Russell found he had a real knack for software, the rare ability to apply development and program design with a practical business mind.

He created several innovative applications that caught the eyes of his professors. Two months after graduating, with some funding help from one of the faculty, he had developed a program for processing accounting transactions aimed at smaller CPA practices that supported small and medium-sized businesses. After building up a base of just over two thousand clients, through very little marketing and a lot of word-of-mouth referrals, he sold the business to a prominent, public software company called Datatel.

They were, and remain, a *Fortune* 5000 powerhouse in the accounting industry. A team at Datatel had learned about his software through the same professor who had provided Russell's initial seed capital. Datatel had been trying to develop a similar solution for several years but had struggled, their size and bureaucracy inhibiting agile development.

Russell learned of their interest after a call from their head of corporate strategy, Charlotte Nguyen, late one evening when he had been setting the alarm and preparing to leave their office, which housed their nimble team of seventeen employees.

He chuckles at the memory, recalling what now seems like the gargantuan flip phone he had taken that notable call from.

"This is Russell," he announced, fumbling the phone, and trying to key the office alarm code into the eye-level wall console.

"I'm Charlotte, Mr. Nowak-McCreary. I lead the mergers and

acquisitions division for Datatel, among other functions." Still in his late twenties, he found it odd when professional people, especially executives, addressed him by his surname.

"Oh!" Russell had remarked. "Datatel is massive. I'm not sure what I could possibly help you with."

"Quite a bit as it turns out," Charlotte replied. "I'll admit that this approach is a little unorthodox. Usually, we would work with one of our investment banking partners on something like this, but I thought the direct approach made sense in this case."

The light bulb had started to flicker for Russell, the contours of a possible motive for her call taking shape.

"Our research team learned about your company about a month ago and we've been doing some probing into your product portfolio and capabilities. Just data in the public domain, of course."

"Okay."

"We're looking to add a solution set exactly like yours to our platform," she continued. "Our development efforts have been, well, let's just say less than effective in trying to create our own."

"Are you saying Datatel is actually interested in buying my company?"

"That is precisely the reason for my call. We're impressed with the depth of your development team and the impressive client base you've built without a ton of investment. We want to move quickly which, candidly, is why I'm approaching you straight on and circumventing the conventional broker method."

The purchase price was a pittance to Datatel but a fortune to Russell. One and a half million dollars. A figure he could not have fathomed when he first started the business. He felt instantly wealthy.

"I have to admit, I'm a bit stunned. I mean, in a good way, of course. It's just unexpected."

"If you're open to a discussion, we'd like to send you an initial letter of intent and meet to discuss our proposal. We would conduct an expedited due-diligence period of fourteen business days."

Along with the purchase agreement, they offered Russell an executive position as a liaison between their client base of accounting firms. Five weeks later, Russell was a full-time employee, and his start-up firm was quickly subsumed and digested into the belly of Datatel's corporate infrastructure.

It took only five years before Russell was promoted to senior vice president, ultimately rising to the position of chief product officer, where he has a team of more than five hundred employees located in Boston, Dallas, and Mumbai.

In the past year, things have become incredibly complicated at Datatel and for Russell in particular. This trip to Toronto was part necessity and part escape. Datatel's troubled past twelve months have him swimming through the murky waters of pressure and ambiguity.

Russell had recently begun reporting directly to Datatel's CEO Sarah Westroes. For years prior, the chief executive role had been held by a long-time employee Cal Morales, who had progressed from a front-line regional sales representative to lead the corporation. Morales had acted as Russell's de facto mentor over the years and was a big promoter of Russell's career advancement and development. When Morales retired, Westroes was named as his successor. Morales still sat on the company's board of directors but remained only peripherally involved in Datatel's affairs.

Westroes was a highly regarded CEO who had achieved almost celebrity status among the corporate elite over the course of her career. At age forty-four, she could analyze detailed financial data, lead a company culture to perform and had an uncanny, almost prescient ability to foresee macro-economic trends and understand exactly where business opportunity lay.

Westroes had spent the first ten years of her professional life climbing the ranks at no less than three top-tier private equity firms.

Then, in her early thirties, she was tapped to take over cygnall.com, a large digital service provider that had swiftly grown during the dot.com boom but slipped into decline after failing to develop its platform from an archaic email and domain services provider.

In less than four fiscal cycles, Westroes had not only turned around the balance sheet, but she also ultimately rebranded the company as CYG Digital Solutions and built it to become the third largest content services social platform in the US, Canada, and the EU. This earned her enormous recognition, including being named *Fortune's* top CEO for two years running shortly after the 2008 Great Recession, which she had also navigated CYG through without losses to either the firm's employee base or its bottom-line.

"She's going to take us to the stratosphere, I'm sure of it," Cal had said when Russell first queried Morales' point of view on the Westroes announcement.

"What do you know about her leadership style?" he had asked.

"Well. Not surprisingly, I've heard she has a no-BS approach," Cal said. "I've also heard she can be blatantly candid and hard driving."

"I read an *Inc.* article a few months ago that described her as having 'vivid intensity.' It also said she was incredibly smart."

"I've heard that too," Cal responded. "Sarah Westroes definitely has the track record to prove it too."

"I have to confess," Russell said, "it's going to be an adjustment. I mean, I'm so acclimated to how we work together and collaborate. It is strange to think of having to get accustomed to a new boss. I've really enjoyed reporting to you."

"I appreciate that, Russell." Morales stated. "Achievement never comes from complacency. I've gotten too comfortable as CEO and I'm aware enough to know it's time."

"Change is the only constant, right?" Russell replied.

"Damn right. It is going to be good for you too, Russell. You are going to be able to learn from a real dynamo. My intuition is that you are going to complement one another extremely well."

"Here's hoping."

"Who knows, you shadow her for a few years, and you could be next in line for the big chair."

Russell laughed. "An appealing yet daunting thought!"

Privately, Russell had wondered how reporting to a new CEO, and especially a power broker like Sarah Westroes, would compare to his long-term relationship with Cal Morales.

In the initial days after her arrival at Datatel, it had occurred to Russell that he was, admittedly, a little star-struck and intimidated by the corporate icon. His early trepidation proved groundless over the first months of her tenure. They developed a positive flow to their communications and work styles. Westroes clearly appreciated Russell's extensive domain expertise, and Russell respected Westroes' incredible depth as a leader. He felt lucky to strategize, plan and manage with someone who seemed to always be dispensing brilliant insights, whether about the economy, the financial markets, or how to manage Datatel's board and its shareholders.

Then, roughly a year ago, things started going sideways.

*

First, there was activist investor Raymond R. Tisdale, who ran a hedge fund bearing his name. Tisdale took a run at stacking Datatel's board of directors with his appointees. This culminated in a protracted, six-month proxy fight where Westroes eventually won the support of most shareholders and the board, a victory and confirmation of the shareholders' faith in her. But the battle came with some wounds. Tisdale had made his campaign to control Datatel both personal and public. And it was Westroes's integrity that Tisdale had taken a direct shot at. Raymond R. himself appeared on no less than five of the major network business channels as the proxy fight heated up.

"I've met Sarah many times and I've watched her premature ascent to the summit," Tisdale had commented to a host on a popular daily, pre-market opening, business segment on CNBC. "With all due respect, she's way out over her skis running a colossal enterprise like Datatel."

"Strong words and hard-hitting criticism coming from a titan like yourself," the host had declared, her obsequious tone scarcely obscured. "Explain why for the audience. What is it that makes Westroes unqualified?"

"Don't get me wrong, she's bright. Bright and capable."

"So why is she 'over her skis'?" the host asked, fingers making air quote signs to the camera.

"When Sarah was at CYG, she led several mergers and acquisitions where she ignored the advice of her senior team and lawyers in due diligence. She made bad deals in my estimation."

"Tell us more."

Tisdale was experienced with the media and came across as credible and reasonable in all his interviews. Referring to Westroes by her first name was both shrewd and effectual. It portrayed their relationship as congenial and reinforced the impression that he knew her intimately. Once he had established this footing, he would pounce with a deftly delivered reproach. It gave him the appearance of a concerned uncle or father, objectively pointing out the shortcomings of a close relative.

"Some insiders shared with me that she was an intimidator and was obsessed with these acquisitions. The companies CYG took over were little more than her personal trophies, and she has a history of overwhelming anyone who raises an objection or legitimate concern with the deals she led." Tisdale paused, mugging for the camera. "She's got an even bigger war chest now at Datatel. The company is sitting on a ton of cash. With that much dry powder at her disposal, I'm concerned she's going do more ill-advised deals for the sake of her ego and light a match to that powder."

The television segments were followed up with quasi-journalistic articles and a social media campaign to reinforce the image of

Westroes as suffering from tunnel vision, an oversized personality, and a Machiavellian leader. One pundit even went so far as to float the innuendo that if her win-at-all-cost tactics were not about her ego, there must be something surreptitious behind her aggressive methods.

In the end, Westroes ran this gauntlet of public trouncing with her usual aplomb and came out the victor, retaining her position as Datatel's CEO, with only residual disfigurement to her reputation.

A few months after Tisdale conceded defeat and moved on to his next target, Westroes and Datatel were thrust back in the news. A business reporter for CNN had been intrigued by the idea that there was more behind Westroes' conduct than simply being shrewd. Some off-the-record interviews with former Datatel employees fanned flames of suspicion over a recent acquisition.

Before the ill-fated Tisdale battle, Sarah had coordinated the takeover of a mid-sized, start-up firm called Jukes, which had developed an AI software capability that could parse through financial reports and conduct ninety percent of the tasks associated with a corporate audit. Like with most software startups, Jukes hadn't completed full development of its solution. What it had completed was a public relations coup. It resulted in almost every accounting and business consulting influencer ordaining Jukes as the future disrupter to the auditing industry through its ability to deliver near-total automation of manual processes. After its third round of venture capital funding, Jukes had gone public with an IPO that many conservative investors quietly deemed to be premature.

Sarah had resolved to acquire Jukes. She led what some considered to be a hasty and single-minded pursuit of the young company, acquiring Jukes weeks before the turmoil with Tisdale had started.

Russell and his peers were blindsided and astonished when the CNN reporter published a full-length article on its website. The journalist had done his research and come to a pejorative conclusion: Sarah Westroes had used manipulation and intimidation to close acquisition deals not because of a massive ego and drive, but to benefit from a complex insider trading scheme.

The investigative article delved into the finances of Westroes and her husband, Derek Paulson, a retired investment banker in global markets. The article traced a shell company in the Bahamas to another corporate entity registered in Panama, which they established as having belonged to Paulson. The ghost company had recently been transferred to Sarah under a new name. The web of transactions was complicated enough that CNN had to use an infographic to show the web of cross-references. In the end, the article raised suspicion that Sarah's shell company had been, covertly, buying up massive quantities of Jukes stock prior to the acquisition.

Russell recalled a conversation with Westroes the day after the CNN article appeared. She had been uncharacteristically cagey and overtly looking for his support. It left little doubt in Russell's mind that she had at least some sense of culpability.

She barreled into his office unannounced the next morning and held up the article on her iPhone for him to see before sharing her disgust.

"After all the trouble with Tisdale, I don't know how I'm supposed to defend myself against this garbage now," she exclaimed, clearly reeling from the idea of another march through the badlands of negative media scrutiny. "I wouldn't be surprised if Tisdale himself is behind this latest horseshit from CNN."

Russell simply conceded, "Yeah, it's far from an ideal situation."

"Now they're bringing Derek into it and dragging us both through the mud," she added, following a theme she quickly adopted, framing the media as inherently parasitic. "I can't tell if they're inferring that he and I concocted this master plan or if I duped him into transferring his company to me. I'm going to have to come out swinging no matter what. Our lawyers are telling me to stay quiet until we form a defense. Of course, their jobs are to be afraid of their own goddamned shadows. I'm itching to get on a prime-time news program and firebomb these rumors directly."

She leaned against one of the leather office chairs on the other side of his desk and stared incredulously at her iPhone, which was still open to the article.

"What do the public relations consultants want you to do?"

"The same," Westroes said with a weary exhale, "cower in a corner until we figure out some kind of silver-tongued, wishy-washy press statement."

"It might make sense to take a breather before jumping into the media fray."

"Fuck that. I'm not a piñata, and I'm not sitting around waiting for everyone to conclude that I'm some sort of criminal."

"It's a tough call, either way," Russell said. There was no point in offering an alternative perspective and risk pushing her toward a higher tide of belligerence.

Sometimes strengths can simultaneously become a limitation. Russell knew that and had tremendous respect for Westroes's business instincts and impetuous drive. He'd observed it work to her advantage in accomplishing some of the most aggressive targets she set for herself and those around her. At times like this though, that intractable quality could become a hazard.

Russell decided to try and nudge her away from the perilous impulse of hastily taking on the media.

"You may want to consider holding off on any immediate media engagements, at least until you've had a chance to address the whole situation with the board."

"There's an emergency meeting with the board tonight," she said. "They sent me a list of questions they want answered and invited me to consult with my own personal attorney before we gather for the inquisition at seven o'clock sharp."

"I'm sure that isn't going to be pleasant, at all," Russell admitted.

"Yeah. It seems like they want to go deep too," she exclaimed. "They specifically asked about the product development cycles and software glitches that came out of the tech due diligence. They're already asking why we didn't question them more thoroughly."

The reference to *we* stood out immediately to Russell and rooted into his subconscious. *Better jog her memory on that one*, he thought. "I know Farouq had tabled some concerns around it at the time," Russell said.

"Right," she said.

The truth was, she had shut down the discussion about the tech report. The due diligence uncovered that Jukes core product was not as market ready as their leadership had suggested. The most recent development cycle had resulted in several bugs that needed to be resolved before the software could ever be released. When Datatel's Chief Technology Officer Farouq Ahmed suggested they should delay the takeover until he had a chance to analyze the finding more exhaustively, she attacked.

"Do you know how many millions we are spending every day on this process?" she had scolded Farouq in front of the senior leadership team, Russell included, sitting around the main boardroom table. She half stood at the head of table, leaning forward in a dark blue designer pantsuit, blond hair pulled tight and oversized, thin wire glasses slid to the tip of her nose. A portrait of gravitas. "Do you really want to *further evaluate* us into a giant expense crater on this? We're already a week behind schedule. Besides, everyone knows software development isn't perfect. Are you suggesting your team isn't competent enough to jump in and fix these glitches on day one?"

Farouq tried to reply, "We can, but—"

"There's no *but*. Either you can or can't. I happen to have faith in our IT team. If anyone wants to suggest spending more unnecessary dollars in analysis-paralysis land, let me know."

That had effectively closed any further debate on the tech due-diligence report.

While Westroes looked back and forth between Russell and the article on her smartphone with exasperation, Russell had decided it wasn't the time to recount that boardroom dialogue for her.

"Let me know if you need any help with the board inquiries before the meeting tonight," he offered.

"Thanks, Russell. Glad I can count on you right now."

⚜

Exactly a week after the article and eight days after that disquieting conversation in Russell's office, the hammer dropped. Minutes after it hit the newsfeeds, every text message, email, and Microsoft Teams chat at Datatel was on fire with news that the Jukes acquisition had now come under scrutiny at the US Department of Justice, which was investigating Westroes for fraud. The SEC was also launching an investigation, and Westroes was facing a potential criminal indictment. Every media outlet carried the story, some speculating that she had pushed the deal through despite signs that Jukes was overvalued. Others more boldly asserted that through her husband's maze of offshore corporations, she made off with a seven-figure payday by riding Jukes meteoric stock climb once word of the deal was made public.

Despite his approbation, Russell had to admit that the evidence was amassing into an incriminating set of facts. As more background to the initial investigative report started to filter into the news updates, it was clear that the CNN team leading the charge had inside government sources leaking them documents that mapped a complex money trail. Russell winced as he read through the breaking updates, tracing the money movement through Panama and the Bahamas down to the literal dollar.

Russell found himself and his peers living in a maelstrom of distraction. The tension inflated and expanded through the office like an unseeable yet unambiguous smog. Sarah stepped down as Datatel's top executive, most certainly at the insistence of the board. Almost every hour of the executive team's time was taken up managing the fallout of what became known as the *Sarah Situation*. He went from one meeting to another, either working with the public relations team, investor relations, or the legal advisers who were already starting to prepare the key players at Datatel for possible depositions.

In parallel, an internal investigation was launched and run by another outside firm, Fares-Tolmken, to ensure that there was no exposure for the company beyond the actions of Westroes and her husband. The Fares-Tolmken team advised transparency and started prepping them for depositions.

At first, the Fares-Tolmken consultants probed each Datatel employee they interviewed with an interrogatory approach. Anyone who worked closely with Westroes and all those who were involved in the Jukes deal, directly or peripherally, were grilled.

As the investigation progressed, Russell found himself in an increasingly problematic position. On the one hand, he continued to feel a misplaced, but undeniable sense of loyalty to Westroes. He also intrinsically understood that her actions had put his entire team and the company in an untenable place. For that, he was incensed at his former boss.

"I still can't wrap my head around it," he told Farouq Ahmed one day as the Fares-Tolmken investigation kicked off. "Sarah's the proverbial bull in a china shop, but this is too much. The time we're dedicating to this inquiry is such a waste."

"No kidding, my friend," said Farouq, who was in charge of the company's sizable IT operation. "I thought she always pissed me off when she was here. Now she's gone, and I'm still annoyed at her," Farouq snarled. "Has your interrogation been scheduled yet?"

"Tuesday bright and early. Eight."

"I'm going under the lights that afternoon." Farouq raised a few sheets of paper between them. "I was up half the night making notes."

Russell had noticed the handwritten comments scrawled in the margins of what looked like a report. It was widely known that Farouq had the eccentric habit of scribbling notes in meetings.

"I admit it, it's a biproduct of my OCD," Farouq had once said of his scribbling. "I get anxious if I don't see my own shorthand all over documents I'm reviewing. I have to write my notes longhand."

"If that's your worst failing, Farouq, I don't think you should even listen to your team tease you about it."

"I don't take it personally. I mean, I do run the technology business unit. Really, they have every right to make fun of me," Farouq had conceded with a good-natured giggle, "They mainly give me a hard time now because I print any proposals or reports they submit electronically, make my notes in pen and then scan the files and email it to them!"

"What have you written all over for the Fares-Tolmken interview there?" Russell asked, pointing to the sheets of paper Farouq held.

"Oh, I printed off some of the meeting summaries from the Jukes days. Trying to jog my memory and make sure I answer their questions as accurately as I can."

"Now I wish I had done that," Russell admitted.

"I'm sure I'm just overpreparing," Farouq said. "Good luck with the cross-examination on Tuesday."

Of course, he had tried to remain unphased as the investigation proceeded, knowing he was innocent of financial malfeasance. If anything, he felt embarrassed. He had attempted to rationalize the situation when the news had first broken about Sarah, telling himself that there must be some other explanation for the allegations. But as the evidence mounted, he found himself feeling increasingly disillusioned and naive. How could someone he respected and admired so genuinely be capable of such unethical behavior? If anyone should have known Sarah was involved in something untoward, it was him, given he had become close, even too close, to her.

When it came time for Russell to sit for his first of five interviews, a slick sheen formed on his palms and his pulse throbbed against his shirt collar.

The interview took place in a small meeting room in Datatel's third floor HR department. Russell had faced off with two Fares-Tolmken interviewers, both young employment lawyers turned corporate investigative professionals. They queried him for over two hours in that first session. There would be follow-up interrogations in weeks to come. The women were pros, bellying little through commentary, but hinting that they did not think Russell's actions or motives were suspect.

The grilling during the first meeting with the lawyers left the two interrogators and Russell exhausted. Jackets were removed and shirt sleeves rolled up.

"Okay, Russell, I think we've got everything we need for today."

"And we want to thank you for your candor and the level of detail you've been able to provide," added Deborah. They had filtered through the detritus of the Jukes deal and Westroes' actions from top to bottom.

Russell observed that both lawyers, while acting relaxed, were still studying him. He continued choosing his words and responses with measured brevity and accuracy, even as the conversation took on a more amicable tenor.

Over the course of four additional interviews, Russell became more familiar with how Judie and Deborah assumed specific roles. Judie focused on questions involving Russell's interactions with his peers and seemed to be particularly curious about whether Westroes' senior executive team had unwittingly succumbed to a form of groupthink, indirectly becoming complicit in the chess game their CEO had allegedly engineered. Deborah homed in on Russell's direct interactions with Westroes herself, ostensibly assessing whether there was any indication of a co-conspiracy.

When the fifth and final interview of the cycle was completed, the discussion had shifted to a line of questioning from both Fares-Tolmken consultants that became more concentrated on Russell's insight and hypotheses, attempting to further identify how Sarah

Westroes had moved the pieces of her own iniquitous algorithms and logic to deceive even her closest advisers and internal auditors.

"There's been a lot of speculation that she rushed the Jukes job and ignored a lot of warning signs among your peers," Deborah divulged during the last session. "Wouldn't you have recognized she was putting her pawns in play?"

"I didn't," Russell stated emphatically. "I mean, if she was steering us to close the deal, I don't remember it being that overt."

"So, it was more subtle?" Judie pressed.

"Honestly, I don't know." Russell squirmed. "If she was manipulating us, it was probably somewhere in between. At times she could be a little intimidating with people. She usually got her way. At the same time, it's not like she browbeat us into submission."

"A lot of your coworkers have said that you were the closest to her. You must have noticed something was awry, off-base, no?" Deborah asked.

Russell's warning system went to high alert.

"I'm not sure anyone is that close to Sarah." He said, attempting to bury a kernel of skepticism in the dialogue. "I always saw her as being aggressive. You know, driving her agenda and not letting anyone make excuses or slow us down. In retrospect, maybe I should have been more observant."

"This all appears to be her crime, not yours," Deborah had said, attempting to assuage his sense of responsibility after the final interview. Despite the reassurances, Russell knew the *Sarah Situation* was still far from over.

✤

The email from Haplich, Hauz, and Zubnig in Toronto, requesting that he finally wrap up the business of his mother's estate, had arrived in his inbox sometime between the fourth and fifth interviews. At first, the idea of leaving Boston to tend to the estate in the middle of the scandal struck him as preposterous. A week later, exhausted and relieved that the interviews had concluded, the idea of escaping to Canada for a week or two seemed more of a fortuitously placed egress from the tension around Datatel, a welcome respite.

It wasn't long after that he found himself booking his long-overdue flight to Toronto.

# 3

As the Airbus approaches the myriad of pinpoint lights of Toronto below, the clouds dissipate, and a quarter-moon emerges like a beacon to guide the plane to safety with its lunar pull. Almost instantly, Russell senses an unpleasant tautness unraveling inside him. The least comfortable facet of his journey, the flight is now officially over.

The plane taxies sluggishly to the gate. Its drizzling and swollen droplets meander down the darkened window. Russell pulls his iPhone from his pants pocket, turns the airplane mode off, and, courtesy of Bell Canada, watches notifications appear on his home screen.

Three texts from Sarah Westroes, increasing in urgency, asking him to call her or let her know when he will be available. The Datatel legal team insisted on a zero-contact policy regarding any communication with Sarah and her husband. Yet, for reasons that any outsider would see as inexplicable, Russell hasn't blocked her number yet and instead simply ignores her calls, voicemails and texts. He is unable to cut all ties with his boss. Their association is too profound, a tangled knot, interwoven threads of emotion, affection, and discretion.

He checks his email and at the top of his inbox is a message from Cal Morales, his mentor. The subject line just reads *Need to Talk ASAP*. Russell scans the uncharacteristically long email from Cal, who is notorious for his four-lines max email preferences.

"Here we go," Russell says to himself with a somnolent sigh

upon reading the message. Cal apparently has updates regarding Sarah Westroes' next moves. The board of directors convened an extemporaneous meeting that morning and discussed some restructuring ideas that involve Russell. Cal's communication style is usually more off-the-cuff. The formality and dimension of this email, however, seems rehearsed.

Rumors had been circulating on the executive floor of Datatel that Russell was being considered as Westroes' replacement. It made sense. He had the professional pedigree, had founded and led his own company before Datatel's acquisition, and probably, most critically given recent events, he was considered controversy free.

"The betting pool is leaning toward to you as the heir apparent," Datatel Chief Financial Officer Tim Connor had recently hinted.

They had just completed a meeting going over the capital expenditure on the latest product release initiative. There were some immaterial budget overruns Connor had wanted to review in advance of the next quarterly investor call. He regularly overprepared for those sessions, never wanting to be caught off guard with a random question intended to disrupt his balanced narrative.

"It's flattering that they think I'm capable of filling Sarah's shoes," Russell had replied to Connor during that boardroom discussion. "She's a tough act to follow."

"That she is," Connor had agreed.

"Anyway, the board isn't likely to opt for any of us on her direct team."

"Why do you think that?"

Russell rubbed his chin stubble thoughtfully. "They may concede that none of us were privy to her actions. In the board's eyes, we have to be a little tainted with the afterglow of it all though."

"Has Cal said that to you?" Connor blurted, knowing Russell's special relationship with the former CEO.

"No, not at all. In fact, Cal has been playing everything close to his vest on this whole conundrum." Russell admitted. "He's been careful to not share any of the board's current thinking. I've barely spoken with him."

"I hope you're wrong about the whole being tainted thing," Connor said. "How could any of us known what Sarah was up to?"

"True. I'm probably thinking inventively and going down numerous paths. I sometimes worry about the possibilities."

Conner had laughed and said, "My money's still on you. You're a safe, stable bet and we need that right now. I guess we'll know soon enough. For what it's worth, I hope it's you. Westroes was a wild card and look where we are now. I trust your instincts, and I know how you think. A preferable outcome in my books."

"I appreciate the show of support," Russell had acknowledged. "I have to try not to worry about it until and unless it becomes a reality."

At any other time in his career, Russell would have been eager to learn more about what the board was thinking. But right now? It all seems like too much. This trip to Canada, wading into the seawaters of his distant past, with the events of the more recent past declining to permit him any peace of mind, depleted him of energy to focus on other matters.

The decision to take this short sabbatical didn't come easy. He had wrestled with it, even wandering over to Farouq's office a few days before his departure to question if he was taking time away at the worst possible moment.

"No way, brother" Farouq declared. "You gotta do it."

Russell had wrinkled half his face in response, conveying his persistent doubt.

"Listen my friend, you've sweated it out for this company," Farouq had tried to reassure. "Everyone knows your commitment to Datatel and the team. And you've been through so much. I mean, your son, Anna. Now all this insanity with Sarah. You deserve the time. You need it."

Recalling the conversation with Farouq and his mention of Joshua and Anna brings a swell of reminiscence and snaps his attention back to the present. Subconsciously, Russell finds himself toggling back to his inbox and confirming Cal's was the last email he's received.

Nothing from Anna.

He reprimands himself silently for even imagining that she might have reached out. Although he'd let her know that he was leaving the country for an unknown amount of time, why would she check to see that he'd arrived or show any level of interest? Forbidden to communicate with Sarah, a part of him wishes he saw Anna's familiar name on his iPhone as he scrolls through his messages.

*

He met Anna around the time of his first promotion on a visit back to London. She was a resident working under his mother's mentorship. He soon learned that Anna had already gained international acclaim for research she had published on transcatheter aortic valve replacement and other minimally invasive procedures in her area of specialty. Anna's long-term aspiration was to help develop robotic assisted surgical techniques that would make open heart surgery virtually obsolete.

Russell quite literally collided with her one day after walking, head down, around a corner in the cardiac unit at St. Bart's, his elbow smacking stridently against the clipboard that she'd held up as a shield.

She was delightful; a striking face under dark, short bangs and dark hair, shaped in a stylish curled mid-length cut and cropped at the back. She had large green eyes that betrayed a fervent spirit and an engaging Scottish accent that sounded carefree and out of place in the stoicism that surrounded her at work. Russell was embarrassed and had stumbled on an apology.

"Sorry, sorry . . . I—"

"You what?" she challenged.

"I just didn't see you, sorry."

"Daydreaming or lost in your own thoughts?"

"Um, neither" Russell had said, shrugging to convey that he felt silly. "I just wasn't paying attention, to be honest."

She broke out into a warm grin. "Aw, I'm just giving you a hard time. No damage to me or my things, so no apology necessary. I can't find fault in a little errant clumsiness at the end of a long day, now, can I?"

"I guess not," he said, smiling back.

"Well, until we, quite literally, run into each other again, be well."

Russell couldn't tell whether she was being dismissive or flirtatious.

As he stood across from her, feeling awkward, Russell noticed that she tilted her head when speaking. Later he learned that this was a habit formed in adolescence. She had a patch of ultra-white skin that traced an uneven track from her right temple to just above her lip. It resembled a rough, inverted triangle. It was something called localized vitiligo, a disease that caused cells to stop producing melanin. Later, after they were on their third or fourth date, she voluntarily shared her experience with vitiligo.

"It first presented when I was thirteen. As a teenager, I was naturally self-conscious about my appearance. I felt like I looked different from everyone else, and I didn't want to draw attention to myself. I was afraid of being bullied or ridiculed because of my skin, so I did my best to blend in."

"That sounds like a terrible time to go through something like that."

"Yes. That's when I developed my torticollis habit," she said with a wry grin, referring to her head tilt. "Sorry, I mean my somewhat unique neck cricks. Torticollis probably isn't a term I should expect you to know. Occupational communication hazard, I'm afraid. I spent hours in front of the mirror trying to find the perfect shade of foundation to match my skin tone and hide the spot. It didn't work though. I always felt like people were either staring at this splotchy thing on my face or avoiding staring at it. As I got older, I wore bright colors and bold patterns, hoping that people would notice my clothes instead of my skin. But no matter how hard I tried, I couldn't escape the fact that I looked different from everyone else."

It wasn't until Anna was in her late twenties that she finally started to feel comfortable with the condition. Some of it was a boost-of-confidence effect from her academic achievements. As she consistently received recognition as the top pre-med student in her year, she began to let go of her fear of being judged and embraced her unique physical differences. She stopped trying to hide her face and started to wear less makeup and, eventually, even wore her hair in a way that revealed the white patch. The head-tilting habit never completely diminished, though, and it was something that Russell thought added to Anna's attractiveness.

That impromptu hallway meeting quickly spurred Anna to action once she learned that Russell was the son of her mentor. A nurse who had witnessed and overheard the brief incident when they'd first collided in the hallway shared the intel with Anna. She wasted no time tracking down Judith to get Russell's phone number.

"Had I known that you were Dr. Judith's son, I would never have been so forgiving after our collision the other day," she said after he'd answered the unrecognized number on his phone.

"Sorry, I'm not sure I know who this is." he replied.

"Well, I'm calling to properly introduce myself and give you the opportunity to do the same. Although, I do hold the upper hand since I know your name, Russell, and you, clearly have no idea who I am."

"That's true," he said, trying to guess her identity.

"I'm Anna."

"The Anna? My mother's Anna?"

"The very one. Not only are you the offspring of my favorite person in the entire world, but you were kind of cute when you got all embarrassed after nearly knocking me over. I've decided to give you the opportunity to make it up to me by taking me out to dinner the next time you are in London. When will that be?"

Very typical Anna.

Their first date happened a month later during his next visit. They braved an emblematic fall evening in London. He met Anna at her Islington flat, and they strode out onto a quiet street lined with tall, elegant townhouses, the wet pavement polished by a mild, dim drizzle. Islington had seen significant regeneration in recent years, transformed from a working-class neighborhood into a fashionable and desirable residential area for the middle income. Anna, a rising figure in cardiac surgery and no longer a student, was now an enlisted member of that income bracket.

They had made loose plans to perhaps see a movie and have dinner—typical but simple. Soon after leaving her flat, Anna mentioned that she had to pick up something she had forgotten at work but let him know they should still be able to make a show. Their pace was deliberate but slow enough to maintain the conversation as they passed cafes, bookstores, and local boutiques lining the high street. He learned that Anna had a keen interest in London and the historical changes in its many boroughs and neighborhoods. She stopped several times to point out and admire the Georgian architecture that characterized the area, and the street art adorning the buildings.

At Angel station, they descended into the Underground and boarded the Northern Line, heading south toward St. Bartholomew's Hospital. The tube was crowded, and they squeezed into two open seats close to the doors amidst the automated mind-the-gap announcements.

Anna continued her narrative, describing the brutalist architecture they'd transitioned into as they made their way through the Barbican Estate, a vast residential complex and, according to Anna, a spectacle of post-war architecture.

At St. Bartholomew's, Russell waited for her outside, standing under the hospital's striking Victorian façade, an imposing presence amidst the modern buildings surrounding it. Watching her walk through the gates when she returned, he was looking forward to the rest of the evening. He found himself becoming rapidly besotted. *Anna is remarkable*, he thought.

"I'm not sure how intent you were on a movie," he said when she approached, "but I'm enjoying talking with you way too much."

"We're sharing thoughts already! Absolutely. You've been to the museum, right? I mean the St. Bart's Museum, right here."

Russell admitted that, despite his mother's senior position at the hospital and his frequent visits there, he had never been to the museum. He was struck with one of those moments of realization that sometimes the simplest experiences directly in front of us are those that we overlook.

Anna's full access security badge meant she could access the museum and she spontaneously grabbed his forearm and pulled him alongside her.

"You have to see it," she insisted. "Your mother will be so impressed that I coerced you into visiting the museum. You may not even know this, but she absolutely adores it."

"Wait a second. You know things about Dr. Judith that I don't even know."

"Many, my friend, more than you could bear to know."

They moved through the museum over the course of the next hour. Russell found himself increasingly drawn to Anna's endless knowledge and impulsive enthusiasm. She was his apt tutor and tour guide. She revealed to him St. Bart's long and storied history as they took in exhibits showcasing the hospital's role in treating victims of the Great Fire of London in 1666 and treating soldiers during the two World Wars. As they left the museum, they mused over the contrast between the hospital's historical significance and the rush of the modern city outside its gates.

Eventually, they found their way to Soho and realized they were almost an hour late for their dinner reservation. It would take another thirty minutes to get to a table. Absorbed in their conversation and developing a sense of connectedness, they decided to walk further East and eat at a place called Sandy's on Seymour Street, which Anna declared to have the best Sicilian-style pizza in the city. He learned that she had been born in Aberdeen, Scotland where she had lived until university. However, she seemed disinclined to talk at length about her childhood and instead spoke extensively of her admiration for her mentor and friend.

"I really never imagined I'd be living in London and definitely not working under someone as famous in the field as Dr. Judith," Anna had said as they huddled in the warmth of their small table. A soft drizzle had persisted all day and beads of water outside curled and bent down the window. "I really didn't think I'd leave Scotland. It wasn't until I recognized that I was constantly ahead of the other kids in science and math that I got the nerve to even consider med school. And then the application to intern at St. Bart's with your mother was the longshot of all longshots!"

"Well, I for one am glad you took the long shot," Russell said. "We may never have met otherwise."

"Ah, but we were always going meet, Russell." She smiled and raised an eyebrow. "After all, fate is fate."

"Fate. A very existential subject to broach on date number one," he quipped.

"Ah, I'm struck by two different things with that statement," she said with an air of pensiveness, her accent increasingly prominent as the lighthearted dialogue continued. "First, it suggests there will be subsequent dates, and I make special note of the plural. I must say, this pleases me greatly based on this first outing."

"Me too. And the second thing?"

"Well, I believe the whole existential conversation should happen early in a relationship," Anna shared. "So, here it is, all laid out on the table for you. I am a scientist first and foremost. I put my faith in knowledge and the pursuit of it. On top of it, growing up Catholic,

I long ago shed the guilt and neurosis that is the foundation of most institutional religions."

"That really is putting it all out on the table."

"Well, now you know. I am an agnostic, at best," she admitted.

"Being raised by a woman of science and reason, I was not really brought up with anything but that to consider. I confess, there were no Sunday masses with my mother, or Bible classes or church, for that matter. So, I guess we have a healthy dose of agnosticism running through our veins."

"Hallelujah!" Anna put her drink down hard on the wooden table.

Their laughter filled the small restaurant. They finished their pizza slowly, continuing to giggle as they discussed the virtues and shortcomings of anchovies, eventually moving on to talk about his life in the States.

---

They dated for six months, with Russell making frequent flights between Boston and London before they eloped to Bermuda. It hadn't been a long courtship, but they were both established in life and experienced enough to know they had a connection that would last. In some ways, their combination satiated a shared desire for a conventional life—hers born from a precarious, unfriendly upbringing, and Russell's from a need to feel safe and consistent. They didn't announce the marriage to anyone until they had returned from their ten-day trip with smiles and suntans.

To celebrate, his mother took them to dinner at an upscale restaurant in Saville Row called Sartoria and insisted on buying them their wedding bands as a gift. It was all very low-key. Everyone was pleased.

"I'm not only proud of you, but I'm also happy for you both," Judith had said as the dinner plates were being gathered by the waiter.

"Well, thank you, Dr. Judith," Anna responded, lifting her glass and toasting the air. "And here's to my two favorite people on the planet. My new family."

Russell stood and gave them both an embrace.

"And to the two toughest, yet most elegant, doctors in my life," he exclaimed, lifting his glass of wine, and following up with a toast of his own.

Once her residency was completed, Anna was placed in her first official role in the United States as a cardiac specialist at Mass General. Years later, after they had practically ruled out having kids, Anna got pregnant. Russell was almost forty then. He felt like he had played by the rules and was reaping life's rewards. He couldn't have been more content.

But contentedness would not last. When he now dares to reminisce, he is still shocked by how things had changed with the suddenness of a lightning strike. The last half-decade pounced on him, sinking its teeth into sinew and bone, leaving him stranded, wounded, and crawling through a mire of self-doubt and angst.

Several months back, Anna and he both attended a ceremony awarding a scholarship in his mother's honor. It is an annual event during which a cardiology intern receives a bursary based on a variety of qualities. Anna had established this yearly award first at St. Bart's and then also through Massachusetts General to memorialize Russell's mother the year after she died.

This was the last time he'd seen Anna. He didn't notice her until he caught her familiar stride approaching under the latticed arch of the hospital chapel. After months of unbroken estrangement, she looked and sounded different; her once-strained features had softened, and he could hear less tension in her voice. Still, Russell knew that despite her improved outward appearance, she would always shoulder that insufferable pain of any cheated mother who cannot forfeit the memory of her lost child. She said hello and brushed an indifferent kiss across his cheek before asking how he was doing. Although her words carried the customary inflections of caring, her ineffable tone was enough to convey the emptiness that lay at their foundation. Her voice reminded him that she could no longer construe any form of feeling toward him.

"You've been well?" she had asked, her eyes darting over his shoulder as if looking for a safe harbor toward which she might escape his company.

"I've been okay," he answered, hating how meek the response sounded.

"I guess work must really be keeping you busy lately."

Russell could say nothing to her in response and merely lowered his head with a grim smile. Anna's question was intended to be biting. His history with Datatel, and particularly Sarah Westroes, was still a raw wound. It was hard to fathom the joy he and Anna had once felt in their life together. And then, with her standing across from him with her familiar head tilt as if to still obscure the signs of vitiligo, nothing but a cold ocean of regret and indifference in the space between.

Russell told her goodbye before quietly withdrawing from her.

As anticipated, Russell enters undeterred through the Canadian customs at Pearson. In the main lobby of Terminal 3, swarms of people wait expectantly at the arrivals area behind a glass partition. He again consults his iPhone to avoid catching anyone's eye and to bypass this conglomeration of other people's relatives and friends. Of course, no one is waiting for him.

Slipping into a restroom outside the baggage carousels, he plucks a tissue from the top of his leather duffle bag and washes his forehead with a splash of frigid water. His reflection gazes back: the brown tuft of thinning but intact, gray-flecked hair; tired eyes; indented cheeks that bear testimony to the weight he has recently shed. He is still wearing the same outfit that he started out in earlier that morning, his tie now pulled loosely around the collar of a white, button-down shirt that is tucked into conservative, unremarkable black khakis.

He had been working from his home office earlier that day but had a few online video calls and decided on more standard business attire. He preferred working from home when he could lately, although he wouldn't go so far as to say that he'd been avoiding the office. He rarely felt eager to commute downtown because of the undercurrents and pure stress permeating Datatel.

Now in Toronto, he surveys a queue of identical, black city cabs parked outside the airport terminal. One veers to a spot directly in front of him, and the driver springs to the curb and tosses Russell's bags in the backseat.

It is a long ride to the downtown Hilton. Russell sits nervously in silence, not wanting to distract the driver who is speeding along Highway 427 and lane-hopping. He's aware of his paranoid tendency. His mother used to attribute it to an overactive imagination, encouraging him to dispel such thoughts before they boil over. Despite his best intentions, Russell has long since surrendered to his neurotic predispositions and recognizes them as one of the many unalterable facts of his life.

Once the cab has delivered him to the hotel amid a blaring cacophony of car horns and braking tires, a sharply attired concierge escorts him to the registration counter. The front desk associate unexpectedly hands him an envelope that had arrived earlier that evening. Russell waits until he is settled in the one-bedroom suite before he peels open the envelope. It bears the familiar insignia of Haplich, Hauz, and Zubnig, and contains a handwritten note welcoming him to Toronto and reconfirming his meeting the following morning at nine o'clock. It appears that, even in this day of instant messaging and texting, they are holding true to Dr. Judith Nowak-McCreary's partiality for old-fashioned correspondence, *a very nice touch,* he thinks.

The note bears the signature of Tony Haplich, Jr., the son of the lawyer to whom his mother entrusted most of her affairs in Canada. Shortly after her funeral, his assistant tracked Russell down to inform him that she had a Canadian will that they would need to discuss and settle. He had received an email with a similar request about every six months since.

Then, a few months ago, he heard from Haplich, Jr. himself. The lawyer called his direct office line and insisted that the matter of the will had to be resolved. He revealed that Russell's mother had left a fair sum of her Canadian assets to several charities, leaving Russell an amount that he did not want to disclose over the phone but that had, apparently, been sitting in escrow for too long. He explained that she had also left him the ten acres for which her estate still held title on Teapot Lake in northern Ontario.

He could hear the undertones as the lawyer divulged this news. Haplich Jr. was concerned that Russell might not want to take possession of the land which would, undoubtedly, cause him or his staff additional complexities in settling his affairs. Russell set the lawyer's mind at ease without hesitation, explaining that he was more than content to work with him to transfer the land.

In fact, it was something he wanted. It was the most important thing his mother could have left him.

"In that case, we can settle your mother's estate by email," he had recommended.

Russell lied and said he had business in Toronto and would plan to meet Haplich Jr. in person. "One of our vendors is headquartered in Mississauga, close to the airport. I'm going to pay them a visit, probably shortly after we meet."

"In that case, I'd be more than happy to go over the details up here in our main office."

Something in him felt obliged to do this in Canada; his mother would have demanded it. Even from beyond the grave, he could feel the tug of her wants and expectations. Taking over the land on Teapot Lake necessitates being there in person.

Russell is determined to see the A-frame cottage situated by the lakefront which transports him back in time to a more enlightened season in his life, one of unspoiled joy and exhilaration. Those happy months before he and his mother left Canada for the United Kingdom figure most prominently in his memory.

During one childhood summer, when he was at the pinnacle of discovery and revelation, Russell's grandfather entered his life and became the closest thing to a role model that his fatherless existence had previously denied him. After that summer, he all but stopped searching for answers to the quandary of his longed-for father and ceased plaguing his mother with questions about him. That summer somehow had remained one of his few enduring sources of strength.

It was a period strangely devoid of contact with his mother, who spent much of her time reading and the last several days of their stay at the cottage traveling to London to interview for what would become her permanent position. But Russell hardly noticed her sporadic departures and returns that summer. He can't help but smile whenever he thinks of how reticent he had been, at first, to leave their cramped apartment in Toronto for some cottage in the wilderness, which the thought alone was enough to spike his anxiety. Familiar territory was more comfortable.

He had appealed to his mother countless times to stay in the city. He resented that his entire summer had been planned on his behalf without even the charade of consultation. Of course, as a child, he couldn't have anticipated the extraordinary season that lay before him. But, as is often the case, the events that ultimately shape themselves into life's milestones are often those to which we assign the least expectations.

# 4

Russell had been eight years old for two weeks, and he still didn't feel the slightest bit different. It was like that every year. He would wait for an upcoming birthday with a lingering sense of anticipation and then, as the day drew closer, with exhilaration. But when the day came, the effect never reached the expected heights. He didn't feel wiser or, for that matter, even older. And this year's birthday looked to be the same as last year's.

Russell was bored as their rusted station wagon rolled along the blistering ribbon of highway. They were entering the fourth hour of the journey north, and his cursory study of the *Popular Mechanics* magazine in his lap had become tedious. Its contents revealed nothing to absorb the wandering interests of an eight-year-old. Besides, he had only asked his mother to purchase the magazine because of the sharp photograph of a jet fighter on its front cover.

That had been hours ago when they stopped at a gas station in a place called Gravenhurst, where the unshaven attendant behind the counter smiled at Judith in a way that made her son feel uncomfortable. Russell was relieved when they left the smell of petrol and the leering attendant behind, gravel crunching under the wheels and dust swirling in the wake of the car as it rejoined the paved highway.

Strangers made Russell uneasy, especially those that stared at his mother. He knew why they did it, though; she was attractive and was conspicuously missing a customary male counterpart. For her sake, he feigned ignorance when a man winked at her or offered her a knowing look. Still, he wasn't blind to these overtures, and secretly he often dreamed of how his father, were he alive, would undoubtedly have deflected their unsolicited advances.

"That should be our last pit stop before we get to the lake," his mother announced, "so don't drink too much soda pop or you'll have to hold it."

"I won't. How much farther is it?"

"According to the map, a long, long way." She smiled. "How's your magazine?"

"It's good. I already read most of the stuff I wanted to."

With Gravenhurst a mere memory, they both settled into a calm daze on the final leg of their voyage along Highway 11. Earlier that day, Russell had become embroiled in a rare argument when he attempted one last stand against the ensuing northern holiday and refused to load his overstuffed suitcase in with a pile of coolers and gym bags already situated in the rear hollow of the station wagon.

"We've talked about this for weeks now, Russell. I'm not going to keep having the same argument two minutes before we are supposed to get on the road," Judith had admonished him with exasperation.

"It's not fair," Russell protested, avoiding his mother's stern eyes. "I just don't want to go. At all."

"I'm well aware of that. And fair doesn't even figure into the equation," Judith said with mounting impatience. "It's non-negotiable. Fair doesn't start to be a factor until you're an adult."

Russell huffed in response.

After this brief debate, his mother's reaction evolved into calculated simplicity; she started the car and locked the doors as if she might drive off without him. Russell weighed if a coaxing smile or witty comment could be used to cause a hairline crack in her hard outer shell. However, once she had set her mind on something and her posture straightened, he knew that it was time to capitulate. The severity of the look she gave him from behind the driver's side window gave him but one option. With a resigned sigh, he swung the last heavy bag onto the heap and slid into the passenger seat. However, as the drive northward progressed, his attachment to the city seemed to diminish with each passing mile.

The two of them had never, for as long as Russell could recall, ventured beyond the periphery of Toronto, except on their occasional visits to her friend's house in Milton. Their world had always consisted of the city's droning engines, illuminated signs, and all the hallmarks of organization practiced by the people who lived there. Now, only hours from home, the rolling landscape outside his window, dotted with infrequent signs of humanity, was as foreign to him as another country.

Russell's imagination projected him into the dense foliage beyond the gravel shoulder of the highway. In an instant, he thought he knew how it would feel to be lost and isolated in this desolate wilderness, the futility of his cries for help, and the creeping fear that would accompany the coming dark. Although he shifted uncomfortably against his seatbelt whenever these thoughts arose, his eyes were drawn continuously to the forest. It was at once unnerving and intriguing. Judith became increasingly relaxed as their car cut a swath through the humid air that rose like steam from the pavement. All spring, as she neared completion of her medical internship, she had become increasingly tense and, by default, Russell had picked up on her anxiety. His mother had been training for her career for as long as he could remember, first as a student at the University of Toronto and then as an intern at St. Michael's Hospital. And as her sacrifices and labors slowly came to fruition during the past months, he took hold of the assurance that his life would be much improved by summer's end.

Back in Toronto, Russell had grown tired of his after-school sitter, Maria, and her limitations as a companion in the hours before his mother returned home, her energies spent from eighteen-hour shifts at the hospital.

The stresses on them both would be eased in the upcoming year, he was certain of it. He had been given a sign. On July 1, her last day at the hospital, Judith had unexpectedly returned home from a celebratory party and woke him from a light sleep. Then, with a tired smile, she guided him through the attic to the coarse roof of their rented duplex on Claremont Street and huddled under a woolen blanket to ward off the cool night. They watched together as the Canada Day fireworks transformed the sky over Lake Ontario into a kaleidoscope of bursting color. It was a good omen.

⚜

Judith was singing as she drove north to the remote lake. It meant that she was calm. It was more humming than actual singing, sometimes punctuated with words to break up the monotony. She sang to him like that every night before tucking him into bed, even if he had already dozed off before her arrival. She would sit at his side, gazing out the window and croon in a murmured hush. Often, he would pretend to be asleep as he listened to her soothing purr, and when she rose from the creaky bed with a peck on his forehead, he would roll onto the warm spot she had left behind and pass thoughtlessly into sleep. He hoped that this ritual wouldn't cease at the cottage.

She and Russell's father had been engaged for two years before marrying, only one month before his sudden death. In those days, she had been a nurse, always craving more knowledge and dreaming of a career as a physician.

Russell's father, Terence McCreary, who had been considerably older than his mother, had taught high school. This was the most concrete information she had revealed to him about his mysterious dad, insisting whenever he asked about him that he, like her, live in the present, not the past. She had remained loyal to his memory, this much he knew.

Only once had she discussed his death with him—on a Christmas morning. Russell had stumbled excitedly into her room and found her crying, a photograph grasped in her quivering hand. It was a picture of a man he did not know—bright eyes and high cheekbones over a tight-lipped smile and a reddish beard. It was then that she told him how he had been clipped by a truck while driving home on a foggy highway, and his car had rolled into a ditch. Nobody's fault, really. Just a tragic, random accident.

Russell's mother offered pensively, "We set a blueprint in life and sometimes things happen that knock us way off that plan," more to herself than to him.

"Not having a dad. It makes me seem . . ." he searched for the words, ". . . not the same as most kids."

That comment elicited a compassionate look from his mother. She had looped her arm across his shoulders.

"Being *the same* is the same thing as *normal*. And who wants to be normal? Booorrring." She smiled, drawing out the last word as long as possible and rolling her eyes.

The fact that she had denied all potential suitors since her husband's death gave Russell a reason to infer that his father had been unique beyond equivocation. Late at night, Russell had watched his mother through his half-open bedroom door when she thought he was asleep. She would listen to the music from their wedding day on his outdated record player—Mozart's Symphony No. 40—as she sat at the bottom of the stairs leading to the ground floor, her arms folded under her and her head resting on her knees.

He couldn't count the number of times he would sneak into her room and retrieve the picture from its secret location beneath the socks on the top shelf of her armoire, trying to get some hint of his father from the cryptograph of that faded snapshot.

She still maintained a warm relationship with his father's family. He saw his Uncle Malcolm and Aunt Elaine once a year. Russell's cousin Kenny was their only offspring with whom he had an ambiguous and often capricious connection. He looked forward to their annual visit to Toronto with unerring skepticism, unable to convince himself that the sanctity of his controlled and dependable existence would not be encroached upon as it had on previous visits. Yet, every year they rolled into town like a tempest, Malcolm boisterous and domineering, Elaine hysterical, and Kenny uncontrollably wild.

However, on Russell's father's side of the family, it was John McCreary, Russell's grandfather, who was a figure veiled in an impregnable cloak of mystery. He had not seen the man since he was five, and those memories were vague. The only prevailing recollection Russell had was that his grandfather had always teasingly referred to him as Rusty. Everyone else, by Judith's decree, addressed him by his birth name, Russell. Use of the nickname was a privilege reserved only for Pops McCreary. He and Judith corresponded most frequently by mail and random phone calls. The tidbits of intelligence he had managed to accumulate on him were spare, gleaned mainly from telephone conversations he had overheard between his mother and Aunt Elaine. Pops spent his winters sheltered in the cabin he had built for himself at Teapot Lake and the summers tending to the fields or making minor repairs to the A-frame cabin.

At one time, Pops had lived in Toronto, working in a government office, and sharing a townhouse with his wife, Nana McCreary, who had died years earlier from heart failure. Soon after her death, Pops had taken to living in a hermit-like state on the land up north, an estuary unto himself, quietly removed from the pull of society's swirling currents.

With the television's standard effigy of a hermit as his only guide, Russell envisioned his father's father as a weather-beaten figure with a long, grizzled beard and misanthropic mannerisms. As he now drew ever closer to meeting him in the flesh, he prayed that this picture would prove inaccurate. In a bid to assuage some of these uncertainties, Russell's mother gave him the abridged version of Pops' life story as they continued on their inaugural northbound drive.

"Do you know what Pops McCreary's first name is?" Judith asked with an upward inflection.

"Um. I don't know."

"I'll give you three guesses. You've probably heard it before."

"I can't remember," Russell groaned dramatically.

"Well? What's your first guess?"

"How about, John?"

"Whoa. First try! Wow. You're an amazing guesser."

Russell smiled. "Maybe I did remember it?"

"I think maybe it was a combination of excellent guessing and some recollection."

A moment passed as Russell considered how he couldn't think of his grandfather as John. He was just Pops McCreary.

"He was born in Ireland and immigrated with his family when he was still a child. He met your grandmother after fighting in World War I on the front-line infantry," she explained. "After the war, he had returned to Canada and worked as a clerk in the Ministry of Defense."

"Oh," said Russell. "What does the Ministry of Defense mean."

His mother smiled. "More things related to the army and the military. He felt there was a mission to protect the country. Actually, he joined the armed forces again many years later during World War II, when he instructed newly recruited medics techniques to rescue injured people in war zones."

"He sounds tough."

"I suppose he is pretty tough, yes," she agreed.

"And a bit scary."

His mother reassured him that Pops McCreary was pensive, thoughtful, and gentle.

Although Russell accepted her words with faith, they did little to appease his growing uncertainty. But he didn't allow his sense of what lay ahead at Teapot Lake to diminish his generally good mood as he drove onward. He cherished these rare moments alone with his mother. She was wearing a long, loose-fitting, summer dress of thin, floral-printed fabric, her chestnut hair liberated from its customary bun and falling across her shoulders.

The steady sun that streamed through the windshield and glinted off the metallic wipers bestowed its golden light upon him and filled the car's interior with welcome warmth. If he could have captured this one moment and spread it across the future, his suspicions about how the rest of the summer would unfold would have faded like a faint autumn breeze.

Russell found most new situations to be intimidating. His mother was only partly culpable in the development of this trait insofar as her means of showing affection was not showering him with kisses or embraces, but rather through concern for his welfare and a desire to safeguard him from harm. After all, her profession was all about mishap and misfortune, so it was only natural that when it came to her only child, potential peril seemed a very real possibility.

Instead of repelling her protective maternal instincts, Russell had adopted them for himself and worried along with her. He knew that it would not be long after reaching the cottage before they both had concocted a list of safety regulations and areas of hazard for him to avoid. However boring, his home in Toronto, where he knew and accepted the designated boundaries and permissible activities, had been his only real sanctum to date.

What he had also inherited from his mother was a penchant for perfectionism, a trait harvested from a long-standing configuration of chromosomes that dominated the Nowak genetic landscape. Judith had been raised in a household of uncompromising strictness and propriety, eventually embracing her parents' own puritanical pursuit of excellence. Her flawless attention to detail and intuitiveness enabled her to graduate from medical school at the top of her class and receive nothing less than accolades from her internship supervisors.

Russell was her protégé by example, apprenticing in the virtues of discipline and diligence by subconsciously following the pattern of her personal achievements. By inference, she instilled in him a propensity to focus on success in all his own pursuits as well. Although she placed no overt demands on him, he was afraid of failing her, of representing the one ingredient that would defile her perfection. He was eager to please and took it upon himself as imperative to do the right thing for fear of disappointing her.

"You don't have to try so hard to be so faultless, Russell," Judith implored on numerous occasions. "I can see that it causes you to be stressed."

"It doesn't make me stressed," he would protest.

"Do you fully comprehend what it is like to be stressed?" she asked.

His response was immediate but pensive for an eight-year-old. "I think so. It's sort of like when you feel worried about stuff, right?"

"Well yes, but it's more like an ongoing worry or nervousness that doesn't go away. See, when you are really focused on something that worries you, a hormone called cortisol is released by the body. It helps provide energy, regulates the immune response, and affects memory and emotions. Cortisol levels rise during stress which is what causes you to feel that anxiety."

"Mom, you're doing it again."

It was not feasible for his mother to carry on a conversation for too long and, concurrently, elude her penchant for absently drifting into what she referred to as her medical tongue.

"All I'm trying to convey is that it's impossible do everything to perfection. I worry that you will make yourself stressed if you overdo it."

"So, you're stressed about it?"

"Ha, ha. Very funny."

He often responded to these parleys by saying, "You're perfect at everything. I'm just trying to be like you, Mom.

Despite the sometimes-melodramatic wanderlust of his imagination and his residence in the shadows cast by his mother's infallibility, Russell's childhood was not as stressful as one might suppose. His mother's love was uncompromising, allegiant, and dependable. He was a loner and an excellent student in virtually every scholastic area. In contrast to other children his age, he was an anomaly, yet he was conspicuously unremarkable.

He had several acquaintances to alleviate the boredom of recess and lunch hours at school, but he was otherwise content to roam within his own province of relative solitude. Although he was energetic and active, always riding his banana-seat bicycle on some neighborhood mission, he shied away from organized team sports since they often required a rough-and-tumble aptitude to which he was disinclined, his mother's voice in his head cautioning against it. He was never envious of other children who lived within the constructs of more traditional, nuclear families. He had never known anything other than the familial duet of him and his mother.

At a quaint village called South River, which was too small to earn recognition on their frayed, Coke-stained Ontario road map, his mother made a sharp right turn and left behind the uniform flatness of the pavement.

The station wagon was ill-equipped to negotiate the meandering, pebbled roadway that led to Teapot Lake, but his mother maintained her composure. He rolled up his window to avoid any airborne stones as they drove deeper into the dense forest. Through a canopy of branches and intertwined leaves, the sun-painted speckles of light marked their passage along the unpaved route.

Once or twice, his mother stopped to consult a sheet bearing the handwritten directions his grandfather had provided in his most recent letter. It seemed that they were not getting anywhere. However, they proceeded slowly along while his mother drummed her fingers on the steering wheel. By the time they finally reached a stout mailbox with the name *McCreary* scratched onto its rusted flank, the late-afternoon heat had yielded to an advancing tide of cool evening shade.

"It looks like we have arrived," his mother proclaimed.

"Finally," said Russell.

"It wasn't that bad, Russell. We didn't rush, we stayed safe and, I for one, enjoyed your company."

He looked up at her sheepishly and said, "Me too."

A sturdy white fence hugged the roadway where the property began, broken only where a gate door swung inward, partially ajar. The station wagon came to a halt beside the fence, and Russell hopped out to open the gate for his mother. The joints in his knees cracked with each step from sitting immobile for too long. He gave the gate a solid shove, and it creaked open tentatively against his palms.

As he turned back to the car, he was suddenly captivated by the stillness of his new surroundings. A breeze as delicate as lace evoked long whispers from the tall grass, awash in a satiny blanket of sunlight that covered the field beyond the fence. Across the road, leaves waltzed lazily with the shadows of neighboring branches, and the earthy scent of the forest mingled with the fragrant perfume of lilacs. Underlying it all was an unadulterated silence that gave Russell a feeling of unqualified calm. He believed he would have remained in that hypnotic state for hours had his mother not blasted the horn in an impatient bid to return him to the car.

The driveway that wandered through the field had been created less by deliberate construction and more by a slow evolution under the wheels of John McCreary's Oldsmobile. A single green ribbon of grass divided two rough gravel ruts as if a chariot had descended briefly from the heavens and etched the undeveloped road into the *terra firma*.

With great concentration, his mother navigated the few isolated potholes that had been left behind from the spring thaw. Soon, the end of the road appeared between the walls of towering grass, and he finally caught his first glimpse of Teapot Lake.

He made a quick, careful study of the terrain. Across the shimmering surface of the water, the opposite shoreline of the lake could hardly be discerned in the fading light. To the right, beyond the field, was a thin peninsula of coniferous bush that jutted into the calm water beside a sandy spot of beach. On his left was a large edifice of smooth rock that rose from the lake like the petrified fossil of some antediluvian monster.

As they approached the cottage, he noticed that it was nestled beside a giant rock at the outer edge of the forest. Despite looking weather-beaten, the abode appeared to be sturdy. A small, railed deck led to a wide bay window that was carved into the cedar wall and faced the lake, reflecting a perfect image of the water.

The alpine slope of the roof engulfed both sides of the structure, its shingled surface all but concealed by a tsunami of pine needles. The trim was painted a yellow that suggested a stratum of brighter color beneath its pale outer layer. The only sign of life was a lazy curl of smoke that ascended from the chimney like an apparition before it faded into the sky.

Their car stopped beside the wall of the cottage, and his mother freed herself from her seatbelt, inhaling her first sample of northern air. He waited until her door was shoved open before unlatching his own. His eyes remained riveted to the wooden front door of the cottage, anticipating the sudden emergence of John "Pops" McCreary. However, by the time they had proceeded to the front of the cabin, the sun-bleached planks of the deck cracking under their feet, the door had not yet opened.

"Go ahead and knock," his mother urged him, "maybe he's fallen asleep."

"I don't want to wake him up," Russell whispered.

"It's okay," his mother promised as he hesitated before stepping forward and drumming gently on the door.

Still, no evidence of movement came from within the cottage. Above the persistent rhythm of shallow waves lapping against the rock, he heard only the lofty chatter of birds as they carried out their early-evening commerce high above the cottage. A nervous squirrel scampered across the deck with an unrecognizable object wedged between its teeth, heading undoubtedly for its private cache. He glanced expectantly at his mother.

"He must have gone for a walk," she suggested. "Let's go in and get settled before he comes back."

The door responded to her shove with a lethargic groan and swung inward to reveal the warm interior of his grandfather's home. Russell took inventory of what would become his home for most of the summer: a cluttered kitchen, dusty windows peeking out from behind checkered drapes, a card table kept company by several worn metal chairs, embers hissing in the fireplace behind a blackened metal screen, an enormous Chesterfield sofa, a closed door hiding what was undoubtedly a bathroom, and an open door revealing a bed that was covered with a sprawling, quilted blanket.

Most of the tiles on the kitchen floor had hairline cracks, while the remainder of the cabin floor was covered with a thin rug. Despite its relatively diminutive size, there appeared to be plenty of room to move about, making the cabin seem deceptively spacious. On a mantelpiece in the main room was a black-and-white photograph of a soldier, whom Russell took to be his grandfather, smiling beside his wife. Next to the photo sat at least half a dozen bottles with used candles protruding from their necks, the multi-colored wax having solidified on the outside.

Although the cabin was kept impeccably clean, it was the type of room that would always seem dusty, if only in its mood. Inside, the smell that came off the cedar walls blended with the fire's smoke and filled the room with the aroma of mild incense.

Russell had just landed his suitcases on top of the bed when he heard the front door swing open and the heavy footsteps behind him. Pops was not at all the grizzled hermit he had envisioned. He strode into the cabin with a smile creasing the corners of his mouth. His skin was pale and wrinkled, with brown splotches covering the bald expanse of his forehead. Although his walk was touched by the prolonged, torpid movements of those in their later years, Russell could still spot the dignity in his gait, no doubt instilled from his years of military parading.

He wore baggy overalls, a faded denim shirt, and rubber waders that extended up his calves. But the most remarkable feature, the one that defied all external signs of aging, were the deep aquamarine eyes that exuded strength despite his aging physique. After rushing to Russell's mother and planting a kiss on her cheek, those penetrating eyes of Pops McCreary scanned the room alertly and finally settled on Russell.

"Rusty, thank God, you're finally here," he exclaimed, wiping a forearm against his temple, and sighing in relief. "I need your immediate assistance. There's some trouble down at the trout stream. Have you been lifting weights?"

Russell shook his head slowly, glancing at his mother for reassurance. This was not the greeting he had expected. His grandfather spoke as though only days had passed since the last time they'd met.

"Well, I hope you've become as strong as you look," he said emphatically. "We've only got a few more hours before dark, and there's a lot of work to do. Did you bring rubber boots?"

Russell shook his head again. He could feel his eyes widening. What could be so urgent that it required his attention? What trouble was awaiting him at the trout stream? His head swam with possibilities.

"You'll have to wear a pair of mine then. Just let me fish them out of the closet."

Russell's mother was smiling at Pops as he strode across the room and slid open the closet door. Russell looked to her with a querying expression, but she offered him only a shrug in return. Then a rubber wader, worn and frayed at its top, flew over his grandfather's shoulder and smacked the wall beside him.

"See if that one fits."

Answering meekly, Russell said, "Okay. I think it will be good."

It was at least four sizes too large. Pops insisted that it was a perfect fit, however, and slung the other in Russell's direction. He slid the other boot easily on his right foot and looked down, feeling ridiculous. The tops came to his knees and when he attempted to walk, his heels slid, making the boots flap against the wooden floorboards. His mother was still smiling.

"Are they alright, Rusty?" Pops asked as Russell trudged toward the kitchen, relearning the art of walking.

"I think so," Russell lied.

"Good man," Pops responded with an affirmative nod of his sun-spotted head. "Let's move out and leave your mother to get herself settled in."

Russell caught him winking in his mother's direction before Pops put his arm over Russell's shoulder and guided him toward the door, his oversized boots beating a cadence on the floor that matched his mood of restrained concern.

The air had cooled considerably with the declining sun, and Russell breathed it contentedly after his daylong confinement in the sweltering car. He headed across the field along a path that was cut through the center of the tall grass, enjoying a tacit silence usually reserved for those accustomed to spending long hours in each other's company. The stalks of grass rose at least six inches above his head so that he could not see anything beyond the pathway. Russell examined his grandfather with quick peripheral glances while they walked side-by-side toward the far side of the field.

Russell speculated whether his father had possessed the same expressive stare, proud demeanor, and self-assured stride. He had seen only that single photograph of his father years before, but he could not remember if the picture had disclosed any suggestion of these qualities. And now, as Russell searched Pops' features for some link to the missing generation, he could not conjure up the faded black-and-white image that had gazed back at him through the secrets of frozen time.

As they neared the gurgling sounds of a river, Pops broke

the silence and asked him about his school year. Russell told him everything: about his teacher, Mrs. Fitzhenry, with the perpetually stale breath; the bullies from the eighth grade that he avoided during recess; and how he was entertaining the notion of learning to play an instrument for the school band.

"I was always a big fan of the saxophone," Pops shared. "I never had a chance to take lessons though."

"Why not?" asked Russell.

"It was a different time when I was your age. There weren't quite as many opportunities to do different things outside of school."

"That doesn't sound very fun."

"Ah. I think we always managed to make our own fun in a way. So, have you picked an instrument you'd like to try?"

"I had been thinking about the drums."

"Ah, percussion instruments. Definitely a good choice."

"Maybe I'll try the saxophone, though."

Pops did not speak to Russell in the patronizing tones employed by most adults who seemed always to address him as though he were still in diapers. Pops knew instinctively what questions Russell wanted to be asked, and when they stopped beside the slow-moving trickle of the stream, Russell was astonished to discover that he had been speaking incessantly.

"There goes Horatio," he heard his grandfather say as they leaned the shovels against the snarled trunk of the immense oak tree under which they had stopped.

"Who?"

"Horatio . . . watch now."

He pointed up at the sprawling network of branches just as the leaves rustled, and a bird, larger than any Russell could have imagined, burst from its refuge in the shady oak. With languid strokes of its impressive wingspan, the heron floated lazily over the field and disappeared silently into the tall grass where a flittering helix of sparrows lifted above the field in deference to their sizable peer.

Over the next few weeks, Russell would learn that his grandfather could, with impeccable exactitude, predict the daily movements of Horatio on the frequent airborne excursions the enormous bird took from his lodging high in the oak tree.

Russell followed his grandfather down a steep embankment that began at the base of the tree. The instant he saw the trout stream below, he understood the nature of the mission that had brought them to its twisting bank. A beaver dam, a structure he recognized from his science classes, had been expertly erected at an oxbow bend in the river. The wall of entwined branches and tightly packed mud had swollen a segment of murky water closest to the lake and reduced the other side to a snaking roadmap of rivulets in the river's bed.

"This is our mission, Rusty. Right here," Pops pointed to the riverbank. "We need to take apart that beaver dam."

"Wow, it's huge." Russel exclaimed.

"That it is. That's why I need your muscle power."

He stared wide-eyed at his grandfather and then shifted his gaze back to the dam.

"We'll take it a bit at a time, Rusty. It's probably going to take a few days before we have it completely removed. But if we don't get started now, the water will keep building and soon it could flood a big portion of the field."

Russell set to work, first shoveling out the mud wedged inside the dam and then removing the soggy branches. His assignment was to run the branches up the embankment and deposit them underneath the oak tree.

Soon, he was short of breath and mosquitoes nipped angrily at his exposed neck, which he slapped repeatedly. By the time the last remnants of the amber sun had dipped below the distant tree line, the trout stream was again flowing freely. Sweating and smiling, Russell and Pops proudly surveyed their success.

Pops complimented Russell, saying, "You're one heck of a dam buster, Rusty McCreary!" and suggested he come back early in the morning to ensure the beavers hadn't raised the dam again.

Pop asked, "Are you up for rising with the sun?"

Russell nodded.

"We meet on the deck at zero-eight-hundred hours after breakfast tomorrow morning."

They both gathered up the shovels and retraced their steps toward the cottage. Tapered bands of orange sun streaked across the receding indigo of twilight, and the sky metamorphosed into night. They walked slowly, Russell's eyes drinking in the collage of overlapping colors that marked the advent of dusk. The sound of his boots turning up loose stones on the pathway was magnified as the forest became still, the babble of its gossipy meadowlarks dulling before the sharp descent of darkness. The first stars had emerged, announcing the arrival of a saffron crescent moon that was sneaking above the horizon. And from far across the mirrored surface of the lake, a solitary loon issued its forlorn falsetto cry.

As they walked, Pops revealed that for the past three summers, the grass, now plush and emerald, had been crisp and heat-scorched and brown from drought. But this spring's gentle rains had imbued the field with fertile wealth.

On that quiet evening, Russell could not have foreseen the same thing happening to him. This flourishing acreage he would share with his grandfather would stir his spirit and cause it to emerge from its protected enclave of boyhood. He would come to love what the rustic cottage, its remote lake, and its sprawling wilderness represented—nature and its ability to cultivate wonder.

It was this mutual reverence for the grandness of the natural world and their significance in it that enveloped Pops and Russell in that reciprocal admiration that only the very young and the very old can share. Pops introduced Russell to his familiar wilderness, and by doing so, set in motion the awareness that nourishes the human soul. In the span of several weeks, Russell formed an everlasting bond amid the willowy rushes, the harmonies of the wind, and the rippling trout stream. From that summer forward, he would always have a spiritual connection with the tranquil spirit of the North Country.

※

Inside the cottage, Judith, who seldom found time to cook, had managed to concoct a piping stew from leftovers she'd found in the refrigerator.

"This is perfect, Judith!" bellowed Pops. "I can't remember the last time I had a home cooked meal made by someone other than myself. It smells outstanding. I can't wait to taste something other than my own cooking."

"I wouldn't get too hopeful just yet," she laughed. "Russell can attest to the fact that I'm not exactly a gastronomical wizard."

"You're a good cook, Mom," he insisted.

"Oh, but you are fibbing now, young man," Judith mocked. "You're always asking if we can have something outside my usual dish rotation."

He smiled sheepishly. It was true. She alternated regularly between roasted chicken, grilled cheese and baked pasta and he occasionally grumbled to have something different. They did have pizza his mother picked up on the last Friday of every month, so that was always something distinctive to look forward to.

"I believe you are just being extra kind about my culinary skills because your grandfather is here," Judith teased.

"Either way, I'm looking forward to this stew!" Pops chimed. "And I would be willing wager that Rusty here is going to inhale his in a few spoonsful. He worked hard out at the river and I'm sure all that fresh air and dam busting have him famished."

Russell nodded energetically.

He ate in silence, contemplating what adventure might be awaiting them the following morning while Pops and Judith caught up on the family news. Once they had finished eating, Russell slipped over to the fireplace, hoping to extend his participation in the evening further. But he was betrayed by an irrepressible yawn and was immediately ushered into the bedroom at the back of the cabin by his mother.

Outside Russell's bedroom window, a symphony of crickets began tuning for their nightly performance accompanied by throaty bullfrogs. He must have checked the battery-operated alarm clock his mother had set on the dresser a dozen times before he was satisfied that it would ring at seven the next morning. With effort, he managed to remain alert until the adults finally retired for the night. He heard his mother creak onto the sofa bed in the main room of the cabin, and, soon after, the shuffle of Pops outside his room. Dim light flickered through the crack in the door, and he glimpsed his grandfather's elongated shadow gliding across the ceiling. Soon, the muffled sounds of running water reached his ears as he listened to him brushing his teeth. Russell drifted into semi-consciousness, listening to his grandfather's movements as he performed the personalized rituals of a lifetime, preparing for bed.

# 5

Russell awoke, got dressed, and stood on the deck at seven-thirty the following morning, waiting for Pops. He had looked into his grandfather's bedroom before stepping past his sleeping mother, filching a slice of bread, slipping into the oversized rubber waders, and heading outdoors. His grandfather's bed sheets had been unruffled and folded neatly into the bottom corners. He had risen before Russell and was somewhere unknown, though he couldn't have gone far; his old boat of a car was parked idly against the far wall of the cabin.

Then he caught the sound of hammering and an echo that reverberated off the surrounding trees. Cautiously, he followed the noise until he found himself at the back of the cabin.

There was his grandfather, sweat-mist forming on a pair of magnified glasses that slid down his nose, the sleeves of his green plaid shirt rolled to the elbows, and a wood-handled ax hanging from his calloused right hand. He breathed heavily through an expanding smile.

"You're up early, Rusty," he greeted Russell between panting breaths. "Feel like helping me chop some wood?"

"I don't know how," Russell replied, eyeing the glinting metal head of the sharp ax, and envisioning a severed finger.

"I'll do the big pieces, and then I'll show you how to cut the kindling, okay?" He said as he swung the ax in a perfect downward arc, splitting a log that sat on the flattened top of a tree stump. Splinters of wood sprayed in all directions.

After he had cut about a dozen large logs, he waved Russell over to his side and guided his fingers around the smooth handle of the ax. Standing with his back to his grandfather, his hands cupped inside his leathery palms, together they brought the ax down and divided the wood into smaller pieces. Then Russell helped pile them under a tarp against the rear wall of the cabin.

"There sure is a lot of wood here," Russell exclaimed, inspecting rows upon rows of various-sized chunks of wood, from whole logs to slivers of freshly cut timber.

"I'll need almost double this by the time winter comes," Pops mused. "It gets bone-chilling cold up here, and I need the fire going full blast from the time I get out of bed until late into the night. There are a few deep freezes in January and February that keep me indoors for at least a couple of weeks each year."

Russell screwed up his nose and asked, "Why do you stay all winter?"

"It's more beautiful than you can imagine." Pops' eyes sparked by a source of light from deep within.

"It must be kind of scary being alone for that long though."

"Over the years, I've become very comfortable with it, Rusty. I know there are many people who don't like the idea of being isolated, especially when it gets cold. I enjoy every season, and I have Horatio to keep me company too. Most people would say I am content in my own company."

"You must be."

"In the winter months, everything is pure and bright. There's absolutely nothing that can compare to the silence of winter. You can almost hear the clouds scuttling across the sky."

He cocked his head as if listening intently for that distant sound before returning to his description of the coldest months in the north, creating for Russell an image of winter on Teapot Lake so vivid that, despite the coppery folds of summer sunlight that stretched across the beckoning eastern sky, he felt a cold shiver penetrate the base of his spine. Russell could feel the bracing, hollow winds penetrate layers of clothing to touch his skin with winter's frigid chill, witness the snow-laden trees, and hear the cracking of their branches under a crystalline lacquer of ice, gazed across the faultless sheet of opaque white that covered the lake as gusts of snow blew like topsoil across its ashen surface.

Russell realized then that his grandfather was a virtuoso of an indefinable magic, a sorcery that enabled him to compose narratives that spawned visions and ignited the imagination. The inanimate came to life, and the ordinary became spectacular.

Once they had finished piling the wood, he made his way to the front of the cottage. Pops had left a thermos on the deck, which he retrieved before guiding Russell toward the water.

The sun was climbing, and Russell worked himself out of the sweatshirt he had donned in the coolness of his bedroom. He stopped at a sandy segment of the lakeshore where the hollow trunk of an enormous, worn tree had been situated close to the waterline. Following his grandfather's example, he wedged his lower back against the gritty log and crossed his outstretched legs in the sand.

The beach sipped at the tiny waves that made it to the shallows beyond his feet. A steady, tepid breath of wind blew narrow wrinkles across the water's skin. A fly landed on the tip of Russell's boot and walked uneasily across the muddy toe until he flicked it away.

From within the depths of his pants pocket, Pops withdrew a small, Tupperware container of sugar. He unscrewed two plastic cups from the top of the thermos, distributed its contents into even portions of steaming tea, and handed Russell a cup. Russell had never tasted tea before, and when the bitter liquid slid across his tongue, it reminded him of swallowing bath water. His grandfather laughed at his grandson's snarl.

"You can't drink tea without a touch of sugar, Rusty," he cajoled. "It's like eating spaghetti without the sauce, an appalling offense against the taste buds."

Russell held the cup out as Pops deposited a generous heap of sugar from the container into both of their cups and stirred them briefly. He rested the spoon across the Tupperware, leaving bronze stains in the sugar that remained.

They sat undisturbed, admiring the steady pitching motions of the silvery lake, a unified symmetry that gave it the appearance of a massive, self-governing creature. That morning, Pops and Russell began a ceremony that they would reenact each day during the brief time they would share at Teapot Lake, an observance that helped forge a bridge between the many decades between them. Each morning, they would make their way down to the granular shore, recline against the log, and finish a cup of sugar-sweetened tea as daybreak gradually dispersed across the expanse of their woodland. Afterwards, they would cross the field through the swaying grass to the trout stream, where they would unfailingly discover that the beavers had coordinated a nocturnal campaign to resurrect the dam.

During Russell's days at the cottage, he followed this routine with regularity until it was simply a habit. Pops would stand at the bottom of the embankment, shaking his head at the perseverance of Russell's adversaries in the battle of attrition that the dam came to represent. Russell would trudge up the steep bank of the river, transporting the saturated, twisted branches while his grandfather pulled the dam apart.

One morning, the small amount of water that had managed to filter through the dam had created a quagmire in the riverbed. Pops was careful where he stepped, and each time Russell disappeared over the lip of the embankment to unload his cargo of branches, he heard the sucking sounds of his boots in the sloppy sediment and feared that as he returned to the riverbed, he would see only the top of his head disappearing into the gurgling muddy soup.

Pops fixed them both a lunch of toasted tomato sandwiches while Russell's mother lounged on the deck, relaxing for the first time in months. Once they had finished washing and drying the dishes in the humidity of the confined kitchen, Pops vanished into the closet and emerged seconds later with two fishing poles. Russell had never seen a live fish other than the occasional pet store goldfish.

"Uh, I've never really gone fishing before," he confessed to Pops.

"That's what is so perfect about you being here this summer," came his grandfather's immediate reply. "There are so many things you never get to experience in the big city. By the time you go back to Toronto, Rusty, you're going to be a bushcraft expert and a survivalist."

"I hope I can do it."

"Of course, you can!"

Russell started to slide on his colossal rubber boots.

Outside, he watched his grandfather crawl under the deck and, shimmying backward, haul an aluminum canoe onto the grass. Its dented hull reflected the sunlight into his eyes.

Once they had dragged it to the beach, Russell sat in the bow, packaged in a crimson lifejacket that smelled like lake water. Pops placed one foot into the unsteady stern and pushed off in the sand with the other, launching them expertly onto the water. He paddled them around the enormous rock, the canoe rolling with each movement of his arms as he guided it into a hidden bay on the other side of the bluffs. A few fallen pines lay half in the water, their broken masts still clinging to the shore. Tall reeds lined the inner curve of the inlet like a sentry of foot soldiers defending the shoreline. As they approached, they scraped faintly against the hull of the gliding canoe.

Pops slowed them to a standstill in the center of the reeds, and brandishing his fishing pole, demonstrated the art of casting.

"We are going be angling for bass," he stated.

"Is that a type of fish? Are they big?"

"A good-sized bass will be about the length of my forearm."

"Whoa. That's big enough for me! I don't know if I could pull that into the boat on my own."

"Like everything, Rusty, we'll do it together. The best way to learn is to do."

He practiced his casting several times more.

"We'll concentrate on this little bay here. Bass abound in the shallow waters close to shore, where they hide in the vegetation, rocks, or submerged logs."

Pops waited patiently as Russell attempted to secure a wiggling rubber worm on the hook, the sun warming his back through his pale T-shirt.

Most of the afternoon had drifted lazily by, and Russell's shoulder was beginning to ache from the repeated casting action before he caught his only bite. With a triumphant cry, Pops reeled it skillfully into the boat.

At first, Russell didn't want to touch the bass writhing on the end of his grandfather's line. But Pops showed him how to grab it behind the neck, and although its oily flesh felt unusual under fingers that had previously experienced the texture of nothing more exotic than a neighborhood dog, Russell impressed himself by not recoiling while he handled the fish.

After a guarded inspection of the bass, its fixed eyes bulging and mouth sucking unprofitably at the air, his grandfather eased it from his hand and gently placed it back in the water. They drifted out of the reeds and began paddling back to the cottage. Could Russell ever have imagined himself performing such a daring feat during the days before his journey up north? Toronto seemed a world away; he sensed a growing detachment from his life in the city. He felt transformed, liberated, and for the first time, uninhibited by his cautious inclinations.

"It's a sign of true good luck that you caught one your very first time fishing, Rusty."

"That's good. Can we go out again tomorrow and catch more?"

"Of course, we can. With your good fortune we're bound to catch a ton."

They fished off the edge of the lake outside the cabin the following morning, and Russell was ecstatic when he reeled in another catch.

"That's a rainbow trout. Outstanding, Rusty!"

"Is that better than the bass?"

Pops pondered the question. "There is no need to compare. You've already become a skillful angler, and any day you catch any type of fish, it's gonna be a good day."

"Yeah!"

"And if I may opine for just a minute, my dear Rusty, I must admit that I do find the flavor of rainbow trout, well, any trout for that matter, much more pleasing to the palate than bass. Basically, it tastes better."

"Why don't we cook it for dinner?"

"A grand recommendation indeed. I will teach you how to gut it, remove the head and filet a fish. Then we'll have our own little fish fry tasting party!"

That afternoon Russell picked his way carefully through the thicket of evergreens behind the cottage on another unannounced mission. He trailed Pops McCreary, who pushed aside the many branches that obstructed their path as they marked their route on the paper-thin bark of every second or third birch tree with a stub of purple chalk. Insects buzzed around their heads in earnest, appetites whetted by their perspiration. They hiked for what must have been miles, sidestepping the many boulders that appeared to have been dropped arbitrarily by some meteoric downpour as they advanced along the ever-changing gradient of the forest floor.

Soon they emerged from the trees into an open meadow. Around the periphery of this confined stretch of wavering grass and wildflowers were thickets that stood as high as his chest.

Before Russell could ask why they had trekked through the underbrush to this hidden grassland, his grandfather smiled, reading his skepticism, and thrust his arm into one of the bushes. When he pulled it back, his fingers came out stained with the vermilion tincture of raspberry juice.

"We'll pick as many as we can, and when we get back to the cottage, we'll make a mouth-watering raspberry pie for your mom," exclaimed Pops while handing Russell a plastic bag out of his baggy pants pocket which, like an illusionist's black hat, never failed to yield the right thing.

Judith had driven into the nearby hamlet of Burke's Falls to stock up on groceries earlier in the day. When Pops and Russell returned to the cottage, she was sitting at the wobbly table reading a letter that had been delivered to the Burke's Falls post office. When Russell paraded through the front door, proudly flaunting the returns of their hours of labor in the raspberry field, she folded the letter promptly and listened as he relayed his excited account of that afternoon's events.

*

Russell was perched on top of the titanic rock beside the cabin that protruded into the water like an overgrown appendage of the forest. If he craned his neck sideways, he could peer down at the weathered shingles of the cottage roof.

He had ascended the cliff slowly, working his way up the gradual slope of rock by grabbing hold of tree trunks and hoisting himself to the peak. His feet now dangled over the crest where, far below, waves curled around the rocks at the base of the precipice. Like the bristled hairs on a kitten's back, innumerable evergreens were raised on the shadowy swells of distant hilltops across the lake. It had been a full week since Russell and his mother had arrived at Pops,' and he had since contentedly accepted the cottage as his temporary home.

"Does anyone else live on the lake?" Russell asked while scanning the shoreline for signs of life.

"There are two other cabins," his grandfather replied, pointing to a rounded curve of ragged shoreline to his left. "They are both on that bay about a mile inland."

"You can see forever from here," Russell stated.

"Hundreds of years ago, this spot was a lookout point for the natives who lived in these woods," Pops McCreary said, embarking on yet another installment in his ongoing chronicle of the prodigal workings and history of his wilderness domain. "They called it lake *Kaywawamog,* which meant *round.*"

"Round Lake?"

"That's right."

"What were they looking out for?" Russell squinted against the sunlight at his grandfather while chewing on a long sliver of grass.

"Iroquois," he said ominously. "The Huron communities that lived up here were in constant fear of them. The Iroquois were warriors and would often come up from the south and attack Huron villages."

"How would they find them?" It would have required little effort to stay hidden within the outlying jungle of bushland before him.

"The Native peoples of North America in this area could read the network of rivers and lakes around us the way you or I would read a road map. Everything they did was connected to the order of nature. There's nowhere you could have hidden from the Iroquois."

As a seagull squawked below him, Pops paused. It glided along the surface of the shimmering lake and disappeared into a crevice in the cliff wall.

"There would always be a guard standing watch on a high peak like this one, ready to warn his people if he heard the Iroquois war chant and saw the enemy canoes racing across the lake toward him," Pops explained.

As Russell's grandfather continued, he could almost see the painted canoes of the Iroquois approaching the shore, preceded by the eerie dirge that would echo like an omen over the murmurs of the wind.

"I think I would rather be an Iroquois than a Huron, Pops." Russell said. At some point in the week, he had unconsciously begun addressing him in this manner without adding their shared last name.

His grandfather gasped in mock exasperation. "But the Iroquois were fierce and ruthless brutes. The Huron were civilized and peaceful."

"Yeah, but who would want to be afraid of being attacked all the time?" Russell asked. "At least if you were an Iroquois, you wouldn't be scared of anything."

Pops laughed and, in a single motion, swept Russell off the ground and into his arms. He lifted him with alarming ease onto his back and carried him down the incline to the cottage. Russell ducked below an elm branch. Riding on his grandfather's shoulder, he placed a palm over his lips and sounded his best rendition of an Iroquois war chant.

Out of breath as they reached the cabin, Pops announced that he had to drive to South River and would be gone until supper. When Russell asked if he could accompany him, his mother interjected and said she wanted him to stay behind with her. At first, he was hurt that his grandfather, who hadn't left his side for an entire week, didn't come to his defense. When he pleaded with his mother, she shot him a stern look that he intuitively understood as a display of her resolve on the matter. Further discussion would be in vain.

He watched in a mournful mood as Pops peeled off his rubber boots in favor of black loafers and retrieved his keys and wallet from a cluttered shelf above the sink. Russell followed him outside and stood beside his behemoth of a car while the engine coughed. His grandfather rolled down the window and waved him over.

"I need to get some supplies for later. We've got a big night ahead of us." Russell stared at him with a questioning gaze.

"We're going on a stakeout," his grandfather winked. "Over by the river. Tonight, the beavers meet their match. You have to stay behind to make the preparations while I'm out rounding up equipment, okay?"

Russell nodded, his distress eased, knowing he was remaining at the cottage for a special purpose. He listened to his grandfather's last-minute instructions, reciting a mental list to himself before the Oldsmobile rolled out of sight: *sleeping bags, sweaters, plastic containers, and a flashlight.* Russell raced back to the cabin and began a frantic search for these items.

He had gathered together everything but the flashlight when his mother summoned him to the deck. He folded the sweaters into the sleeping bag and searched the closet one last time for Pops' flashlight before scampering onto the deck. Outside, his mother examined him over her glasses before closing the book she'd been immersed in for two days.

"I want to talk to you for a minute, Russell." Her voice conveyed that it was a serious matter. She motioned for him to sit. Russell plopped down and looked up at her as his stomach quivered, certain that some terrible news was forthcoming. "You seem to be enjoying your holiday so far?"

He nodded.

"How do you feel about spending a few days alone with Pops?" she asked.

A week earlier, Russell would have shuddered at the thought. His mother was the only constant in his life, and the prospect of her absence would have been most unthinkable. But he had spent nearly every minute of his days at the cottage with his grandfather, and the prospect of having him all to himself for any number of days was appealing. Remarkably, his mother's question inspired no worrisome response, only anticipation and an almost guilty enthusiasm.

"I think I'd be okay," Russell replied, sparing his mother's feelings by tempering his excitement. "Why? Where are you going?"

"In the spring when I was wrapping up my internship, I applied for positions everywhere I thought I might have a chance at getting hired." She faced him squarely. "The other day I received a letter from London, in England, from a great hospital there. They want to interview me for a permanent position in cardiology."

"Is that hearts?" Russell asked. His mother tended to occasionally employ terms well beyond his eight-year-old vocabulary.

She smiled and nodded. The significance of this announcement escaped Russell's immediate attention. He was preoccupied with thoughts about the next several days, particularly the "stake out" that his grandfather had alluded to earlier.

It wasn't until later that morning that his mother's revelation would coax the inevitable questions simmering in his subconscious all day. A job in London would mean he must forfeit everything he currently relied on, leave his life behind, and adjust to a new home, new school, and new classmates, not to mention a new city. That sense of bubbling anxiety with which he was so well acquainted would creep into his thoughts like an old archenemy, inching closer, threatening a wholesale assault.

He asked her a few questions about London: Where was it? Would it be big like Toronto? However, he only half paid attention to her enthusiastic responses. He assured her that England sounded like it would be okay as he listened for the sounds of Pops' car grumbling toward the cottage.

As Judith returned to reading her book, he told her that he was going for a walk down by the water. Her customary admonishing glance told him to be careful, but there was something unusual in her expression, a masked incredulity. The desire to venture from the cabin on his own for a short while was an unanticipated development for them both. But he had become so comfortable, so pacified by his surroundings, that he felt no hesitation at the thought of being alone for a short while and breaking away from the safe folds of her skirt.

The fact that he had not asked his mother to accompany him registered in the look she gave him. He recognized but could not fully appreciate the composed sadness, which briefly visited the outer fringes of her smile as she patted him on the arm and ushered him to the steps with a wave.

# 6

In the hotel room in downtown Toronto, Russell awakens from a fitful sleep. A dream returns in a choppy jumble. He is in a vast room, empty except for a wooden table upon which sits a pencil and paper. He kneels beside the table and, with the pencil, signs his name repeatedly, like a disobedient student being forced to write repeated lines during after-school detention. He experiments with different slants and scratches, trying to make his signature perfect, but even once he has filled the page with these sundry inscriptions of his name, he examines each, and none seems to be his own. Each scribble looks like a stranger's attempt to impersonate him. Eventually, he runs out of paper, and with great urgency, he charges across the room and continues writing his name on the walls, frantic and obsessed, until even those are filled.

How is it that the sight of his own signature does not become the most abhorrent sight imaginable to him? He signs everything and everyone away from himself. It is his personalized signatures that endorse the disjunctions of his life, the goodbyes, and the sorrowful partings.

Months earlier, Russell put his handwritten authorization to divorce papers dissolving his marriage. And on this trip, he will apply his signature to the notarized papers that will stamp the official end of his mother's life. It's not the least bit extraordinary that he would dream about a room filled with the intrusive sight of his imperfect autograph.

He decides to leave Toronto soon after his business with the lawyer is complete. He plans to rent a car and leave for Teapot Lake first thing the following morning. Maybe tonight he will have dinner in the hotel lounge and then head over to the movie theaters a few blocks north, across from the Eaton Center. He needs to get out of the hotel room and let his mind escape, lose himself momentarily in a movie plot and ward off these difficult thoughts that keep tugging at the threads, pulling him apart. He'll never entirely annul his loneliness. At least soon, he'll be at Teapot Lake, far from the indifferent world, where solitude might prove to be the panacea he requires and not the source of his undoing.

He rolls onto his elbow and reaches over with his other hand, lifting his iPhone from the night table beside his bed. Scrolling past the typical early morning junk mail and spam, he finds another email from Cal near the top of his inbox, boldfaced and marked urgent in capitals. He touches the message and starts reading.

*Need to talk before noon today. There's a BOD meeting this afternoon and I need to discuss a few things with you before it. It can't wait, Russell. Call me as soon as you get this, please.* It was signed *CM*, further conveying his earnestness.

Russell swipes over his calendar. He has a bit of time before he must be at the office of Haplich, Hauz, and Zubnig.

*Will call in 20 minutes,* he writes back hurriedly.

He orders coffee and a bowl of fruit from room service and then showers and dresses before calling Cal. Russell leans back in the chair, takes a deep breath.

"If I didn't know any better, I'd think you're trying to dodge me," Cal answers with a good-natured crack. "How's Toronto?"

"It's been a long time since I've been here, Cal. To be honest, it's hard to digest just how massive the city is now."

"Well, I'm glad you made it up there. I know getting these last few knots tied off with your mother's estate has been hanging out there for quite a while."

"Yeah, that's an understatement, isn't it?" he laughs.

"Seems a bit risky, though. I mean, up there by yourself in the woods. Not my cup of tea."

"I'm looking forward to a bit of time with no distractions. And up until my twenties, I was a real enthusiast."

"Oh, really?"

"Yeah, I used to go canoeing and backpacking all the time. The more remote the better. Somehow as I got older and busier, I just stopped being motivated to do it. Strange."

"And now at your tender age," Morales chides, "you still think you can handle it?"

"I better be able to, or I'll be stuck with nothing but hundreds of miles of forest around me and no one to hear my calls for help."

"Switching subjects, have you seen the latest news on Sarah?" Cal asks, jumping right into news of Datatel.

"No," Russell admits. "I glanced at some headlines this morning but didn't see anything on her or the company."

"Our former CEO and infamous Ms. Westroes is not, as they used to call it, front page material anymore. She did make a headline a little further down screen in the *Wall Street Journal* though."

Russell emits another sigh.

"It appears the latest casualty of her deceptions is true love itself. Apparently, she is officially estranged from Derek. Despite all his public attestations of support for her, they are headed for the matrimonial wrecking yard."

Russell thinks carefully about how to respond. When it comes to Sarah's relationship with Derek, he needs to be judicious with his comments. "Well, Sarah's always been the best at being one maneuver ahead of everyone. Maybe she saw he was going to turn against her since they could end up both facing charges."

"Reading between the lines, she may look to cut some sort of deal and claim that she and Derek were both behind the scheme. Share the punishment," Cal speculates. "The reports state that she and her attorneys have been meeting with the DOJ."

"I guess you're right," Russell states. "True love is the next casualty."

"Agreed, and I read a stat once that twenty percent of CEO's are either narcissists or sociopaths, or something like that."

"I think you safely fell in the eighty percent majority then."

"Ha! Well, I'm glad you put me in the majority on that one!" Cal snorts.

"We've all had a ton of success and grown the company directly because Sarah drives her agenda and never backs down," Russell adds, still feeling the occasional need to acknowledge her redeeming qualities. "I know she's been advised to take a back seat and not create waves until she knows for certain if there's going to be an indictment. But it would be completely unlike her to not respond by fighting everyone to the death."

"Yep. She probably needs to learn that war isn't the only option. Better to have different responses depending on which end of the gun barrel you're looking at. I have to be a hundred percent frank with you, Russell, no matter what moves she makes, I don't see her coming out the other end of this one with anything but a jumpsuit and an extended vacation in at least minimum security."

Russell instinctively knows that Cal is right. Even if she manages to avoid prison, this will damage her deeply and where it matters most to Sarah Westroes—her ability to pursue her career and her public personae.

There is a pause in the conversation. Russell knows this means the tone and subject are imminently about to change.

"Speaking of CEOs," Russell's former boss and mentor starts. "I think you have a pretty good idea why I've been so eager to speak with you."

Russell lets the statement linger.

"The board has asked me to approach you to let you know they are interested in appointing you. They think you're the right person to take the big chair, Russell."

"I suspected this might be coming," Russell sighs. He's been considering how he might address an offer for the CEO. "Listen, Cal. It really is an honor to even be considered for this and I'm grateful that the board and you recognize the contributions I've—"

"You can cut the bullshit with me, Russell," Cal interrupts. "We know each other better than that. It sounds like you're launching into a with-regrets speech."

Russell laughs. "Yeah, you're right. To be honest, a few years ago I would have been asking you to sign the paperwork today and starting tomorrow."

"You've been through the ringer, no one would debate that," Cal says. "I know you probably see a new challenge like this as too much weight after everything you've been through. I warned the board you may see it that way, and who could blame you?"

"Thanks, Cal."

"At the same time, I must admit, it's possible this could be just what you need. Every time I faced a life crisis, I threw myself into a new project and focused on changing my environment. I'm sure a therapist would say it's avoidance, but I always found a new set of goals and circumstances helped me feel like I was steadily improving something around me."

"I can see that, Cal."

The discussion lapses into an awkward silence.

After a moment, Russell says, "It's a lot to process right now. I'm trying to take a bit of a break and walk through some childhood memories while I'm up here. Maybe ground myself in my best summer up north here when I was just a kid. I feel like I owe it to myself to focus on that exclusively. It's hard to try and probe through all the possibilities of taking on the CEO position in parallel."

"Well, and that's where the sticky part comes into play," Cal confesses. "They don't want to wait for an answer. I completely get where you are and why you need this trip and this time. So, I feel like a bit of an asshole even putting time pressure on you."

"Nah, you're just being responsible and conveying the board's offer. I don't take it personally at all . . . not coming from you, Cal."

"They feel it's important to demonstrate to the shareholders that we have a plan. They don't want to appear to be treading water or indecisive in any way," says Cal. "And you're the real deal. You've got the bloodline at Datatel. You're a respected leader in the organization, you've run the biggest, most critical P&Ls at the company and always grow the bottom-line. And you don't crave the limelight, so you don't come with any public image preconceptions."

"I bet that's a big part of the equation," Russell scoffs. "The last thing you and the board want is anyone controversial occupying the C-suite right now."

"I'd love to be able to tell them that you are at least considering it and will have an answer in the next couple of days when I'm at this afternoon's meeting," Cal says, nudging him closer to a commitment.

"I don't see how I can come to a conclusion on it right now. There are so many implications for me personally and for the company, I'm not in the head space to work it all out right now. Which means I'm probably not the right person, right now, correct?"

"You are the right person, Russell. I know it, the board knows it and, I think at any other time, in any other circumstances, you'd see it too."

More seconds of silence ensue.

"I have an idea," Cal finally offers, breaking the stillness of the call. "And this is just between you and me, okay?"

"Of course," Russell answers.

"I haven't talked with the board members about this so I don't even know how they would take it. So don't take it as firm. What if you were to mull it over during the next couple of days and think about accepting on an interim basis? The board would appear to be taking conclusive action in appointing a new leader, you could get some time to see how the role fits. We announce you as interim CEO while the board considers the long-term and gives you a chance to build out the strategy for the next phase of Datatel's growth. Everyone can exit the arrangement gracefully if you determine it really isn't the right time for you."

"You don't think that would seem sort of half-assed?" Russell asks.

"Not at all. It happens all the time. Some might see it as being non-committal in the early days, but that will diminish after the first couple of quarters, especially after you drive the kind of performance and stability I know you would."

Russell thinks it over for a moment. He knows Cal is unlikely to let him go without some form of promise to consider the offer.

"Okay. That's fair. I'll think about whether this could work. I have to caution you that I'm probably leaning toward declining the offer, but I promise to give it some serious consideration and get back to you."

"Deal."

"I'll reach out before the end of the week," Russell commits.

"That works," Cal says. "I've got to run, I'm late for a meeting with the legal team. Now that is probably the real definition of *avoidance*!"

They end the call and Russell quickly checks the time. He'll be late for his appointment with the lawyer if he doesn't leave soon. To no avail, he makes every effort to push any reflection on the discussion with Cal or the CEO opportunity out of his immediate thoughts.

It is one of those times he could use Anna's perspective. He knows exactly what she would have done if they were still together. She would have insisted they open a bottle of wine, sit together in their family room, and deconstruct the decision systematically, breaking it down into its various fragments. Anna always defaulted to the scientific method to solve real life problems or dilemmas. She would walk him through each possible outcome of taking or not taking the CEO role and test several hypothetical scenarios to see if the balance of probability tipped in one direction or another. If anything, he could have relied on her to provide more clarity.

As he walks from the elevator and through the hotel lobby, he is aware of the vacancy that he feels since the knot slipped both with

Anna and, admittedly, in his convoluted relationship with Sarah.

※

In hindsight, Russell can see the mistakes that left him and Anna susceptible to their own collapse, yet a part of him still believes that their marriage could have worked.

He cannot use what happened to their only child as an excuse. Joshua was not the glue that held them together, as children so often become for many couples. It would be much easier for Russell to reconcile himself to the fact of their separation if he could reposition the blame on that tragedy, the chance subtraction of his son from this world, which can be attributed to nothing more than the cruelty of fate. What happened to Joshua is certainly the catalyst of their breakdown, dragging into the light the full accumulation of their inadequacies, but it is not the sole reason behind it.

Together, they should have grown from his loss and strengthened the bonds between them through the memory of their boy. Instead, they allowed their grief to become a wedge between them, forever sundering the very lifeblood of their love for each other.

The first thing that attracted him to Anna was that she possessed a fearlessness that he lacks. He relies on the women in his life for this virtue. Where he wavers, both Anna and his mother forged ahead. And so, when they were a couple, Anna navigated them through the swells while he perched himself on the bow and contemplated the dark billows of life, always scanning for the storms he imagined to be just beyond every horizon.

On many occasions, Russell also guesses that Anna's strength, unlike his mother's, may be less a natural trait than an artificial mechanism that she triggers to disavow her private demons and doubts. Often, she deludes herself into the belief that she can somehow control the events of her life with the same surgical exactness that she applies in her profession. She approaches her existence as something to be shaped and molded by her own self-determination. Where Russell is burdened by fatalism, Anna brazenly and almost desperately disregards anything undermining the notion that it is she alone who regulates the unfolding of her life.

When Joshua was stolen from them, through circumstances they could neither control nor alter, the wall of denial Anna built around her was crushed under an insupportable tonnage of grief. And in the end, the only response she could muster from the powder of her crushed self was unremitting rage.

In the months following the accident, Russell grasped that this anger, the rage that eventually took hold and became the central dynamic of Anna's being, simmered in her for most of her life. She prevailed over a childhood that debilitated her brother and sisters. Now she can do nothing but retaliate with hostility toward an unjust and indifferent world.

She had been tricked into believing that the debts owed to her own personal hell in the years before she fled, first to London and then with Russell to the United States, had been paid in full. She had longed to supply her child with the sheltered upbringing she had been denied. And, when he was killed in a senseless mishap, she not only lamented the possibilities that would never flourish and take form to develop into Joshua's personality, but also became enraged at life itself for denying her the therapeutic effects that nurturing her only child promised.

It was not until their honeymoon that Anna revealed to Russell these stark, inner valleys of pain. It was a hurt that had been dredged during her adolescence by a father who wreaked his own brand of domestic savagery on both his wife and children. Russell had learned very little of her past in the months prior to their wedding. The subject of her family seldom came up during their brief engagement.

He had deduced that her father was the reason she had fled Scotland for London, and that because of her relationship with her family, she preferred to be estranged from them. And later, she had the protection of the Atlantic Ocean between them. She would email her mother occasionally and made a video call with her every year but had no contact with her father or siblings.

At first, Russell had wanted to learn more about Anna's childhood and her reasons for escaping, both to satisfy his curiosity and to know as much as he could about the woman with whom he had fallen in love, but he kept his inquiries to a minimum. Anna did not want to tarnish the happiness of their marriage with stories of her dark past. She promised she would provide him with the unabridged summary after they had been wed.

"I know that one day soon I'll have to tell you about my family and why I left," she said one night when the subject had come up inadvertently. "But it has to be at the right time. Thinking about them makes me sad. I want you to know every detail, Russell, but right now I just want us to enjoy ourselves."

"I can wait," he reassured. "I know enough to know that it won't be easy for you."

She smiled sadly. "You don't know half of it."

It was not until they spent a few days strolling the pink beaches of Bermuda during their honeymoon, far from the daily calamity that came with her internship and demanding medical career, that Anna's mind became unobstructed and focused on what she wanted to say. She felt clear-headed and ready to divulge a secret story that had remained hidden, never revealed, safely stored in the impregnable fortress of her memory.

It happened on a day during the best years of his life with Anna. He can remember every minute, as if by a lapse in the rigid rules of time.

They were on the fifth day of their vacation, glowing in the fresh exhilaration of their newfound status as a married couple. They had gone all out and emptied their bank accounts to stay in one of Bermuda's choice chalets, the Harbor Castle Resort, and it was proving to be worth every dime. It was an enormous country inn, set on a sprawling tract of impossibly manicured lawn, with rows of perfectly shaped hedges that sloped down to where they blended with the sky and the calm, lime-colored ocean surf. The inn was like a castle, regally situated atop its grassy promontory. Adorned with oriental rugs, antique furniture, and ceilings that seemed higher and more ostentatiously painted than the Sistine Chapel, the inn made all its guests feel as if they had mistakenly been selected to enter an unfamiliar world of privilege.

They woke up in their room's four-poster bed that morning, with the breakfast they had pre-ordered waiting for them on their private balcony. After breakfast, they asked the concierge where they might find a secluded beach to spend the afternoon. So far, the uniformed retiree who seemed never to leave the front desk had proven indispensable in providing them with guidance on various day trips. He had a peculiar custom of praising every tourist attraction on the island by proclaiming it to be "seismic." When they had inquired on their first night at the inn about a restaurant they had seen in a travel brochure, he endorsed it, claiming excitedly, "You'll have to sample the seafood bisque, my friends. It's seismic!" The shopping in Hamilton was also 'seismic,' and the countryside coach tour was recommended as 'absolutely seismic.'

On this day, however, their friend, who seemed to be either of East or West Indian descent, went well beyond the typical level of hospitality they had become accustomed to over the past days. They were delighted when he not only drafted them a detailed map leading to a private beach called Buccaneer's Inlet but also secured the rental of a moped and ordered them a special picnic luncheon from the kitchen.

# 7

Buccaneer's Inlet turned out to be a ribbon of coral shoreline that Russell and Anna reached by squeezing between two giant boulders beside a seldom-used roadway roughly four miles from the inn. They spent the entire afternoon alone, listening to the lone lyric of a song dispatched with each breaking wave by the turquoise ocean. They ate their lunch on a blanket, giggling as they declared the salmon pâté, fresh strawberries, and partially chilled Zinfandel to be undeniably seismic.

After lunch, they spent several hours wandering barefoot in the foaming surf. In later years, when Russell would search for warm memories of their time together, they would almost always be culled from the sharp images of this day.

In the months preceding the wedding, Anna had grown her hair to shoulder-length. Since their arrival in Bermuda, the sun had lit the tips into golden ringlets. Her skin had turned a soft bronze, and everything from her flecked green eyes to her graceful fawn-like movements seemed to radiate health and comeliness. But it was the candid delight in her smile during that intoxicating, Pacific afternoon that lent Anna the diaphanous beauty that springs to mind whenever Russell searches for those mental pictures of her likeness.

They left the beach as soon as the sun began to set and decided to stay at the inn for dinner. The restaurant was situated at the back of the colonial house on a two-tiered terrazzo terrace bordered with a waist-high balustrade of flagstone and wrought iron. The pungent salt air rose from the ocean, ascended the impeccable gradient of the lawn, and fused with the teasing aromas that drifted out of the kitchen. Diners were erupting in pockets of laughter, clinking crystal wine goblets above the candelabra or praising the cuisine in hushed whispers around them. Russell and Anna were oblivious to it all, focusing only on one another and on the flawless day they were sharing together. They feasted on canapés of salmon topped with dill cream cheese, garlic sautéed escargots with chanterelle mushrooms, and wild duck that had been braised in a gentle port sauce and sprinkled with juniper berries. Taking their half-finished bottle of wine with them, they left the restaurant soon after dinner.

They decided to go a few blocks to the oceanside. The night was warm, infused with an almost imperceptible drop of silky mist. They walked silently down a darkened street under a motionless canopy of trees; the dimly lit homes monitoring their midnight passage, like sentries providing a reassuring sense of security.

It was one of those rare and unambiguous moments when, looking back, it seems as though time was suspended just for them. As they neared the water's edge, the slow rhythmic sound of the waves began to match the cadence of their steps. They came to the end of the street and the opening to a walking path became visible in the dim light. Their shoulders touched briefly, and Anna's sun-kissed skin felt at once cool and soft. They caught each other's eye and, without vocalizing their intent, continued toward the path.

The outline of gray dogwood bushes could barely be discerned at the edges of the trail as Russell and Anna turned toward the ocean. The water soon became visible through gaps in the foliage. They rounded the curve and were met with an almost surreal scene—the moon, a rich, ginger orb hovered over the water, casting a band of orange fire across the ocean surface to the shoreline. It was as though they were being pulled into this ethereal moment by some inexplicable yet commanding force, as elemental and prevailing as the draw of ocean tides themselves. At that moment, Russell could not have been more profoundly and fully in love.

A short time later, in the quiet of their suite, Russell and Anna lay naked on the majestic bed with the French windows open to a warm breeze, their tired bodies cleansed by the light of a single candle on the bedside table. Anna lay her head across his chest and slept lightly for a few minutes before turning and kissing him gently. He tasted tears on her cheek and pulled back, stroking a loose strand of hair from her face.

"Why are you crying?" Russell whispered.

"I'm just so completely happy," she said softly. "I guess I've always been afraid to believe that I'd ever get here."

"I know you haven't always been able to believe it," Russell said, trying to gauge her expression, "but I promise I'll try to make our future a better place for you."

"You don't have to try, Russell. Just be with me, that's enough. I suppose it's unreasonable for me to keep my past from you any longer, though."

Russell shrugged.

"I've often been a little envious of you, you know," Anna began. She rolled onto her back, and Russell stroked her arm beside him. "Of the fact that you never knew your father. That he's never been a part of your life."

Puzzled, Russell replied, "Sometimes I think it's the most difficult thing I've had to deal with."

"Trust me, if he were anything like my father, you'd prefer your connection with him be limited to a couple of old photographs."

Anna had never gone beyond these caustic statements. Tonight, she would clarify the meaning behind the hard edges of her sarcasm.

"Did he beat you?" Russell finally asked.

"Oh, not me, or my sisters for that matter. It would have been morally reprehensible for him to cuff one of his daughters. Somehow, he seemed to think that smacking his wife or pummeling his son was well within the bounds of decency, though," she said. "No, when it came to Elise and Karen, my older sisters, or myself, he chose to demean us verbally. His lectures could elicit more pain than a thousand bruises. Either way, he managed to damage all of us, physically and psychologically. My brother got it the worst."

Gabe was the oldest of the Doyle children, and his father's preferred target. Nine times out of ten, it was Gabe who ended up with the bruises, regardless of who had originally enraged their father. If one of the girls had failed to clean the living room or empty the cat's litter box, it somehow always came down to Gabe's shortcoming.

"Why the hell don't you keep things in check around here when I'm out?" their father would scream at his son upon coming home in a drunken daze, reeking of booze and finding that some duty had been neglected. "You're the man of the house when I'm not here! I'll not have this place go to pot just because of your incompetence, you hear me? Learn to be a fucking man!"

Then, in an explosion of fury, he would set about to teach his eldest his vision of what manhood entailed, usually with a volley of punches that wouldn't cease until the boy was in tears or Anna's father became too exhausted to continue.

"Why do you think he was so abusive? Just because of the alcohol?"

Anna laughed without a trace of levity.

"Who knows? Probably learned it from his own father. I don't think he had an ideal childhood. His parents were hard-core alcoholics, too. Whenever he drank, which was pretty much all the time, he brought such tension to that house. When he was around, it'd be like tiptoeing across a landmine, trying to circumvent his moods, and never knowing what might trigger his temper."

"That sounds awful. I'm so sorry, Anna."

"It was awful. I think the thing that hurt me the most, though, was the sense of betrayal that arose from his inconsistency. He would go through periods of sobriety, usually no longer than a couple of days, but enough to coax us into believing that maybe he had quit the bottle and things would begin to calm down. When he wasn't drunk, he'd be just like a regular father; he talked to us and joked around, without even recognizing the damage he'd inflicted during his most recent bout. He'd always make these grand promises to stay sober. `I swear, I've touched my last ounce,' I heard him tell my mother over and over."

"But he never quit?" Russell asked, knowing the answer.

Anna just closed her eyes and grunted.

"I don't believe he ever meant to quit. He was devoted to his drink and, to tell you the truth, I think he got a secret thrill out of his maliciousness. I believe he liked to think of himself as the overlord of his own little empire. The pledges he made to stop were just his cruelest forms of mockery. Once he inevitably started in on his next binge, we'd just sit around waiting for the abuse to begin, for him to turn back into the heartless mean bastard that he became."

She paused.

"Usually, he would start with the silent treatment. He'd single one of us out for some minor infraction—like interrupting him or accidentally leaving the lights on in the bathroom—and forbid anyone else in the house to speak to that family member for weeks at a time. We unknowingly developed our own codes and gestures to communicate when he was at home. As he got deeper into it and graduated to hard liquor from beer, the abuse escalated."

Financially and psychologically dependent on her husband, Anna's mother had been incapable of either controlling or fleeing the fierce rage of Jack Doyle. The only periods of peace came when he was at the window and door factory where he had been employed since he was eighteen, the same year the two of them had married.

Over the years, Anna's sisters adapted themselves to their father's ways by learning to assume the role of dispassionate observers.

"I don't hate them for it," Anna explained, lying on her side and plucking imaginary hairs off the pillowcase. "I can understand why they became so numb to the disaster that was acted out in front of them practically every day. After a while, the temptation to shut yourself down and live in denial is too great, especially when my mother's refusal to acknowledge our predicament served as a model. I was different from both of them, though. I found it impossible to dupe myself into considering any of it to be normal or acceptable. I grew up never really knowing either of my sisters because of that difference. They pretended it didn't exist—the secret torments that we all suffered and that defined us—and I was the exact opposite. I couldn't let go of it."

It was through her brother, Gabe, and the gentle ministrations she would routinely provide to him after a session with their father that engendered Anna's calling to medicine. She discovered within herself, through the careful application of soothing salves and the calming words she offered to her eldest sibling, that a nurturing side emerged and helped her to restore some sense of order and harmony to the vestiges of their troubled lives. She became a mender of wounds, both physical and emotional.

"Back in the woodlot, behind our house, there was this enormous tree that Gabe would retreat to after he had beaten him," she said, her voice distant. "I've always been afraid of heights, so I'd usually follow him out to the tree and try to coax him down. Eventually, he'd come down, and I'd sneak him through the backdoor and into my room where I could check the damage our father had caused. I remember this one time, though, when I was twelve and Gabe was almost seventeen. We'd been eating dinner in absolute silence. All of us were tuned in to the undercurrents and sensed that my father was ready to lash out. We sat there just hoping we could make it through the night without an incident. Any sound, from a stomach growling to a fork hitting the floorboards, could make you jump out of your seat. My father broke the silence by telling Gabe to fetch him his fourth or fifth glass of straight Scotch. `Not too much ice, remember,' he ordered."

Anna mimicked her father. As she did so, the lilting timber of her accent was transmuted into something slurred and guttural.

"Gabe went into the kitchen and came back with an empty bottle in his hands and the usual supplicating expression on his face. My father took one look at him and snorted loudly. `You been into my bottle, son?' Gabe didn't deny it. He was far too frightened to say anything in his defense. He just sat back down and stared at his dinner. Without saying a word, my father took the bottle from Gabe's hand and placed it right on his plate, in the middle of his food.

"I remember every detail so clearly. The red-and-white checked tablecloth, the familiar insignias and letters that were embossed on the label of the bottle, sitting there in my brother's mashed potatoes. He waited until everyone but Gabe had finished eating, and my mother and I were clearing off the dishes. Gabe rose to help us, and my father's hand shot out and pushed him back down into his chair. `I asked you a question?' he said. In a quivering voice, Gabe answered, 'The last thing I'd ever want to drink is—' He didn't get a chance to finish the sentence. My father jumped halfway out of his chair, snatched the neck of the bottle, and shattered it against my brother's jaw. The rest of us just stood there and watched, witnessing but not really believing what had just happened. I noticed that Gabe's chin was bleeding just before he sprinted out of the dining room and outside, clutching his hands to his face.

"My father started to go after him but stumbled and instead turned to my mother, slapped her across the cheek, and screamed at her to clean up the mess before he stutter-stepped out the door. I grabbed a napkin off the table and ran after Gabe, with my mother yelling after me to stay out of the view of the Bartletts, the family who lived next door.

"This time, Gabe wouldn't come down from the tree. I begged him from twenty feet below. I could see that the gash under his chin was bad. I started climbing, and he helped me up by telling me exactly which notches to put my feet on, and which branches to grab onto."

"Up there, in his sanctuary of leaves and sturdy branches, he wrapped his arms around my shoulders and held me so tightly that I couldn't breathe. It was a while before I realized he was crying, and it terrified me. He'd never broken down and shed tears before, at least not in my presence. 'Promise me you'll never leave me, Anna. Give me your word. I haven't got anyone but you,' he whispered to me. I told him I'd promise only if he came down and let me clean his chin. He fell asleep weeping on the edge of my mattress. That was the only time I ever saw Gabe cry."

Anna's father used to scold her for the attention she rendered to her older brother, referring to her as Florence Nightingale and throwing coins at her over his morning newspaper, teasing that he'd gladly employ her as Gabe's nurse. Whenever Anna hinted about her aspirations to become a doctor, her father ridiculed her, which in the end only served to galvanize her resolve.

The same pattern of abuse remained until the Doyle children were old enough to move out. Both of Anna's sisters married immediately out of high school. Anna knew that matrimony was simply the most efficient and readily available compromise for them. Their respective grooms were perceived as heroes, delivering them from the house of horrors in which they'd been incarcerated for so long. She went to university in Glasgow to study sciences shortly after her seventeenth birthday, her eyes still set on medical school. To everyone but Anna's disbelief, Gabe remained at home and went to work in the same factory as his father.

"At the time, I practically begged him to leave, to at least move in with a couple of his old schoolmates that he still hung around with," she explained. "But he just said that everything was fine, that he could handle it. I think he stayed to protect my mother. He couldn't leave her to fend for herself."

A long pause ensued before Anna continued. Russell waited, saying nothing because he sensed that there was even more to this sordid tale of woe.

Finally, she said, "The longer he stayed at home for my mother's sake, the more Gabe came to hate her because of it."

It was when Anna was completing her final year of med school that one last catastrophe shattered the already decaying connection she held with her family, when something inside her beloved brother broke down and prompted a pathological border crossing.

"It was all over the national news. Three teenage girls raped over a six-month period in their homes in Fraserburgh, a town close to Aberdeen. People were panicking. There were all sorts of stories in the newspaper about how people had started locking their doors and windows and sleeping with hatchets under their beds. Gabe was arrested shortly after the last attack. His foreman at work had called the police after overhearing a couple of Gabe's coworkers chiding him about his likeness to the artist's sketches of the attacker appearing in the local newspapers. Once he was in custody, Gabe confessed to sexually assaulting another girl who until then had kept the attack to herself. My father's depravity had come full circle. I remember when my mother called me at my dorm to warn me before I saw it on the news. I spent half an hour puking into my sheets. I couldn't use the common washroom at the end of the hall, or everyone would have asked me to explain, not that they didn't find out anyway."

Russell felt her breath in deeply as he lay beside her, stunned and unable to comment. He couldn't imagine learning of such horrible depravities.

"I applied everywhere to finish out my internship far away. I got lucky and was accepted at St. Bart's and left for London that summer. I haven't seen any of them since. I couldn't even bring myself to visit Gabe in prison. On the one hand, I feel so sorry for him. But whenever I think of those poor girls that he attacked and their ruined lives, it just nullifies everything he meant to me. I have to keep forcing myself to remember Gabe as the sweet, sorrowful, frightened boy I held way up in the branches of that tree. That was my brother."

"I don't know what to say," Russell whispered.

"How could you? There's nothing I can say either, other than to acknowledge that it happened and that it is behind me. I take comfort in the fact that it's part of a life that doesn't exist for me any longer, the life I left when I flew out of Glasgow years ago. It's almost as if it belonged to someone else."

In the years of marriage that followed their honeymoon, Russell and Anna never again rummaged through the unsorted miscellany of her years in Scotland. It was the set of unique circumstances—the days spent in each other's company, the beautiful backdrop of Bermuda, the closeness of their bodies, and the tranquilizing warmth of the wine. All of it allowed Anna to lay herself open and expose the crouching, tormented girl that would be forever entombed within her.

In retrospect, Russell realized that he should have persuaded Anna to confront her past, to extricate her child-self from the place of abandonment that was her dark birthright. Without Anna's acknowledgment and healing, he had fallen in love with and married Anna's silhouette, her two-dimensional self that he could behold but neither touch nor heal.

After telling him the full story, Anna cried for a short time, and then fell asleep. Russell got up to blow out the candle and stood for quite a long time at the open door to their balcony. The full moon hovered high above the water, seeming to gaze in admiration at its own elongated reflection in the rolling flux of the ocean. He was aware of Anna's motionless shape in his peripheral vision, and his mind kept returning to her. He was puzzled and felt unsettled by how Anna could live with all she had survived. But most of all, he hurt for her, imagining the shame and helplessness she must have endured throughout the prolonged suffering of her youth.

Anna woke up a few hours before sunrise when Russell crept back onto the bed to join her. As if casually brushing away the heart-wrenching account of her past, she rolled over and tickled him playfully under his ribs. Laughing and trying to wrestle her off of him, Russell told Anna that he loved her.

"How much?" she said, throwing herself onto his chest.

"So much . . . it's seismic!"

In the soft pale of early, pre-dawn shadows, they embraced one another and made love, consciously melting into an intimacy so genuine that Russell's heart ached when he recalled it. If only they had managed to preserve this same awareness, the willing surrender, and tenderness for each other, they might have fared better than they had over the decade of their marriage. Russell's thoughts drifted back to the woman he cried with and caressed in the muted light of that morning as he thought of what might have been.

# 8

A brisk wind had been escalating since noon, and it was now strong enough to bend the pasture grass away from the water. Russell felt tiny stings on his face as he passed through its sharp tips whipping against his skin. An osprey lifted into the open air before him and glided toward a rendezvous with the buffered calm of the forest.

When he reached the shore, the peal of the wind and the commotion of breaking waves amplified into a steady roar. He imagined each wave, swelling and rising, swallowing him whole if he waded into the water. Above the lake, an armada of broken clouds paraded toward the western hills, their destinies driven by the vagaries of the winds.

Russell concentrated on this setting around him, partially to block out contemplating his mother's trip to England and its possible upshot. Every few minutes, he would strain to discern the sound of Pops' car crunching on the gravel driveway. He looked forward to his return.

He stood as close to the lake as he could without getting his feet wet. A twisted and waterlogged branch had been deposited onto the beveled surface of the beach, and it snapped in two when he picked it up. He traced a wandering pattern in the sand with the tip of the branch and stood watch as the waves washed it into obscurity. Although he was acutely aware of his isolation—no boats appeared on the water, and no signs of humanity emerged from the shoreline that ringed the lake—he was untroubled by the solitude. He felt only a momentary sense of humility, and with it, veneration for whatever force had created this wondrous, impermanent scene composed of the sapphire sky, rolling water, and bounteous verdure, to which he was the lone witness. And in this, the first true spiritual glimmer of his young life, he had discovered an inclination that he would carry with him into adulthood—a sense of solace he derived from moments spent alone in places such as this.

As he grew older, he would seek out quiet spots in the woods or unfrequented hilltops in the countryside. Part of his spirit would forever yearn to travel back to this very moment, with the wind pushing his hair back, the sun shimmering off Teapot Lake, and the future as boundless and indefinite as the sky above him.

A rustling noise startled him out of his reverie. He turned to see Pops emerging from the grass and marching across the sand toward him, surprised that the boy had not detected his arrival.

"So, this is where you were hiding. Great place to be off by yourself for a spell," he said, as if he had read Russell's mind. "Here, I brought something for you."

He handed Russell a plain cardboard box, which he tore into immediately. His hands touched something rough and tubular, and he pulled the heavy object to his chest. It was a pair of binoculars. He popped the black plastic covers off the lenses and lifted them to his eyes but saw nothing but a blur of colors.

"Now you'll have a better chance of spotting those Iroquois," Pops winked and then began demonstrating how to increase or decrease the level of magnification. Russell couldn't wait to sit atop his rock and scan the distant shoreline. Just as he was about to thank his grandfather for the gift, Pops stopped suddenly and tapped Russell on the shoulder. He pointed toward the trout stream behind him. "Look, we're just in time to watch Horatio again."

"Thank you, Pops, these are awesome!"

Russell lowered the binoculars in time to see the heron emerge from his palatial oak. With his naked eye, he followed the path of the giant bird for a brief period before adjusting the focus and finding an enlarged Horatio in the lenses.

"Right now, every field mouse is exchanging whispers with every piece of grass, negotiating an agreement to keep hidden for just a few minutes while Horatio circles above them, looking for lunch," Pops explained in a hushed tone as if sharing with Russell the details of a conspiracy. Although he giggled at his grandfather's muse, he marveled at how he could narrate the ceremonies of nature in a way that piqued his interest. Instead of reducing the world around him to cold facts, Pops McCreary elevated it to the level of magic, one that played itself out in front of his eyes daily. Russell kept the binoculars trained on Horatio, who made one sweep across the field and then flew out over the lake while his grandfather's words annotated the bird's every move.

"Horatio's calling down to the water now, requesting that it provide him with some nourishment. And right about now, a fish is swimming along the bottom of the lake that hears his call and is climbing to the surface. Can you see the way Horatio is circling that one spot? He's thanking the fish for its sacrifice, and the fish is letting the sun sparkle off his back so that Horatio knows exactly where to dive. Watch now—"

The heron seemed to stop in mid-flight for a moment before it dove toward the water and disappeared below the surface without even a splash. A split second later, he reappeared with a thin, silvery fish wriggling in his beak. Russell watched through his binoculars with a mixture of horror and wonder as Horatio snapped his head back and swallowed the fish whole. He then lifted himself off the water and flew unhurriedly back to his private lodging in the oak tree.

The heron's exhibition, punctuated by his grandfather's erudite narration, would be anchored forever in Russell's memory as an enduring parable for life itself. It had opened his eyes to how nature's inescapable workings could be at once heartbreaking and awe-inspiring. In a way, it had prepared him for what Pops would tell him next.

"Are you ready for the stakeout tonight?" his grandfather asked as they turned together and walked along the sandy shore.

"I think so," Russell replied.

"We just can't let them continue to build up the dam like that, Rusty." He stopped and faced Russell, looking down directly into his eyes. "If they did, the field would become so flooded that it would start killing off the grass and the animals that live in this green pasture. Every time they build the dam up again, it threatens all the wildlife around the river, including Horatio and all the mice and insects that live in the grass. Sometimes, the only option you have is to eliminate the threat by getting rid of what's causing it."

"You mean killing them?" Russell blurted.

"Unfortunately, it's the only thing we can do. I bought some bullets when I was in town. I'm going to need to clean my rifle. Tonight, we'll sit down by the river and wait for them to come out of the dam. You'll have to be my lookout, Rusty. We'll probably be up pretty late, and I'm so glad I have your help."

Russell nodded, and Pops tussled his hair as they resumed walking.

"Will I need the binoculars?" Russell asked.

"I don't know if they'll do you much good at midnight," he laughed, "but bring them just in case. You never can be too prepared."

The idea of staying up long past his usual summer bedtime of ten o'clock was exciting enough without the added thrill of being his grandfather's lookout on the stakeout. But his enthusiasm was tempered by the thought of shooting the beavers, regardless of how necessary it might be. Russell couldn't reconcile himself to the idea of killing anything, let alone his worthy antagonists. Their crafty dam building had produced so many enjoyable mornings for him and his grandfather. However, he trusted that his Pops knew how best to deal with the dilemma, so he said nothing to him that would reveal his inner turmoil. Silently, though, he prayed that, on this night, the beavers would stay far away from the trout stream.

Later that evening, as the forest outside the cabin window

darkened, Pops and Russell loaded a pack with the gear they had gathered earlier in the day. Russell's mother had been busy preparing for her trip overseas and her interview at St. Bartholomew's. She would leave before dawn to drive back to Toronto, where she would board a mid-afternoon flight to London.

Before Pops and Russell left for the trout stream, she gave them her standard instructions to be careful, and this time added, "No wandering off unless your grandfather is with you, understood?"

Once they agreed, she went to bed in Russell's room so that they would not disturb her upon their late return.

Outside, a slight chill permeated the night air. The shrill music of what sounded like a hundred thousand frogs greeted them as they neared the trout stream in the dark. Pops swung the flashlight beam along the pathway while Russell held his hand and walked behind him. Slung across his shoulder was the rifle Russell had hoped he wouldn't bring. Russell carried a backpack that held two lightweight folding chairs and their sleeping bags.

Having never been in such a densely forested location at this late hour before, he felt a trickle of fright ripple through him when he turned his head and, instead of identifying the familiar shapes of the grass, saw nothing but a dense wall of pitch black. He breathed a heavy sigh of relief when he arrived at the base of the oak tree where they began setting up for the night.

For the first hour, they sat on their chairs with the sleeping bags draped across their legs and drank water-weakened tea from a thermos that was stationed on the ground between them. Pops' rifle sat on his lap, but Russell consistently forced his eyes away from it. Each time he heard a tiny splash from the river or the sound of a twig breaking, he arched his spine and peered down toward the river while he trained the flashlight on the dam. Although they repeated this process many times, it was midnight before they spotted one of the beavers.

They had been whispering, talking about the wolves that Russell's grandfather sometimes heard baying at the star-glittered night sky on cold winter nights when something agitated the weeds at the far side of the river. Hair stood on the back of Russell's neck as he swung the flashlight beam just in time to see the glistening fur of an enormous beaver as it slid into the water with a branch between its teeth.

"Do you see him?" Pops asked in a hushed voice as he stood and positioned the rifle against his shoulder.

"I'm not sure," Russell whispered back. "Maybe it's a raccoon."

In the darkness, the penumbra of his grandfather's shadowy figure froze for a brief instant, and Russell could tell that he had turned back to look at him. Then, he again faced the trout stream and took careful aim at the beaver as Russell tried to follow it with the flashlight. The swimming animal alerted to their presence.

Before Pops McCreary could fire off a round, Russell heard a thunderous crack as the beaver smacked its tail violently against the water and disappeared into the murky water.

"He must have heard our hearts beating or saw the flashlight beam," Pops said as he returned to his chair and placed the rifle across his lap once again.

Russell could read the hint of disappointment in his tone but couldn't bring himself to share in it. He couldn't reveal that he was privately pleased that the beaver had slipped away, unharmed. And now that he had witnessed the animal swimming unsuspectingly toward its fortified shelter, the thought of ending its life became unthinkable. Russell began speaking to his grandfather in a slightly amplified whisper and shifted in his chair sporadically in the hopes of covertly forewarning their quarry that danger was at hand.

"I doubt we'll see any more of them tonight," Pops said.

🌿

The combination of the cool night air, the tension uncoiling its fist from his heart, and the late hour made Russell's eyes suddenly heavy. He tilted his head as far back as it would go, observing the sky through an opening in the canopy of the forest. The stars blinked with the brightness of diamonds set against the black velvet of night. He had never known that so many stars could be found in the night sky. At home, in Toronto, minimal light from only the brightest usually managed to break through the nimbus of city lights. But there, in the north, with no manufactured light to interfere, Russell had the feeling that if his arm were just slightly longer, he could reach up and swipe a handful from the heavens without anyone taking notice.

"There must be a million stars in that spot," he said to his grandfather, pointing to the nebula that marked the source of the Milky Way. "Maybe trillions."

"There are more than you and I could count in a lifetime. Every time I find myself out on a clear night like this, I think of the sky I once saw in the middle of the Atlantic Ocean."

Russell studied his face through the dim light, not knowing if he was about to embark on one of his mythical tales. However, he quickly determined by his expression that his memory was transporting him back to a bygone season in his life. Russell waited patiently for him to continue.

"I should have been terrified," he said, shaking his head. "I was on a battleship heading to Europe for the war. But I was only a young man and wasn't even thinking about the ordeal that lay waiting for me overseas. I remember that there had been a wicked storm during the day that had broken up just as evening fell. Even though I was exhausted from the rolling and pitching of the ship, I couldn't sleep that night, and I climbed up to the deck at about two in the morning and took in the salty sea air. It was so dark that I couldn't even see to the end of the ship, and I was completely alone. No matter which direction I looked, I couldn't tell where the ocean ended and the sky began. It was the most exquisite sight I think I'll ever see. The stars stretched above me from horizon to horizon and reflected so perfectly off the water that it seemed as though we had left the earth and were floating through the galaxies. I've never since experienced anything that could fill me with such an extraordinary feeling as on that night. I wasn't just a person looking up at the constellations. I was a part of the universe."

Listening to his grandfather's faraway words only added to Russell's already sleepy state. He was certain that he had plodded back to the cottage soon after his grandfather's reminiscence. He must have been steered through a thickening cloud of fatigue by Pops' guiding hands because when he awoke in the early morning hours, he had no idea when or how he had arrived at the pull-out sofa bed.

He did, however, remember how he had been woken from his sleep. He had been dreaming a cryptic sequence of invasive images—enormous beavers slinking into the ocean, and shooting stars that turned suddenly into whistling bullets that were just as quickly transformed into a swarm of birds circling overhead. As he hovered in semi-consciousness, his mind eventually settled on his mother's trip to England.

Having awakened in a somewhat agitated mental state, Russell found it impossible to annul the anxiety that had been hatched in his dream world. He began to imagine what his life would be like if his mother and he did, in fact, move across the ocean all the way to England. And his imagination foretold troubling scenarios. He visualized a schoolyard overrun with bullies and indifferent peers whose circles he couldn't break into. He saw interminable hours spent at home alone while his mother worked the long hours typical of her profession. He pictured a neighborhood too dangerous and hostile to explore on his bicycle. Finally, the procession of foreboding scenes became too much for him to bear, and he slipped hurriedly from the sofa bed in the living room and tiptoed to where his mother was sleeping.

She stuttered awake once he had given her shoulder a slight shake. Rolling toward him, she cleared her throat and asked, "Is everything okay?"

"Couldn't sleep," he whispered.

His mother understood immediately.

"What's bothering you, Russell?"

"If we go to London," he paused to make sure she hadn't drifted back to sleep, "do you think Pops could come with us?"

She propped a pillow against the wall and sat up.

"Do you think your grandfather would want to come with us? I think he's pretty content up here at the lake, don't you?"

Russell shrugged, knowing she was right.

"Don't concern yourself too much with London, Russell. There's absolutely no sense in worrying about things you have no control over. Just try to enjoy the rest of your summer. And remember, there's nothing stopping you from coming back up here next year."

His mother always seemed to have indisputable answers. However, even at his young age, Russell understood that there were only a finite number of summers that would be available for Pops and him to share. Nonetheless, the thought of returning to the cottage next summer gave rise to a faint trace of optimism.

"You think he ever gets lonely up here?" Russell asked after a moment.

"I think everyone gets lonely sometimes," his mother replied, "whether you're surrounded by people or living alone in a cabin. I guess most people couldn't live all by themselves up here without going a little stir crazy, but your Pops McCreary is a rare breed. He's more at home in the bush than he would be in any city. When he was about your age, his father bought this land, and their family would use the cabin as a summer home. Having you up here has been good for him. I can tell it makes him think of the times he and his father spent up here every summer."

Russell's mother slid back under the sheets while she spoke, indicating that it was time for their conversation to end.

"His life hasn't been easy, by any means. I think living at the cabin gives your grandfather the peace of mind he didn't have throughout most of his years."

Although Russell was curious to learn what she meant by this, a surge of drowsiness rolled up on him, and he was forced to postpone his inquiry. It would be years before he would cull the answers from his mother through a slow exhumation of facts and the many conversations they would have about his grandfather. And he would come to understand why his mother didn't burden him that night with the details of Pops' past tribulations.

In the time they had spent together, Russell had come to admire Pops McCreary's carefree spirit and demeanor. But he had not always been the lighthearted man with whom Russell had shared most of his summer. Adversity had exacted its toll on him. Over the years, Russell would be able to chisel a full and accurate portrait of his grandfather from his mother's memories.

John McCreary's childhood years had been mostly idyllic. Born into a well-to-do family that didn't lose its assets until the early years of the Depression, his first years in Canada were filled with prosperity and comfort. The younger of two children, he grew up sheltered and provided for by both his parents and his older brother, William. At an early age, Russell's family recognized that his grandfather, John Robert McCreary, had a gift for storytelling. He could hold almost anyone, from children his own age to adults fifty years his senior, in rapt attention when parlaying a tale composed amid the proving grounds of his unbridled imagination. So impressed were John's parents with his talent that they sent him to a secondary school in Montreal that specialized in creative writing and the dramatic arts, convinced that their son would become an author or playwright. Unfortunately, their hopes for John failed to actualize. In 1918, brothers John and William became soldiers.

According to Judith, who would wait until he was an adult himself before passing on these particulars, William had felt but one duty in going overseas to fight—to protect his younger brother from harm. He made certain that he and John were inducted into the same regiment so that he could keep close watch over him as he always had. Near the end of their tour of duty, William, who always made sure that he marched at least ten paces ahead of his younger brother, stepped on a land mine and was killed instantly.

When John McCreary returned from Europe some months after his brother's death, he was in a state of grief so acute that he had to be institutionalized. He would never fully recover from the millstone of blame he bore for William's death. By the time he was released from a veteran's hospital, the brilliant writing career that had once awaited him had been smothered by sorrow. Such it was for so many soldiers who had returned from the battlegrounds of the First World War.

On a Saturday in August 1926, John McCreary stopped at a small used bookstore nestled between a department store and a hotel in downtown Toronto. There he met his future wife, Nancy Wetherton, who was working as a clerk. Nancy had witnessed the emotional demise of her cousin upon his return from the war and immediately recognized the hurt festering deep within John. Ultimately, it was her compassion and tenderness that would lead John through the labyrinth of his atrophied spirit. They married after a short courtship and eventually had two sons, Russell's father, Terence, and his Uncle Malcolm.

The Depression took its toll on John and Nancy's family. During the 1930s, before John was hired back to the armed forces as a military trainer at the outset of the Second World War, the abyss of emotional despair beset him once again. Barely surviving, he and Nancy grappled with the uncertainties that invariably accompany economic hardship, worries about having enough food to sustain their family, struggles with menial jobs to pay the rent, and stresses about their two young sons during giftless Christmas seasons.

Later, after Russell's father, Terence, and Nana McCreary had passed away, John McCreary came to live at the cabin. He once said to Russell's mother that he couldn't bear the idea of wasting away in some small apartment in Toronto, surrounded by trinkets and keepsakes that could only remind him of the past. At the lake, he could maintain an armistice with the past and push back the bleak memories that threatened to close in around him.

Of course, in the time Russell knew Pops, he could see none of these things. The myopia of childhood impaired his ability to see the hardships that had marked their passage in the deep grooves of his face, to recognize the injuries that he carried behind his cheerful grin, or to foresee the legacy he would leave Russell. He could not know that one day, he, like his grandfather, would attempt to flee from his grief by returning to the more edifying memories that abided at Teapot Lake.

---

Russell sat on the bed, growing tired at his mother's side until her breathing became slow and protracted, and he knew she had fallen asleep again. Then he slid onto the cool floor and returned to the darkened main room of the cabin. He lay awake under the warm comforter for a long time.

When he woke, it was almost noon. His mother had left hours before, and Pops was sitting at the small metal table. He was nursing a steaming cup of tea and shuffling a deck of cards. Russell rubbed his eyes and sat up on the sofa bed. The springs deep within the mattress popped and squealed as soon as he shifted his weight.

Noticing that Russell had finally come to life, his grandfather looked up from his cards and smiled.

"Always have to keep a deck of cards handy for days like this one," he said and tilted his head in the direction of the window.

Until now, Russell hadn't heard the rain drumming on the roof. A steady drizzle of water streamed down the filmy face of the bay window. The trees outside the cabin sagged toward the ground, their boughs heavy and drenched, and the rain dripped off every leaf and pine needle and formed cloudy puddles on the ground. The lake was the color of milk under a sky filled with clouds.

Russell played cards with his grandfather for most of the afternoon. Pops taught him the basics of poker, but he beat Russell on almost every hand. With a great amount of affection, he attempted to show Russell how to maintain an expressionless, stoic stare that he called his "poker face." However, Russell's attempts to emulate him resulted in nothing more than giggles from both. It was finally agreed that Russell's poker face needed practice.

Later, as the rain subsided, Russell gathered what raspberries remained from their outing two days before and, after mashing them with a fork, spread the puree onto slices of bread and polished off an entire loaf in less than twenty minutes.

Just as he thought the entire day would pass without an opportunity to head outdoors, the consistent pattering on the roof began to slow to a sluggish drizzle, and they decided to go for a hike. Pops found a yellow rain slicker for Russell that was at least four sizes too large. He rolled up the sleeves and helped him into it and laughed with unconcealed glee at the sight of Russell, his oversized boots hidden under an equally oversized slicker that fell to his ankles.

They walked for an hour along the dirt road that led back toward South River. Russell thought of his mother and himself passing through that little crossroads town when they first ventured to the cabin. That now seemed like a distant memory. Although it had been only two-and-a-half weeks since he last traveled this roadway, it seemed that he had been at the lake for months.

Contentedly, he took hold of the rubber sleeve of Pops' slicker and sauntered along the rain-drenched road at his side.

"Shoulders back, soldier!" Pops roared playfully.

Russell imagined that, with that deep voice, Pops could make the starlings that darted around the forest snap to attention on the nearest branch.

"We have a long march ahead of us. Hup-two, hup-two . . ."

Following his lead, Russell did his best to march up the roadway in his enormous boots. The sun had broken through the parting clouds, and the air was muggy and pressing with the leftover moisture. Buzzing insects could be heard throughout the forest, which seemed to be coming back to life in the wake of the passing downpour. A pair of dragonflies that had settled on the gravel in front of them danced away as they advanced on their resting spot. The interlaced grasses and ferns that sprouted from the ground were sturdy and swollen with renewed vigor. From high above, the branches released droplets of rainwater on them as they passed beneath them, remnants from the afternoon showers.

After a mile or so of following the roadway, they veered into the underbrush on a worn and muddy footpath. The path was overgrown with the rich vegetation of the forest, and Russell felt wet tickles on his face as he walked deeper into the woods. Before long, they arrived at a hidden inlet at the westernmost tip of Teapot Lake where the water was shallow and unruffled by the breeze.

"Soldier!" Pops bellowed.

"Yes, sir," Russell said, playing along.

"I can't HEAR you!"

Laughing, Russell shouted, "Yes, SIR!"

Pops ordered Russell to get into the water as quickly as possible. Russell hurriedly removed his yellow slicker and struggled with his boots as his grandfather quickly disrobed and raced him to be the first one in the water. The skin on his torso was so white it appeared almost translucent, and it was loose and wrinkled, like a sheet of paper that had been crinkled into a ball and then opened up and pressed flat again. The veins in his legs were a map of blue highways, threaded from the backs of his knees to his ankles. For a moment, the sight of this aged body surprised Russell; he had, over the last couple of weeks, almost forgotten that his grandfather was elderly.

Russell ran a few feet into the lake, the muddy bottom oozing between his toes, with his grandfather close at his heels and splashing him. Once the water had come to his waist, he dove headfirst into it and came up splashing back at him.

They swam and splashed around in the cool water for almost an hour before lying on a flat rock to dry off under the sun. The few clouds that had lingered into the late afternoon reflected off the still water of the inlet. Occasionally, the sun would disappear behind them, and their shadows would glide across the lake as though some species of bird of unimaginable size and proportion were soaring above them.

Pops directed Russell's attention toward a point on the far side of the lake and said, "That's where we'll be heading for a little overnight excursion soon."

"Why?"

"We're going on an adventure, Rusty. An out-trip," he explained, his voice sounding ominous. "We're taking the canoe down a wild river that starts at that point and leads to Manitou Lake. It's a dangerous route, but that river has met its match in us, Rusty. Once we've made it to Manitou Lake, where the river ends about three miles downstream, we'll set up camp and spend the night on Hunter's Island, roughing it."

The hills across the lake seemed foreboding and feral, and he couldn't help but think of a geography lesson film that showed an expedition down the Amazon River, where exotic animals and insects kept the crew on alert. He imagined this nameless river as a northern replica of those uncharted parts of the mighty Amazon.

He waded through the water and dressed efficiently, flapping his arms to keep the mosquitoes and black flies at bay. The walk back to the cabin was slow. The sunlight had been rinsed from the roadway by the shade of late afternoon, and the air had cooled considerably. They spoke almost exclusively of the upcoming canoe trip, his grandfather answering a barrage of questions with careful consideration. When Russell asked whether bears existed on Hunter's Island, his grandfather said he didn't know, but added that if they built a good campfire, they were certain to stay away from them.

"Are there any whitewater rapids on the river?"

"There are!"

Russell immediately stopped in his tracks, eyes wide. "Are you serious?"

"Yes, Rusty," his grandfather replied, "but don't worry, we will go around them."

"How?" Russell asked, trying to picture how they would canoe around a raging torrent of white river.

"We're going to portage."

"We're going to what?"

"Portage," he repeated. "It means we are going to put the canoe over our heads, on our shoulders, and walk through the woods around the rapids."

"That sounds like it will be pretty hard."

At that, Pops suggested Russell do some push-ups over the next couple of days to ready himself for the grueling trip. When Russell asked if they should bring extra food with them, in case they didn't catch any fish or it rained, his grandfather proclaimed that the boy's thinking proved that he was a natural camper, planning for every eventuality and taking all necessary precautions.

While Pops prepared supper, Russell spent a few moments alone on the deck, scrutinizing the far side of the lake through his binoculars. He couldn't locate the mouth of the river that would take them to Manitou Lake. He ate his dinner that night with a brisk fire behind him, built to vanquish the cabin's moist chill. Between mouthfuls of spaghetti, he compiled a list of gear he would need on the camping trip, with his grandfather keeping record on a pad of yellow paper.

Later, when the sun had dropped below the horizon and the trees appeared as one-dimensional shadows, they left the cottage once again and made their way across the field to wait for the beavers. The night air was sultry and heavy, hovering over the field and mixing with the damp scent of their perspiration. They walked to the riverbank and sat in the lawn chairs that had been left there overnight. Looking into the clearing above him, Russell noticed that tonight, the stars were barely visible beyond the hazy mist lingering above the treetops.

It was late in the evening before one of the beavers emerged. Russell had been scanning the riverbed with the flashlight, convinced that his presence on the previous night had warned off the animals for good. Suddenly, he heard the sharp click of Pops' gun being cocked, cutting through the dead silence of midnight.

"There . . . over to the left . . . right there," he whispered. He was crouched low with the rifle positioned against his shoulder, inching toward the river. "Keep the light on him."

With every muscle in Russell's stomach stiffening, he found the beaver in the flashlight beam. The huge animal was crawling along the shoreline, a small branch wedged between its teeth. The forest seemed to have become motionless, as though it were itself quieted into the same paralysis of fear that gripped his heart. The only sounds that could be heard were those of the beaver brushing through the weeds that lined the riverbank. Here was the culmination of two nights of patience, his quarry lined up perfectly in the crosshairs. His grandfather became still as he aimed the rifle at the lumbering target, and Russell's mortification about what was about to occur became complete.

"Hold it steady," his grandfather instructed. "I think we've got him."

Russell replied with a shaky "Okay."

It may have been the tremulous wavering of his voice or something more profound—perhaps an unexpressed but trusted recognition between he and his grandfather—but somehow, his grandfather sensed his dismay. He stopped short, just as it appeared he was ready to pull the trigger. He did not look back at Russell as he let the rifle fall to his side. At that moment, Russell could have thrown his arms around his waist. Instead, he sat in a stupefied state of relief, unable to move. He still had the flashlight leveled at the beaver, and his grandfather stood in the same spot observing it for what seemed like a long time.

Slowly, he made his way back to Russell's side, and without a word passing between them, they sat together and watched as their pardoned victim slid quietly into the water and swam downriver toward the dam.

# 9

Over the course of that one summer with Pops McCreary, Russell enjoyed a taste of what life with a father might have been like, a bittersweet sip from the cup of the impossible. Russell's grandfather was the only key to what he has always timidly regarded as the secret fraternity of manhood, and when he dwells on his memory too intensely, he is overcome with a peculiar sadness that cannot be dispelled.

During that summer on the lake, Russell had tried only once to gain some knowledge of his own father. During a hike on a particularly rainy afternoon, he asked Pops about his father and what he had been like. Pops sat silent as tears had formed in the corners of his eyes.

"He was a terrific son, and he would have been a terrific father, Rusty," was all he said, his voice cracking. Russell had never again broached the subject, although he was aching to know more. The thought of his grandfather hurting was too much.

Lately, though, as with a great many things, Russell's perspective softened. He attempts to rescue every happy moment or pleasant reminiscence that he can pull from the rapids of his childhood memories, hoping that, with enough of them, he can piece together some sense of his identity to rebuild himself out of the debris of his past.

Since being back in Toronto, recollections of his mother have been washing over him like waves, crossing a great ocean of time. No surprise. He knew that by returning here, he would be subjecting himself to a difficult assignment in facing those waves. It's mainly why he procrastinated for so long to make this trip.

Russell is escorted into the lavishly appointed office of Tony Haplich Jr. He sits for only a few seconds before the lawyer greets him and guides him across the hardwood floors of the waiting area and into his office at nine o'clock sharp. Once seated comfortably, Tony wastes little time before producing an original copy of Judith's will. The document is old and thinning, but the familiar loops and curves of his mother's exquisitely refined handwriting grace the page.

"Penmanship is a reflection of the personality behind it," Russell's mother would often say, helping him with his homework at the kitchen table in their apartment where, as a child, he had just begun learning to write. On the weekends, they would always work together in that corner of the kitchen, on an old sewing machine table that wobbled if they neglected to insert a folded piece of cardboard under one leg. Without variation, she insisted on writing everything longhand, from her medical reports to her own will and testament. No word processors, no typewriters. They left no personal mark on what was being written, she maintained. Russell remembered his mother's patient attempts to assist him in amending the wandering and crowded scrawl of his own imperfect script, something he never quite managed to master.

"Don't hold the pencil so stiffly," she would instruct, her breath tickling the back of his neck as she leaned over his shoulder to check his work. "You can't hold onto anything too tightly, Russell, even your pencil. Just keep at it. You're getting better."

Regardless of what task Russell was attempting, perfecting his handwriting, learning to play the oboe, or simply peeling potatoes before dinner, his mother always approached him on the most favorable side of encouragement. That he never seemed to be satisfied with his own performance, regardless of how trivial the endeavor, didn't dampen her efforts to inspire him. In her eyes, it was the improvement that counted, the incremental steps toward perfection than the actual reaching of it.

"From all I've heard, your mother was one in a million," Haplich, Jr. says as he shuffles through some papers on his desk. "My father used to say that he wished all of his clients were as thorough as she was. Said he would have been left without any work to do himself."

Russell smiles and adds that it sounds as if he knew her well.

"What is your father doing these days?" Russell asks.

"Retired. Spends his summers up here visiting his kids and winters down in Belize. He seems to be enjoying himself. Of course, who wouldn't under those harsh conditions?" Haplich, Jr. says with a snort. "Listen, I'm sorry if I sounded a little overzealous on the phone. It's just that the last few estate closures I've overseen have ended up in court, and I wanted to make sure we didn't time out on closing this up."

Russell assures him that it was nothing warranting an apology.

"If you decide to sell the land up north, don't hesitate to call me. I'll gladly handle the sale for you from here," he offers. His hands turn to the ceiling for a moment, as if he were holding in his fingers a priceless glass orb. "Cottage country is starting to expand pretty far north, but that land is still pretty remote. I'm sure we could find a buyer eventually though, maybe someone who wants the roughing it experience, or maybe someone who wants to use it as a fishing or hunting camp."

"Thanks. I've taken a leave of absence for now. I'm thinking of heading up to the lake and staying there for a bit . . . just playing it by ear. I'll see how I feel about selling when it's closer to the end of the year."

"I wanted to offer you my condolences . . . ummm . . . regarding your son. My father told me about it the last time we spoke."

Russell nods his thanks without saying a word.

At that point, the lawyer, whom Russell has judged to be about five years older than himself from the white that flecks his high hairline, hesitates almost ceremoniously before pointing out where he should sign to conclude the paperwork. He swallows back his discomfort at the sight of his mother's words and quickly acknowledges everything laid out in the document by hurriedly adding his own name to the bottom of it.

It is then that he notices the folds of framed photographs covering the mahogany surface of a little hutch beside the lawyer's desk, the largest of which is a shot of him and his wife with their two daughters, smiling from a living room sofa. The perfect family. Russell knew that out of simple courtesy, he should ask the man about his daughters, but he can't bring himself to do it. Numb, he keeps glancing at the picture until the meeting ends.

His business with the law firm concluded, Russell walks toward Claremont Street, just west of downtown Toronto and hesitates before continuing to the upper story apartment where he lived for the first eight years of his life. The street looks different; the undeveloped saplings that had once lined the front lawns have bloomed into voluptuous trees, providing the neighborhood with an imperturbable, shady calm. The elementary school on the corner has closed for the summer and the playground beside it is vacant, attended only by a few gulls that sit atop the slide and pick nervously at their plumage. He wants to walk to the playground and swing on the hanging tire to reawaken the youthful spirits of the schoolyard.

He meanders down the row of rust-colored brickwork homes until he can stand outside the one that once housed him and his mother. He had even considered ringing the doorbell and asking the current inhabitants if he may wander around the apartment for a few moments. But he can't bring himself to continue beyond the corner on which he is rooted. The protective and faint-hearted part of him won't permit him to proceed into these depths of remembrance. Suddenly, he is sharply aware of the sweat that is causing his shirt to cling to his back, and the jittery lather descending into his stomach. He is all at once so unsettled that he turns quickly and almost runs back down the street toward the busy intersection of College and Bathurst.

Just beyond Bathurst, Russell finds that the Venus Café has somehow survived the reorganizations and vagaries of the local economy. It's been decades since he has passed along this street and the café where he and his mother would eat breakfast every Sunday morning. He's pleased to see that, unlike several other personal landmarks, this establishment alone has withstood the punishments of the world outside its dusty windows.

He swings the door open, and a bell chimes to announce his entry. It's as though he has stepped instantly back in time. The same tattered leather stools line the Formica breakfast bar, behind which a surprising number of cooks and wait staff jockey and pirouette around the stovetops, yelling orders to each other. The smells of cooking oil and coffee greet him as he makes his way down the narrow corridor of patrons and wedges himself onto a stool between a young executive who is fixated on his smartphone and an older man who picks at his breakfast and contemplates nothing beyond the ketchup bottle in front of him.

A server appears almost instantly and pours Russell a cup of coffee.

She peers through funky, oversized glasses and asks him, "What are you having this morning?" as if he were a regular. She is young, has sleeve tattoos down both her arms and bears a smile that exudes warmth.

"I'll have two eggs over easy and brown toast, please."

She shouts the order over her shoulder to the line cooks, itemizing the same breakfast he routinely ordered when he came to this place as a kid. If his mother, who was as much a creature of habit as him, were there she would have ordered a bowl of mixed fruit and a cup of tea. They used to sit together after breakfast and talk about the week ahead, both eyeing the future with their different hopes and worries.

"It'll be up in a few minutes, sir," the waitress says while scribbling the order on a dog-eared pad.

"Thanks," he answers absently.

He had always hoped to one day complete this tour of his old childhood haunts, either with his son, Joshua, when he was old enough to appreciate it, or, at one time he had thought it was a trip to take with Anna—a more lighthearted, nostalgic holiday. Judith's words come to him with a swell of irony.

*"Don't reflect too much on what lies in the past or the future, Russell, because the past is in your rearview mirror and the future will look completely different when you get there."*

Could he have imagined that he would one day return to Toronto, return to Teapot Lake in this crippled mental state? Could he have guessed that he would have failed so miserably, failed himself, failed Anna and Joshua, and, even in her final moments, failed his mother? And what could he have done to change it, to alter the course of events to come, and to avoid becoming the person he is today? Nothing. He could have done little to change the genesis, the harsh hand dealt by fate that took Joshua. And it's that inevitability that is maddening.

Had he lived by his mother's example, he may have been better able to withstand all that has happened. But, instead of learning from his mother, instead of drawing from her strength, he always relied on her to be his backbone. He has been remiss in confronting his weaknesses, not fully studying those assailable components of his character, not peering into the portal of his soul, and accepting that he might find impotence where there ought to be self-reliance. And that is why fear has dominated so much of his existence, a fear of being left without those people who define him, of being where he is now, unprotected, and alone and forced to face the reality of his own shortcomings. His mother conquered her fears and frailties and planted her personal flag of triumph on their highest peaks. And when adversity hit, she was able to manage it and go on. However, when fate settled on him as its next target, he became its submissive victim. He crumpled under its rising fist and responded with an ever-deepening well of self-pity.

Having studied the device of his own psyche, Russell struggles to admit that he is as much to blame for his shortcomings as fate. He has lived his academic and professional life in the same mode, balancing known facts with unknown puzzle pieces to make decisions with as little risk in the mix as possible. It just hasn't applied to the complexities of human experience. He now appreciates that emotion, memory, and the unforeseen consequences of the past leave us all with a psychological imbalance that often contradicts logic. There are simply more unknown pieces than known facts, and the puzzle is never complete in real life.

⚜

Several days before her death, Judith had been lying in the hospital, thin and weak from the chemotherapy. Her skin had taken on a yellowish tone that seemed to presage her body's readiness to capitulate.

After retiring from what had been an incredible career both as practitioner and teacher at St. Bart's, she had left London for Massachusetts, determined to be closer to her grandson. She continued to teach part-time and dabbled in medical research.

Although she seemed to enjoy the changing seasons and pace of New England and was content, she still pined for London, which held a deep intimacy that came from familiarity, whether she was emerging from familiar Westminster tube stations or walking streets imbued with history that even centuries of rain couldn't wash away.

It was an afternoon visit to her bedside when Judith tried to confide in him, to purge the only feelings of remorse that she had carried with her through her years. He had listened carefully, straining to hear her raspy words but also believing her regrets to be unfounded, so he didn't respond with the compassion and forgiveness she clearly sought. That was only days before she'd passed away, and now it was too late to go back and hold her and tell her that it was all right, that she had his understanding, no matter how unnecessary it was for her to ask for it. He had relived that conversation often in his mind.

"Here, I brought you some tea," he had announced as he walked into her hospital room that afternoon. It was a Wednesday. Since she had entered the more intensive phases of her treatment, he had taken one afternoon off work every week to sit with her, mostly in silence, from noon until visiting hours ended at seven o'clock in the evening.

"I put a little honey in it for you."

"Too hot . . . can't swallow," she whispered, her eyes sunken, her features looking prematurely skeletal, bleakly foretelling the future.

"We'll let it cool down a bit then," he said.

Then her hand had come up and settled on the stainless-steel rung of the bedside. He put his fingers around it and held on to her, feeling nothing but her tiny bones. These spells were the worst for her, every five weeks, as her body battled the aftershocks of the latest dose of chemo. In the last year, Judith's looks had been pitiably transformed; the graying hair she had always coiled into a tight bun at the top of her crown had fallen out, she wore a kerchief to cover her bare scalp, and her visage of calmness had been displaced with a tautness that accompanied her steady fight against the disease.

She had overcome the hurdles that face any single mother, excelling in a career that had traditionally excluded women, and pursuing that career at a time when the odds were against her eventual success as a surgeon who would be honored by her fellow physicians for her contributions to the field of cardiology.

Achievement was something that had been ingrained in her since childhood. Her parents, Stan and Ella Nowak, had crossed the Atlantic from Poland before the Second World War and manufactured a life for themselves and their daughter, confronting and overcoming the barriers of language and culture that face all immigrants.

In Poland, Russell's grandfather had apprenticed for a brief time as a tailor, and, once in Canada, he set about creating an opportunity out of his limited experience and sheer resolve. By the time North America had been drawn into the war, Stan Nowak was running a garment factory with thirty-seven employees. Never turning their backs on who they were, his grandparents worked together on the floor with their employees, sewing, packaging, and shipping the clothes they produced in the cloistered heat of the factory floor. Even after the post-war boom, when the business grew exponentially and with it their hard-won prosperity, they continued to labor alongside their workers.

Naturally, the lessons of their endurance were passed along to their only daughter. With an austerity that some might even classify as fanatical, they reared her from the same canons of discipline that governed their own lives, supplying their love through a rigorously enforced desire to see their offspring succeed.

Growing up, Russell's mother did not receive the softer elements of nurturing. Judith was raised by people who never had the luxury of exploring those deep channels of emotion that run through each of us. Consequently, although she was neither insensitive nor incapable of intimacy, Judith was rarely one to verbalize her feelings. Her emotions were always a secondary consideration in the rigidly defined lives of her lineage.

Several years earlier, Judith had participated as a member of a team of combined heart specialists and pharmaceutical company representatives that was in the process of developing a revolutionary drug, one that could help clear constricted arteries during a severe angina attack. At a formal dinner held to celebrate the team's work, she had been singled out and commended for her lifelong commitment to medicine. As speaker after speaker offered toasts in her honor, the dinner became a tribute to his mother, and, in an unintended way, it came to mark the pinnacle of her career.

Russell had attended the event with Anna, a testimonial to the closeness they shared with Dr. Judith. Both fought back tears as they spoke about her selfless pursuits, constant drive, and remarkable contributions. Russell was proud of the woman who had given him and many of her patients the gift of life.

As the post banquet dance commenced, Russell twisted through the crowd where he caught his mother's arm and, with exaggerated formality, requested the first dance. They waltzed clumsily with each other, eventually getting in step, and spinning smoothly among the other dancers. At the end of the song, Russell performed a very unskilled turn-and-dip from which Judith, her face bright and flushed, came up laughing. Fun had been missing from so much of her very serious life. It was at once enlightening and heartbreaking to see her so enthralled and carefree on that festive evening.

Holding her shriveled hand in the hospital room, Russell found it difficult to accept that this was the same spirited woman who had glided across that dance floor so recently.

"You know why I never remarried?" she said in a voice so hoarse that the words themselves sounded chafed and sore. She held onto his hand as tightly as she could, but her eyes were turned toward the window. "I always thought I could do a better job raising you on my own. That no one would have sufficed or could have been as good as your real father. It really was an arrogant way of thinking, selfish on my part."

"Mom," Russell said, patting the top of her hand and letting her know she needn't go on. But she wanted to. He should have recognized that these old memories needed to be released with the greatest delicacy and examined with even greater care.

"I always felt that it would have slighted what your father had meant to me, what we'd meant to each other," she said, still gazing at the window. "I could never have loved anyone that powerfully again. Not even after all these years."

Her grip tightened around his fingers.

"It was wrong of me, you know, to deny you a father, thinking that somehow, I could do it all myself. I used to always wonder if you recognized his features when you looked at yourself in the mirror, if you longed for him every time you saw your own reflection. But I could never come out and ask you. I didn't talk about him very often because I didn't want you focusing on what was missing in your life."

She coughed weakly. "It's funny how we can make our decisions in life with such confidence, but then we never really get to evaluate them until their consequences are set in stone."

"Mom," Russell whispered, "you've never made a bad decision in your life."

"It helps to hear you say that. It's still something I can't help but regret on some level. Your father was a wonderful person. In so many ways, your Grandfather McCreary reminded me of him."

This is the first time Russell had heard this parallel. "Tell me more, how was he like him?"

"Your short summer with Pops McCreary was something I held as very special," she continued. "I felt so bad having to pull you away. Seeing the two of you together was like a glance into what your life would have been like with your dad. They not only looked very similar, but the way he listened and talked with you, the way he made you feel like you were the only person in the room wherever you were. That was your father. I could never have sufficiently described him in words compared to that time you had with your grandfather."

A long period of silence ensued as Russell sat still, intensely contemplating what his mother had just shared. He listened to the monotonous, two-toned wail of an ambulance pulling up to the emergency entrance twelve floors below.

"Lately, I've been thinking a lot about God," Judith continued. "I suppose it's almost comical for someone as sick as me to start contemplating religion. I've often been surprised at the intensity of other people's faith, especially those whom I've watched facing death. I don't know how many times I've stood aside and listened to a minister or a nun administering the Last Rites to a patient without it stirring any spiritual sentiments within me. I sometimes wish I'd learned to put my trust in something more than the tangible, what I could see and touch and fix with my own hands. Now, it almost seems too late. I never learned to think about myself in terms of my own spiritual side . . . my soul. I wish I knew how, now that nothing can prolong my life, not even the poison they're pumping into me."

"Don't say that," Russell started. "You're going to get better. That's the only thing you need to put your faith in right now."

"Tell me you'll pray for me, Russell," Judith said sadly. "When I'm gone, promise me you'll do that."

"I promise. Just try to rest for a while," he said, feeling uncomfortable, almost annoyed. "You're upsetting yourself. Remember what you used to tell me all the time? 'Don't think too much. Don't drive yourself silly.'"

She had managed a weary smile before rolling toward the window and closing her eyes. Assuming she had fallen asleep, Russell had lifted his jacket from the back of a chair and tiptoed to the door, making sure to close it gently. He never returned to that conversation and her regrets about her decision to remain single. He never got another chance to hold his mother's hand and assure her that he felt nothing wanting in life, and that her choice to raise him alone had been a noble one.

On the night following the death of Dr. Judith Nowak-McCreary, Russell found himself inside a church for only the second time in his life. Anna had been raised Catholic, and although she had long since abandoned faith in religion, she had nonetheless been almost superstitious about Joshua being christened. They arranged for a ceremony that took place at the Old South Church, a nineteenth-century structure that sat on Boylston Street across from Boston's public library building. The church seemed out of place, with its copper-plated patina and its bell tower situated demurely below the many sleek, glass-faced office buildings of downtown Boston.

On that night, having left the hospital to make the funeral arrangements and contact almost everyone who had known his mother with the unwelcome news of her passing, Russell made a special trip to the Old South Church through one of the misty spring rains that blanket the New England seaboard that time of year.

Inside the silence of the imposing and prodigiously stain-glassed church, he had knelt in a pew in the back row. A few people wandered in after him and sat in an area off to the right of the altar. He was not sure that he prayed for his mother in the way she had wanted, he knew very little about the mechanics of invocation, and his mind kept returning to those prayers he had heard previously in this very spot.

He recalled how, at Joshua's baptism, a choir had sung during the ceremony. He remembered that the old pipe organ had been so powerful it shook the wooden pews. The church choir in unison sang a sublime Latin hymn that seemed to sail to the high ceilings of the church like a consecrated dictum lifted from the lips of God himself. Listening to that extraordinary chorus back then, he had no trouble offering his own private benediction for the health and happiness of his newborn son.

But on this day, in the suppressed silence, he had no idea how to offer a prayer for his mother. Instead, Russell knelt in the dim, incense-scented quiet of the church and wept, grieving the loss of one of the finest human beings he would ever know.

# 10

Having finished his breakfast at the Venus Café and engulfed in memories he can't place comfortably in the lost time buried deep within, Russell takes another taxi back to his hotel. After checking out, he arranges with the concierge to rent a vehicle for thirty days. He's uncertain that he will be at the lake for that long. Nonetheless, the idea of being gone for almost a month brings him a sense of solace he hasn't felt in ages. Even if he is back in Boston in a week to sign the job offer and take over as Datatel's CEO, the thought of a long hiatus in the northern woods needs to remain intact for now.

His mentor Cal Morales hadn't waited long to reach out after their last conversation. Just as Russell was finishing his breakfast, Cal emailed. It was another uncharacteristically long one. In it, Cal acknowledged that he understood Russell's reservations but quickly reminded him that he was the most experienced leader at Datatel, with an impeccably clean record. He also admitted that the interim CEO option was a bold proposition. He described Datatel as a grand ship, navigating treacherous waters where the sea can be unpredictable and unforgiving. He wrote about how critical it was that they have a captain who possesses the steady hand and sound judgment to guide them through breakers. To Russell, it was overkill.

*That was quite a vivid metaphor, Cal,* he wrote in his reply, *I promise I'm considering it with the seriousness it deserves and will be in touch soon. And I appreciate your confidence in me.*

His rental is a Volkswagen Atlas SE. His preference for SUV's has crossed the border with him. Who knows, the trail into the cottage at

Teapot Lake could be a disaster and the 4x4 will be welcome if that is what transpires. It takes more than an hour to meander through clogged traffic up the Don Valley Parkway and then across the ETR tollway to Highway 400. And then it is as if his mind starts to clear alongside the dissipating congestion and swarm of vehicles.

The picture of Tony Haplich, Jr.'s family awakens in his thoughts as the sound of the wind outside the SUV builds to a steady hum. Such a picture-perfect family portrait. Haplich was clearly gratified and proud of his daughters, his smile beaming through the glass cover of the photograph.

The view outside the VW's windshield slowly transforms from the cityscape of north Toronto to rolling hills, covered in lush, pea green trees under a sky dotted with only a few errant clouds. Russell attempts to focus on the highway, however, his mind wonders to Cal and his indomitable urgency regarding the CEO role, or to Haplich's framed family photo, which inevitably leads to Joshua.

His son is always there, no more than a thin, broken thread away from present thoughts.

Joshua's birth was by far the most fulfilling event of Russell's life. He imagined that it must be the same for every parent, the startling moment of revelation when they find themselves looking down at the wrinkled, reddened face and tiny, curled fists of their minutes-old newborn. It was a moment of absolute purity, encompassing everything that he was—his needs, his apprehensions, and his hopes for the future. He learned instantly about his own vulnerability and the frailty of life itself, as the primal impulse to safeguard his child took form and established permanent roots.

For the first few nights, Russell had refused to remove himself from the warm comfort of the hospital maternity ward until he received several stern reprimands from the nursing staff. He held Joshua in the same rocking chair for hours, amid the wailing and bawling of the other infants, content with nothing more than holding him close to his chest and feeling his warm, clean breath on his neck.

These initial protective stirrings never abated. He noticed that with most parents, there seemed to be a gradual release, an extending of the invisible circumference in which they'd permit their child to stray. Although he would have eventually been forced to do the same, he didn't know if he could have been comfortable letting his son out of sight. He had a recurring dream since Joshua's accident in which he was a full-grown teenager, strolling alone across endless prairie grassland toward some unseen danger that only Russell could perceive. He always seemed to wake before the nightmare concluded, his arms flailing wildly as if he was desperately trying to claw his way back into that oblique dream world to rescue him. To this day, Russell's undiminished attachment to Joshua still overwhelms him.

During Joshua's first year, Russell spent very little time away from him, both of his own choice and necessity. Anna, forever the dedicated workaholic, took only three weeks maternity leave before returning part-time. During the week, their home was a whirlwind of activity. Russell would come home from work each day, leave the car running in the driveway, and brush a quick kiss onto Anna's forehead in a frenetic changing of the guard before she hurried out the door on her way to the evening shift. Then, for hours, he would have Joshua to himself.

The nightly assignment of playing, feeding, changing, and putting him to sleep quickly became an established part of Russell's routine. When Joshua started to crawl, they would play a rudimentary game of hide-and-seek around the sofa, his lively giggles filling the otherwise silent home. Each night, Russell bathed him in a tub full of floating toys, where Joshua would squeal and splash and leave them both soaked. And each evening, Joshua would doze in Russell's arms as he watched an endless stream of news programs from an armchair in their living room, the volume on the television turned down low.

Once Russell was certain that he'd fallen asleep, he'd carry him gently to his room and stroke his soft, reddish-brown hair before sneaking back downstairs. It became a ritual that they shared right up until the very last night of Joshua's life.

Russell found himself wishing that his mother had been able to see Joshua grow. Judith's illness robbed her of the time she yearned to spend with him during his early childhood. It was a thin consolation knowing that she could at least hold him in her arms during his first months of life. He liked to think that his mother would have been proud of the father he'd become.

When Joshua turned three, Russell and Anna decided to move out of the city. The commute was tolerable, and, like so many new parents, they foresaw the day they would want a backyard area and neighborhood for Joshua to grow up in. Add to that Russell's overprotective desire to find a safe neighborhood in which to settle, one with dependable schools and low crime, and Needham fit the bill perfectly.

They bought a modest cottage that backed onto an as-of-yet-undeveloped tract of farmland. The unpretentious gray brick bungalow, with pale blue shutters and hardwood floors, suited their needs, and the quiet residential street in the north end of the village seemed like an ideal place to raise a family.

During their first night in their new home, amid a labyrinthine assembly of boxes, Russell had sat alone at the fireplace late into the night. Earlier in the day, Joshua had slipped and cut his hand on a jagged piece of metal, and the copious amount of blood made Russell think it was a deep cut. But on close inspection, he found it was only minor. As Russell was pressing a cloth to the wound, Anna had emerged from the garage, saw the blood, and swooped in and grabbed him. She cleaned and dressed the cut, then patted Joshua on his back and suggested that he needed to be careful in the future. Russell thought he saw a mildly accusatory glare from his wife, but he decided to dismiss it and avoid any conflict on their first day in the new house. Later, stretched out on several cushions that were still sheathed in their plastic wrapping, Russell set aside his half-finished bottle of water and fell into a light sleep in the dwindling warmth of the fireplace.

That night, he was abruptly awakened from a disturbing dream by Anna, who gently shook his shoulders.

"I started to wonder if you'd forgotten where the bedroom was," she said, once he'd opened his eyes. "Although, you look so comfortable out here, I think I'll join you."

Russell shifted his weight to make room for her as she lay down and rested her head on his chest. The fire found a dry portion of tinder and was resurrected for a few seconds. It was March. Outside, an implacable late-winter wind purred around the corners of the house.

After a short time, Anna turned to gaze at Russell in the dim light.

"I can always tell when your wheels are spinning. What are you thinking about?"

He sighed. "Just being here, having this house . . . our first real home. It all happened so quickly. I can't believe Joshua is already three. I mean, he's almost having full-on conversations with us."

"I know," Anna said, patting Russell's arm. "You watch him changing and slowly becoming aware of himself. It makes you wish you could savor every moment of it, slow down the clock."

"I can't help thinking, you know, that it could all be snatched away from me in a heartbeat—you, Joshua, our home. Everything has worked out so effortlessly, and I'm afraid some sort of reckoning must be around the corner. Like some force of nature might decide it's handed out more than my ration of happiness and decide to tip the scales against me."

"It's no wonder you'd think that way, Russell. You missed out on having a father, so fatherhood, your family, they've naturally become the things you value most. I think we all face the same sort of paradox at some point. As soon as we gain or achieve whatever it is we believe we've always wanted from life, the fear of losing it can make us crazy," she continued. "I went through it myself when I was almost finished interning and had to work the ER rotation. After a while, everyone gets used to the despairing atmosphere of the place. But the one thing I never stopped being aware of was the fragility of life, how suddenly everything can change or vanish."

The wind howled with renewed zeal. Anna picked up the bottle off the floor and trickled the remaining water onto her tongue.

Russell touched her arm and said, "I don't know. It almost makes our lives seem that much more laughable, all our planning for the future, aspiring for this or that—"

"Most people would probably say that it makes it seem that much more precious, but I know what you mean," Anna injected. "It sounds like banal advice, but the best you can do is try to be grateful for everything without concerning yourself too much with what tomorrow's designs are going to look like."

They lay together until the fire had extinguished. Then, in the darkness, they fumbled down the hall toward their bedroom. Russell heard Anna fall onto the mattress they'd thrown haphazardly on the floor, having had no time after the move to set up the bed frame. He stopped on the way to check on Joshua. Already the pleasant scents of his child had permeated his new bedroom, and he was still for a moment, enjoying them while he stood by his sleeping form. Russell placed a soft kiss on Joshua's forehead, adjusted the blinds, and retreated into the hallway. This was the ideal Russell had envisioned, but an existence that left him battling to suppress his fears and neuroses. He sought security in a conventional blueprint, erecting the stock architecture of a safe, middle-class life, where the preservation of profession, home, and family became his sole, self-defining objective. He held tight to the numbing suburban code of existence, believing in its fallacy, that he could remain unscathed by ill fortune by inconspicuously sticking to an unoriginal script.

Shortly after moving to Needham, Anna went back to working the twelve-hour days that had been typical prior to Joshua's infancy. Fortunately, Joshua was always in proximity at a daycare center contiguous to the medical clinic. Anna checked in on him two or three times a day and called Russell at work each noon hour with an update. This pattern continued even as Joshua grew, and they had settled comfortably into their daily routines.

It was around Joshua's fourth birthday and, ironically, after one such report from Anna, that Russell received a somewhat cryptic message in his voicemail one afternoon. It was immediately odd to him, since voicemails were rare; most emailed him knowing that his track record on response time to recorded messages was terribly slow. One such message startled him to such an extent that he came close to questioning his comfortable career at Datatel.

It was an unfamiliar male voice, a person whose name he no longer recalls, requesting that he contact someone named Elizabeth Alamotti to discuss a proposal that might interest him. A phone number with a New York City area code. No supplementary details were given. Puzzled, Russell checked the previous quarterly sales reports to see if they had signed any new clients in New York, but nothing obvious leaped off his laptop screen.

Datatel occupied the top three floors of the Chamber of Commerce Building in Boston's financial district. The penthouse housed the executives; the seventeenth floor, directly below, was allocated for the IT team, which was famous for its overwrought staff and frantic pace. A person unfamiliar with this environment might walk out the elevator doors onto the seventeenth floor and conclude that he or she had stepped into the hub of a stock exchange or trading floor.

Later that day, Russell had almost forgotten about the cryptic voicemail until he found himself in the tumult of the seventeenth floor. After attending a meeting on a new software product that was behind its planned launch schedule, he had ferreted out Farouq Ahmed.

Farouq was one of those perpetually jovial people whose demeanor seemed to confirm all the clichés linking jolliness to obesity. His fleshy jowls formed into a ritual smile when he saw Russell weaving around the modular office desks toward him. He had huge, brown eyes that gave him a permanently surprised, deer-caught-in-headlights kind of expression. The average career span at any one company in his domain of the software development world usually lasted just a few years. With more than thirty years of combined service between them, Farouq and Russell were, at that time, considered to be the patriarchs of Datatel—or, less affectionately, as lifers.

"You are slumming this afternoon," Farouq exclaimed as Russell approached. "To what do we owe the honor of an executive visit?"

"Another meeting on the Project Z product release you can't seem to get off the ground," Russell quipped.

"Ask any one of them," he said, extending a chubby arm toward the rest of the floor, "I'm certain you'll hear nothing but optimism. We'll be ready for launch by early next month."

They discussed the launch in more detail and Russell shared the details of the meeting that had just concluded.

"Actually, early next month will work out well," Russell said. "We have a new social media campaign launching next week and we don't want to hit the clients and sales prospects with too much content all at once."

"Sometimes even delays end up working out, no?" Farouq offered with a chortle.

"By the way, have you gotten any strange voicemails today?" Russell asked.

"Voicemail? I wouldn't know. I don't think I've checked my voicemail in three years."

"Join the club," Russell laughed, "it's probably some salesperson trying to get through to me. It was a New York number."

"Well, if someone is trying to pitch some sort of product out of New York, send them my way," Farouq said. "I could use a trip to the Big Apple. Haven't been there in ages, and I used to take in a Broadway show at least once a year."

"I'll send them your way then . . . anything to get another sales rep off my plate."

"I have to get back to the grind here. Let me know once you've solved the mystery," Farouq said, winking as he reinstated his bulk into his desk chair and turned his attention to the four giant monitors on his desk. "I have a target date to meet!"

As soon as Russell returned to his office desk, he dialed the number he'd scribbled under *Eliz A.* on a notepad. It rang five times before he received Ms. Alamotti's voicemail, which gave no clues about the name or type of company she represented. Instead of disconnecting, he left a return message to say that he was returning the call and would be in the office until about six. He left his email as well.

# 11

Elizabeth Alamotti called back and formally introduced herself, apparently ignoring the suggested email route.

"I'm a partner with a New York-based executive search firm called Glynroche," she explained without hesitation. "I've been working on a confidential file for one of the largest mobile technology companies in the Northeast. They develop global networking systems for banking and telecommunications companies. We're looking for a new chief product officer, and your name and profile came to us through a database search."

"Ah, how can I help you with that?" Russell answered, mildly relieved it wasn't someone pushing a product or service on him.

"Well, we're interested in you for the position." Alamotti explained. "I've sent a short, mutual non-disclosure and confidentiality agreement for you to look at and sign electronically. If you can take a look and sign it, I'll be able to give you more details."

"I see," Russell said. "But to tell you the truth, I'm not really looking to leave my current role. I've had a good run at Datatel, and I like to think I have some more runway with my career here."

"It never hurts to look at what else is out there," Alamotti persisted, "and if it isn't of interest to you, maybe there will be someone in your network you may want to consider referring the opportunity to, right?"

Russell checked his email and quickly reviewed the agreement she had just sent him. It covered pretty much all the standard clauses, so he clicked to add his initials and the date.

"Okay, I've executed the NDA," he told her.

"Excellent. Thank you very much, Mr. Nowak-McC—"

"Russell is just fine," he interrupted. "The hyphenated last name can be a mouthful, and we don't need to be overly formal."

Alamotti laughed. "I like it, Russell. Are you familiar with Syncron Systems?"

"Yes. I'm quite familiar with them," he said. Syncron was one of several large but relatively uncelebrated system integration firms in the country. They had built a sizable business mostly out of the public eye. The fact that Syncron would approach him regarding an opportunity piqued Russell's interest. Within the industry, they had a reputation as the up-and-coming disruptor with a fast-moving culture and focus on innovation.

"Basically, the company has claimed a significant corner of the mobile communications market, even beyond its projections. As a result, Syncron is currently undergoing a major transition," she continued. Her voice was pleasant and betrayed a soft, Midwest accent that was professional and straight to the point. "The company is in the infant stages of restructuring, actually, more like a complete management overhaul, something I've been told your company has also undergone over the last couple of years."

"We made some major changes about eighteen months ago and are on the other side of those initiatives now," Russell said.

"It's also been revealed to me that you headed up a new product group during the restructuring initiatives within your own organization and transformed your development team."

"I'm considered somewhat of a veteran around here, so it was nice to be tapped for a big project to bring us into the next phase of our growth."

She laughed. "I hardly think at your age you could be considered an old-timer."

"Apparently, you aren't a diehard hockey fan," he joked. "Growing up in Toronto and now living in Boston, hockey is a must-watch sport for me. In some fields, being in your forties is about ten years over the hill."

"I confess, I'm not a sports fan," Alamotti said, "but I'll make you a deal. Come to New York to meet me and the Syncron execs for a preliminary interview, and we'll throw a couple of Rangers tickets your way."

He thanked her for the offer and started to explain that he wasn't in the position to entertain the notion of uprooting his family to New York, but she cut in before he could finish objecting.

"I'll be upfront with you," Alamotti said. "For the first year, you'd have to spend a fair amount of time in the city. But they'd set you up in corporate living accommodations in Manhattan and fly you home every weekend. And, of course, Syncron has offices in Chicago and Denver that you'd be required to visit, but maybe you could build some family vacations around them. After that, they'd likely only need you in the head office for a few days a week."

"One thing I'm guessing you don't know about me is my aversion to air travel," he remarked jokingly.

"Then I'll make you deal number two," she offered. "Come to a prelim interview and we'll get you here on the Acela train. First-class return."

He took a moment to consider it. She was definitely pulling out all the stops to make this happen.

"I'd be lying if I said I was just a little intrigued."

"Then let's set a date," she added.

Russell agreed to meet Elizabeth Alamotti the following Friday on the condition that they scheduled an early morning rendezvous. He figured he could catch the high-speed train into New York on Thursday night and be back in Boston no later than the following evening. Alamotti gave him Syncron's corporate head office address on East 53rd Street and sent him her address and cell phone number by email. Russell noticed her firm's title at the bottom of the note: *Partner, Glynroche & Associates, Executive Talent Consultants.*

When Russell recounted the conversation that evening for Anna, she was enthusiastic. Russell was slightly taken aback, particularly since after a few hours of deliberation following the phone call he had pretty much talked himself out of even contemplating an offer from Syncron.

"I don't think you should abandon the idea until you've seen what they're proposing," Anna said when he told her how he was feeling. They were sitting at the dining room table finishing the pizza they'd ordered. Anna had come home early and put Joshua to bed a few hours beforehand.

He'd charged onto Russell's lap, planted a sloppy kiss on his cheek, and uttered his standard "goose-nye." This valediction had been part of their nightly routine since Joshua had first been learning to talk and hadn't quite mastered pronouncing the letter *d*.

"Goose-nye," he would say after Russell had tucked him into bed and wished him good night. It had invariably delighted Joshua to see the grin that would emerge on his father's face.

"And another goose-nye, back at ya," Russell would chuckle, "I hope the geese sleep well too."

As a toddler just beginning to grasp the meaning of words, Joshua didn't comprehend what his father meant, but would always giggle at this statement. The playful nighttime custom continued long after Joshua grasped the phonetics and meaning of their repeated sequence.

"I don't know if I like the idea of being carted off all over the country, though. And there's no refuting it; it would entail being away from you and Joshua at least a few days a week," Russell said. "I keep seeing this image of myself sitting in a drab hotel room, spending hours on FaceTime calls with both of you and being inconsolably lonely."

Anna laughed affectionately and said, "There's always some sacrifices to be made... just look at my occupation. I'd at least mull it over if I were you. Lately, you've talked a lot about wanting some new challenges."

Over the few months before Elizabeth Alamotti's call, and after the major project he had completed in restructuring parts of the Datatel organization, Russell had settled into a position of professional ennui, content to ride the crests of his past successes within the company, rather than eyeing the future aggressively.

The call from Alamotti made him think that maybe he was getting more restless than he wanted to admit; maybe an invitation to join Syncron wasn't as untimely as he'd made it out to be. It would mean a change of venue, a whole new outfit with new responsibilities, and, inarguably, a notable step up into a handsome tax bracket. Anna was probably right. It would be premature to dismiss the prospect without researching it further.

The electronic tickets arrived the next morning, along with a reservation statement for a single night's stay at the Plaza. Syncron was evidently sparing no expense. Russell wondered who his competition might be, how many others they were interviewing, if anyone. Preoccupied with the upcoming interview, he spent the remainder of the week contributing minimally at work and left for the train station on Thursday afternoon without even glancing at the growing batch of neglected messages in his inbox.

The sky outside the first-class cabin was an uninspiring, unbroken gray that converged at an indiscernible point with the foggy, snow-spotted horizon. Russell easily ignored the murky scenery whipping past and concentrated on a *Fortune* magazine article about Syncron that he'd downloaded to his iPhone. The more he read, the more appealing it became to potentially connect himself to an enterprising outfit like Syncron. Once he had finished the article Russell hit the recline button at the side of his chair, leaned back, and considered his growing excitement over Friday's interview.

By the time the train ground into Penn Station, it was dark outside. As they drew nearer to the city, the charged glow of the Manhattan skyline reflected off the clouds like an artificial imitation of dawn.

The following morning, looking like anything but a native New Yorker in a navy blazer, white, button-down shirt, and tan pants, Russell strode out of the hotel where he met a throng of other easily identifiable interlopers. He had decided not to wear a suit after reading that Syncron's executives prided themselves on informal corporate culture. Business casual was the norm; ties and cufflinks and any old school reserved dress was passe.

Earlier, after he had shaved, he had called down to room service and ordered a coffee and a croissant. Standing at his window, high above the configuration of concrete and glass that traced the margins of Manhattan, he sipped his coffee and tried to picture himself in the world below. From his lofty vantage point, it looked like any other metropolitan vista. He could have been persuaded that the scene below was a snapshot of downtown Boston or another familiar city.

He slid into the back of an Uber sedan that had been pre-ordered by Glynroche & Associates and Syncron and checked to make certain that the driver had the correct address at the north end of Central Park, at 100th Street and Madison Avenue.

The plan for the morning was to meet with Alamotti for about ninety minutes, attend an hour-long lunch meeting with the senior vice president of Human Resources, then participate in an hour-long panel interview with Syncron's CEO and CFO. He knew that the day would be intense, but for some reason, despite knowing these details in advance, he felt only a minimal tug of anxiety.

The Uber driver weaved them through the morning traffic and delivered Russell in plenty of time outside a modern-looking office building. The lobby was filled with the clatter of footsteps as the morning professional crowd made its way to meetings while balancing coffees with smartphones and backpacks. He took the elevator to the fifty-third floor and arrived at Syncron's well-appointed reception area. The receptionist took his name and sent word of his arrival to Elizabeth Alamotti via their internal chat messenger. He was asked to have a seat and offered a cup of coffee or a glass of water.

Alamotti walked confidently across the reception floor with her hand extended. Russell estimated her to be in her mid-fifties and found her quite attractive. She oozed confidence and her skin was a beautiful brown hue. She stood less than six feet tall in her heels; her jet-black, straightened hair came to a line of bangs just above her eyebrows. She wore stylish colored glasses and he noticed immediately that they matched the burgundy belt that cinched her close-cut, dark pantsuit.

"Nice to finally meet you in person," he said.

"I've reserved an office for us to meet this morning." She smiled. "We can go around the corner and get settled."

Their initial interview went well. She was clearly an experienced professional. The conversation kept a natural and easy current as she directed a well-paced set of inquiries regarding his experience and perspectives. It was clear to Russell that, while she came across as conducting a transparent and informal discussion, she was continuously analyzing and assessing their dialogue and his body language.

He was surprised by how quickly the time had passed when he heard a soft knock on the door. A smartly dressed executive assistant let them know that his lunch appointment with Dennis Garratty, the head of Human Resources, was set to start.

The remainder of the afternoon went extremely well. His lunch meeting was very casual, and Garratty turned out to be an affable HR veteran with an easygoing demeanor, thin, reddish hair and matching goatee. Russell's meeting with the CEO David Milner and CFO Abigail Ross, was postponed until three o'clock because they were prepping for a senior leadership team meeting.

Milner turned out to be a sincere and plainspoken Texan. Russell had read his bio online and knew his story of founding the company, eventually buying out his partners and raising over $500 million in private equity funding from one of the major five PE firms in the country. Adhering to the casual dress code, he wore jeans and a golf shirt with a navy blazer. He and Ross played a bit of a good cop, bad cop, mixing tough questions with softballs to test Russell's composure.

The interview lasted forty-five minutes longer than scheduled, which he took as a positive sign. Russell had an opportunity to ask numerous questions about the challenges of the role, the future vision of the company, and its overall culture. He slowly started to feel increasingly comfortable with the thought of joining Syncron.

It was the end of the day, and employees were starting to make their way across the reception area as Russell waited for his wrap-up meeting with Alamotti.

"How was the rest of the day?" she asked.

"Excellent," Russell replied. "It's been a full day, but well worth it."

"I'm glad to hear it." She had a soft leather laptop bag over her shoulder and a jacket draped over her forearm. "Since it's so much later than we'd scheduled, I thought we could grab a drink and debrief down the street."

It wasn't a question. Russell nodded as she described a restaurant called Brass that was in the penthouse of the neighboring building.

"It has a quiet bar where we can catch up without too many distractions," she explained.

Outside, the night air was slightly cool, and the sound of horns throbbed as the mounting end-of-day Manhattan traffic squeezed itself through the streets. They traversed a pedestrian walkway, narrowly escaping a collision with a passing bicycle courier, clearly rushing recklessly to make a final delivery. They entered another building.

"So, any misgivings or concerns?" Alamotti asked while they rode the elevator. "I know you were a little tentative the first time we spoke. How are you feeling after meeting the main players?"

Not wanting to seem too eager, Russell said, "I'm glad I made the trip. I'm impressed. I do have a few lingering questions but, for the most part, I have a good feeling about the company."

"More questions?" Elizabeth winked and said, "Sounds like we have plenty to talk about. Maybe we'll have to stretch this into dinner."

The sliding doors chimed as they opened, revealing a brightly lit lounge decorated in a sparse, post-modern style. They were seated in a corner, in plush low-riding chairs, away from the large mahogany bar that held a crowd of post-workday investment banker types. She ordered a martini and Russell had a vodka tonic.

They spent a solid hour going over a few outstanding questions Russell had, including the potential for advancement, the possibility of an acquisition by a bigger firm, and timelines to fill the position.

"So, Russell, what will it take to get you in the role?"

Russell answered calmly. "I hadn't really gotten to the point where I've got a baseline set in terms of compensation and the overall package. I need to consider the time commitment commuting to New York, getting back and forth to Boston, and other factors. I'd also like to find out more about what sort of equity I might be offered over time."

"I'm sure they'll make it all worth your while," she replied, her large brown eyes squinting slightly as she took a sip of her drink.

"My wife's career is just taking off," Russell said before giving her a detailed summary of Anna's career and aspirations. "Our son, Joshua, is pretty comfortable in his daycare routine too—it would be tough—no, let me correct that, practically impossible—to tear them away from Boston. The commuting is the biggest part I'm wrestling with to be honest."

Alamotti laughed and seemed to contemplate this for a minute. "You're made for the role Russell. I know that's presumptuous, but I have a high degree of confidence that you're going to get an offer and jump at it."

"Sounds good. Thank you, Elizabeth."

They decided to order a light dinner. As they chatted, the conversation drifted from their careers to their college days and the people in their networks they might know in common. She joked that being the offspring of a Sicilian father and a Kenyan mother, she had an affinity for Italian cuisine but stayed thin because she'd been raised to practice communal sharing.

She had been divorced for three years from her second husband. Her first marriage, in her early twenties, had lasted less than a year. Her second husband was ten years her senior and desperately wanted to have a child, but she was heavily focused on her career and confessed that she had always wanted to wait for the overwhelming urge to procreate.

"I'll admit it, I've always been married to my work," Alamotti stated with a wry grin. "I know it sounds like a cliché. But since the divorce, I've just doubled down on doing what I love and I can't lie, I've been productive and it's paying dividends."

"You're clearly good at your profession," Russell said. "You've got me thinking about the Synchron job, and until you reached out to me, I wasn't anywhere close to looking for something new."

"Interesting," she replied and tilted her martini glass toward him in a unilateral toast. "And you're right, I'm damn good at it."

Russell smiled and raised his own glass in her direction.

# 12

The heat persists without relief as Russell drives up Highway 11, leaving Toronto behind. The sun has been beating down on the Atlas SE since morning, but still he turned off the air conditioning after passing through Gravenhurst.

For the past two hours, he has driven with the driver's side window rolled down, allowing warm air to billow into the rental vehicle. Despite his forehead glistening with a glaze of perspiration, he refuses to close the window and cool down. He wants to feel every mile of this drive up north, to smell and taste his journey. The muggy air blowing past his ear seems fitting.

Upon pulling into the town of Gravenhurst, Russell is surprised to find himself disappointed. The small town has changed dramatically, having kept pace with progress, as if the shades had been drawn on the past and could not be unfastened again. Part of him had hoped that the town had stayed the same, his mental picture an image etched decades before.

Even the small burger stand that Russell and his mother had stopped at on their way up north over thirty years ago had expanded into a massive and popular enterprise with a large park and a walking bridge that now extended over the highway so that southbound vehicles could access it.

He follows the directions on his iPhone and takes an exit ramp outside of Gravenhurst toward a resort called the Bangor Lodge. He'd reserved a small cottage at the resort online that morning. After all his travels, the meeting in Toronto and the long drive north, he thinks a night at the lodge will get him in the right mindset and help him rest enough to make the remaining journey to Teapot Lake late the following morning.

Bangor Lodge lives up to its online reviews. It consists of a main resort building with hotel room accommodation, a restaurant and pool as well as ten tiny home-styled rustic cottages along the shoreline. He's immediately pleased that he selected one of the cottages since they provide a bit of privacy and a nice view of the lake on which the resort is situated.

The check-in process is simple, and after he registers and gets the key to cottage seven, he sits in one of two Adirondack chairs on the small deck outside the unit, overlooking the slowly graying and subduing lake surface.

His mind wanders again to his most recent conversation with Cal Morales. He's aware that he is increasingly leaning toward taking the CEO position. Russell knows these types of opportunities don't come up often. Yes, in a way he would be capitalizing on Sarah Westroes' self-induced misfortunes, but he knows he has poured a lot of his brainpower and time into the company. He would not suffer from any form of impostor syndrome; he knows the company, knows its history and has proven that he can move critical and strategic initiatives forward to stimulate continuous growth of their brand and products. He is a safe choice for Datatel, the logical pick as Cal has said.

As the sun retreats fully and light dims in the sky above his cottage, he retrieves a thin blanket from inside. A pleasant chill has suffused the clean lakeside air. One thing that Cal said keeps repeating in these thoughts. His former boss suggested that throwing himself into the job of CEO might be cathartic. Cal relayed that he had also leveraged his work as a form of therapy.

His iPhone beams as he picks it up and pulls up his email, forcing him to squint as it contrasts with the lowering light around him. He starts writing an email to Cal informing him that he is going to accept the CEO offer, but he pauses after crafting a sentence suggesting that he doesn't need to consider the interim role and that he'd prefer to jump in with both feet.

Just as quickly, he decides it's getting too late, and the email is too important. He saves the partially finished message into his drafts figuring he'll finish it after he makes his way to cabin and settles in at Teapot Lake the next day.

Farouq has forwarded him a link. It's an article about Westroes corroborating that Sarah had filed for a divorce from Derek Paulson. She continued to deny that she played any role in the machinations of a fraudulent plan.

The journalist pointed out contradictory evidence showing financial transactions to offshore accounts that she held. At a minimum, the story suggests she will be indicted for wire fraud under the US Foreign Corrupt Practices Act. Westroes would also be prohibited from taking any executive positions in a public corporation for twenty years, essentially ending any career aspirations she might entertain around a reentry into the business world. The article also made mention of some meetings her legal team had apparently set up with the DOJ, speculating that she may be attempting to enter a plea deal.

Russell can't help but succumb to a feeling of disgrace. How could he have believed in her so unhesitatingly? She had impressed him so completely with her undeniable acumen and talent for corporate strategy that he was blinded by it. And, in the end, he had fallen for her in every way imaginable.

Flummoxed at the idea that Sarah is corrupt, he questions if it can really be true that she is now brashly orchestrating another series of moves to save herself and potentially consign her ex-husband into the mix, pouring elixirs into her self-dug abyss, fervently hoping for some magic escape.

And hadn't she convinced him that her and Derek's marriage had been disintegrating to the point they largely avoided one another?

The fact that Russell had believed this, without any doubts about her character, made him question his own judgment. And here he is, preparing himself to take on the biggest responsibility in Datatel. He has to trust his competency in assessing people's character. Exhausted, he shuffles into the cottage and lies down to sleep with these thoughts still front-of-mind.

He listens to the nighttime sounds of the forest outside the cottage. Despite being tired, he can't seem to sleep; an inchoate association of facts begins taking shape into untainted rumination. It has to do with the article Farouq just sent him. There was a quote from one of Sarah's attorneys. *What was it?*

Russell pushes a round, plastic button on the electric cord of a small lamp that sits on the bedside table and picks up his iPhone, and finds the lawyer's statement:

*"Ms. Westroes is seeking to discuss options with the Department of Justice, despite insisting that she is innocent of all the claims against her. We, her legal representatives, have advised her that, while the evidence is largely circumstantial, the refusal of the third-party consultant she retained during the Jukes acquisition to testify, or offer supporting evidence, leaves us in the unfortunate position of being unable to properly prove her innocence."*

He had forgotten about the firm Sarah had brought in on the Jukes deal. The purpose of the firm's contract with Sarah and Datatel was precisely to avoid the type of peril she now faced. The big five consulting firms and national law firms had started in recent years offering their services as consultants to executives and corporate officers of Fortune 1000 companies engaging in significant M&A transactions. The sole purpose of the consultant's role was to shadow the CEO and corporate officers and ensure compliance through the acquisition process. The thinking behind the process was that, on top of the internal legal teams, investment banks and financial advisers that participated in a sizable deal, the executives would have a safety net, protecting them from liability.

It started coming back to Russell piecemeal. There had been some mention, either from Sarah herself, or secondhand, about the independent party, who stayed largely in the background, an embedded figure during the development and conclusion of the Jukes deal. It was Derek, her husband, Russell had heard, who insisted on the third-party service. Sarah had been dismissive at first.

"I've done more than a few these," she had declared with a glib wave of her hand, "I don't need my own overpaid, personal Jiminy Cricket telling me how to do my job under the auspices of protecting me from myself."

Eventually, however, she acquiesced. Thinking back, Russell recalls that he'd been mildly bewildered by her selection of a consultant. It had been a law firm, he remembers, but one that had only recently begun offering that category of service. He had only met the principal partner once or twice and couldn't recall many details other than the fact that he had thick, black hair, wore Buddy Holly-style glasses, and had dressed casually, usually in jeans and a T-shirt and maybe a thin blazer the few times he came to the office.

Rolling over and resetting his pillows, he reaches over and dims the lamp again. In the darkness, he again labors to fall asleep. A troubling question keeps him from slipping quietly into rest. *Why would the consultant refuse to support Sarah?* It was incomprehensible. That was precisely his role in the entire equation.

His phone alarm wakes him early the next morning. Across the lake the sun has barely peeked over the tree line. The coffee maker in the tiny home kitchen brews him a steaming cup and he steps back out onto the deck and walks to the shoreline. The resort is still quiet. There are a few guests walking along a path that hugs the edge of the lake and he picks up the sound of the resort's employees moving chairs up by the pool.

Gentle waves come up to greet him as the sun crests a hill of trees and the lake is suddenly animated in the unsullied first shafts of daylight. Russell is reminded of the canoe trip his grandfather and he took during his summer in this part of Canada. He imagines him and Pops McCreary gliding along this lake in the early hours of the breaking day. He pictures them coasting over the top of the lake in their red canoe, superimposed in his mind's eye as a bonded, single shape, man, boy, canoe drifting against the unspoiled scene before him.

It's surprising to him that he hasn't come up to the Canadian north even once since that summer. That childhood summer plays so often and prominently in his memories, yet he never returned to it.

It leads him to think about Joshua. Had he lived, would Russell have brought his son up here to the cabin? He must believe he would have been impelled by the urge to share his experience with Pops and introduce him to the backwoods and rough country of the Canadian north. As he ponders the thought of Joshua being at his side, maybe as an eight-year-old himself, the illusory silhouette of himself and Pops in the distance transfigures into him and Joshua. His imagination runs away from him and, looking at his feet, Russell realizes that he has dropped his tin coffee mug. Tears form in the creases of his eyes, and he sighs intensely. It is an image he can't loosen from his mind, and it is one that brings with it a groundswell of sorrow.

# 13

Joshua's loss was abrupt and random.

It had been a temperamental late spring in Boston, the weather fluctuating between tepid rainy days with bouts of stifling humidity and spells of dry, blazing heat. But the day it happened was perfect, featuring a restrained but consistent breeze that carried the scents of summer throughout the city, the sun ducking behind soft cumulus clouds and a warmth that presaged the oncoming cool of autumn.

The day before, Russell had made a call to Elizabeth Alamotti and laid out his requests for the Syncron team. If they met his requirements for compensation and shares in the company, he would take the role. He had taken the train to New York one additional time to complete more interviews and he had become increasingly impressed with the Syncron team and the firm's direction and presumed he would be starting in the role by the start of the company's fourth quarter in October.

He had also contemplated how he would resign at Datatel. It would be hard to leave the company he had been so invested in, and he knew that they would take his notice hard. Nonetheless, the role at Syncron had dominated his thoughts for the past couple of weeks, and he was getting excited.

"We're going for a picnic in the city, boys," Anna announced that morning, with a hand on Russell's shoulder and a kiss blown across the breakfast table at Joshua. It was a Saturday, and they had slept in. Joshua was still heavy-eyed and quiet, waking himself by playing with a bowl of oatmeal. "I've decided, no objections permitted, we leave at eleven-thirty on the mark."

Anna had left her job at the clinic and returned to Mass General. She was working tirelessly at the hospital. Budget cuts and an increased caseload, coupled with her ambitious drive to move from the operating room to a prestigious administrative position, had been commanding a heavy commitment of hours at work. This Saturday represented a rare respite for them both, and the idea of spending a slow day in the sunshine with their son was more than welcome.

"Mommy has spoken," Russell said to Joshua. "What do you think of an afternoon in the park?"

"Good," he beamed, displaying a thumbs-up without looking up from his plastic breakfast bowl.

At four and a half years old, Joshua's personality had begun to truly blossom with his own brand of humor, teasing, and playfulness. He was pensive at times and, even at his young age, unflappable in his preference for occasional downtime to play quietly on his own. The expansion of his vocabulary had seemed like an overnight event, and it astonished Russell that suddenly he seemed to be having animated and expressive conversations with his adorable son.

Joshua's attachment to his mother was palpable and profound. For almost all things requiring comfort, he turned to her and craved her attention whenever she was near. Russell had evolved comfortably in the fun role and designated heroic savior from anything fearsome that may have skulked outside the brick walls of their home.

Russell and Anna adored their son and were determined to permit him his childhood by not introducing him to any of their adult anxieties. Their love for him was limitless.

Russell would have given anything for a glimpse into what that Saturday would have in store; he would have sacrificed his own life to have prevented that tragic outcome. In his mind he had failed in his most basic obligation to his son only two short hours after he had made him smile with his thumb cavalierly pointing to the ceiling above a messy bowl of oatmeal.

The rest of that morning often returns to Russell's mind as a jumble of moments, like pieces of a puzzle scattered across a table. He has never tried to piece together the events of the morning in chronological order. The non-sequential mismatch somehow sits more comfortably in his memory.

He remembers driving the car into the city, stopping briefly at a department store because he'd forgotten to pack a picnic blanket, seeing Joshua strapped into his booster seat, hearing him humming a song from a popular children's television show. *What was the song again?* Russell can never remember it, even though the sound of his voice is unforgettable; enjoying the sensation of the hot outdoor air seeping into the car through the open windows; noticing the traffic slowing to a crawl as they neared downtown; parking on a side street and walking with Joshua swinging between their hands they held together; crossing one of the bridges over Storrow Drive, where they took off their sandals and dipped their toes in the Charles River; and listening to Joshua question how the sailboats could possibly move with so little wind.

And then, their worlds imploding. Russell remembers watching Joshua run up an embankment, laughing with Anna at the sight of mud smeared on the back of his shorts; noticing, suddenly, that he would not stop running even as they screamed after him to do so; watching, with horror, as his back and shoulders disappeared over the crest of the hill, unaware of the perils on the other side; racing up the hill after him, blood pounding in his ears, and recognizing that he would not reach him in time; hearing Anna wail as the high-pitched sound of braking tires pierced the air and, then . . . muffled silence as the world around him went numb.

Later, Russell would recount these events many times for the police and a seemingly endless number of insurance investigators. They had been playing a simple game of tag. Joshua had run up the embankment. No guardrail existed to protect pedestrians from vehicles that traveled along the street. Joshua kept looking behind him as his daddy chased him. Having fun and laughing, he must not have registered the instantaneous change in Russell's voice and expression. He ran onto the road. The vehicle that hit him stopped in time but was subsequently rear-ended by a minivan. The collision knocked Joshua, who by then had frozen in fear in the middle of the road, ten feet from the point of impact.

The site of his son's crumpled form, lying on the hot pavement will, Russell suspects, cause him to shake and weep for the rest of his days. He remembers running to him and crouching. Somewhere behind him, a man's voice was yelling as he called 911.

Someone else touched Russell's shoulder and told him that he should not move him. He held Joshua's face in his hands. His eyes were closed, his long, dark eyelashes unmoving. A scrape appeared across his right temple, but it was not bleeding heavily. Russell put his lips to his mouth and could feel the faintest of breath escaping from his nostrils onto the skin under his nose.

"He's breathing!" Russell tried to yell, but it came out a cracked whisper. It was then that he realized that Anna was standing far behind him, at least a car length's distance. She was taking in the scene but not moving, frozen in place like a stone sculpture.

The ambulance seemed to arrive within seconds, although Russell had no idea how much time had elapsed. He watched the paramedics move briskly, but not frantically, as they strapped Joshua's limbs to a board and enfolded him in a blanket.

For some reason, the only sound Russell could remember was that of the board being clipped into place in the tight but organized hold of the ambulance. An oxygen mask was strapped to his little boy's face. Anna and Russell were guided by the paramedics to sit beside Joshua. Anna immediately placed her head on the blanket above Joshua's feet and stared, unblinking, at his face. They did not speak at all from the moment the siren sounded to the point where an emergency nurse ushered them to an empty, private waiting room, as Joshua was pushed through swinging, stainless-steel doors.

The room was small and set aside from the public waiting room in a manner that made it all too obvious that this was reserved for the loved ones of patients in the most serious of conditions. Two oil paintings of cloud-darkened countryside sat above a worn sofa. Anna sat on the sofa, at the end farthest from the door. It was as if she was trying to distance herself as much as possible from whatever news of Joshua's state would present itself through that door. Instinctively, she had already discerned that it would be the worst news possible; she had braced for it and was silently, solitarily preparing for the impact.

Conversely, Russell sat in a chair next to the door and stared continuously at the knob, waiting for it to show the slightest movement. For at least an hour, he repeatedly opened the door and peered down the hallway for anyone who may be coming to give them an update. In between, he would put his hand on Anna's thigh and squeeze while whispering unconvincingly, "He's going to be okay . . . he has to be."

At one point, the quiet and waiting became too much. Russell opened the door and made his way toward the emergency triage windows. He was shocked to see the industrial-size clock over the left shoulder of the nurse's uniform. The clock read twenty-five minutes after five in the afternoon. It had been at least five hours since they'd arrived at the hospital. During that time, a number of nurses had visited the room to provide short updates.

While they spoke in reassuring tones, they offered little in the way of details or prognosis. Each time one would leave, it was as if all the oxygen was sucked from the room with them. At the triage station, Russell begged the nurse in a hushed tone to please send for someone to see them, his voice splintered and hoarse as he spelled Joshua's name.

Anna had not moved a muscle while Russell had been out of the room. He remembers looking at her as he re-entered the room and then feeling all vestiges of composure disintegrate before her.

"I couldn't—" he cried out. "I couldn't get to him. I should never have—"

The door swung open. A young doctor with a shaved head and at least two days of chin stubble, entered the room and gently closed the door behind him.

He introduced himself as Dr. Greg Shapiro, a neurology surgeon who had been paged by the attending emergency physician. He had spent the past three hours with Joshua.

"I'm afraid I don't have good news."

Those seven words remained suspended. Anna, having often delivered the worst of news to family members, immediately comprehended their meaning. For the first time in hours, she moved. Her hands went to her face as she leaned forward and released a wail full of hopelessness and wretched sorrow.

Russell listened and tried to but could not process what the doctor was saying. Joshua on life-support, a summary explanation of brain death, options limited, the sensitive, but necessary, discussion of organ donation. The young surgeon's words were clear enough, but Russell refused to acknowledge them. It simply couldn't be real. It had been only that morning that they had been seated at the breakfast table together, laughing and making plans for the afternoon.

A week earlier, Joshua had played a rough and rambling concert on the toy piano they'd put under the tree this past Christmas. Russell pictured the countless times Joshua had run to him and thrown his arms around his neck when he picked him up at daycare. Now, his son, his sweet, exquisite boy, was not going to see another day? It wasn't possible.

Russell's intellect struggled to process information that his heart was simply incapable of managing. His psyche seemed to find itself unwittingly locked in a room, a space he did not seek entry to with any awareness, a door he didn't knock on, a room that he didn't cut a key or pick a lock to access. Disoriented, Russell found his mind was trapped in such a place for what must have been hours after Joshua's condition had been described to them. Russell didn't snap out of this state until a nurse entered the room, held Anna's hand, and told them they could see their son.

"He's just around the corner. He's in a private room, and you can stay for as long as you need to," she said solemnly.

He couldn't catch his breath. But, somehow, Russell followed the nurse out of the waiting room, through the sliding doors where they had taken Joshua many hours before, and to a stained-wood doorway with a stainless-steel, L-shaped door handle. Anna walked with her hand on the nurse's elbow, her steps hesitant.

Before they had entered the ICU room where Joshua lay, Russell could hear the rhythmic tempo of the breathing apparatus interrupted regularly by the pulsing beep of a heart monitor. The mechanical sounds seemed to find definition and meaning when coupled with the tubes and wires attached to Joshua's face and chest. The intrusive machinery disturbed Russell. Yet, he looked peaceful. They had cleaned the scrape on Joshua's forehead and, were it not for the heap of plastic hoses amassed above his chest, Russell would have sworn that his boy was simply taking one of his usual afternoon naps.

Russell went to him first, a steady, salty stream of tears stinging his face. He kissed Joshua's eyelids and watched his tears crawl down the boy's long, curled lashes. Joshua had Anna's eyelashes, dark and thick. Anna called them his "fans." She used to play with him in her arms, putting his face to hers and asking him to flutter his eyes and cool her. Joshua loved this game and always obliged with a look of deep concentration, followed by minutes of blinking. Russell took in the deepest breath he could force and inhaled the familiar aroma of his son's skin.

After a while, Russell tore himself away, held Anna tightly for a moment, and retreated to a stiff leather armchair in the corner of the room. Anna sat beside Joshua and ran her hand continuously through his hair. She did not speak but just looked intently at Joshua's face with defeated eyes.

They had been forewarned earlier that the doctors would have to turn off the life-support systems within a certain timeframe to harvest Joshua's organs. And, at about ten minutes before midnight, the same nurse who had ushered them to Joshua's bedside slipped into the room. She placed a hand on Anna's shoulder and, looking directly at Russell, said, "It's time."

After he nodded, the nurse began her preparations. Russell watched from what seemed like miles away as she carried out a choreographed routine she had doubtlessly performed too many times. The care with which she went about pushing buttons on various electronic components, removing the breathing tube from Joshua's nose, disconnecting the wires and suction cups from his torso seemed almost like a religious sacrament. Were it not for the desperate circumstances, the procedure might have been seen as a beautiful and sanctified dance of passage.

Russell knew that this was, and would forever remain, the absolute darkest moment of his life. He was overwrought with a need to hold Anna close to him, but he couldn't go to her. He recognized that she had immediately retreated into herself, and he suspected that she would turn away from his embrace.

When the nurse was finished, she motioned to Anna to sit in the armchair. Gently, she slipped one forearm under Joshua's knees and another under his shoulder. She lifted him delicately and placed him on Anna's lap. Russell stood beside his wife and rested one hand where her shoulder met the back of her neck, immediately noticing her skin was cold and taut. With the other hand, he held Joshua's tiny and unmoving wrist so that he could feel the very thin pulse that still stirred within him.

They stayed in that position for another hour. Anna held their son and rocked him. She hummed portions of Joshua's favorite bedtime songs and stroked his cheek until the last air he would breathe was pressed from his lungs, and his body went still in her arms.

Russell buried his face in the nape of Joshua's neck, overcome with a heaving and uncontrolled weeping as he half-whispered, half-gasped, over and over, "I'm so sorry . . . I'm so sorry . . . I'm so sorry . . ."

# 14

As he and Pops McCreary cut a decisive path across Teapot Lake, a fog rose from the water. Young Russell felt like an explorer who had discovered an untouched nirvana. It was as though, in the chilled early morning hush, they were the only souls on the planet.

Nothing stirred. Birds had yet begun to sing their daily melodies, not even the faintest hint of a whispered breeze touched their ears. The only sound was the rhythm of their paddles dipping into the water, murmuring calmly with a soft gurgle each time they pierced the glassy surface.

Russell had been roused from a deep sleep at precisely five o'clock in the morning. He woke slowly at first and then, when he realized this was the day of their expedition, he shuffled off with the speed and alacrity of an athlete. Their canoe trip to Manitou Lake: camping overnight, sleeping in a tent, and venturing into the wilderness. He had been beside himself for days, bristling with anticipation and some degree of uncertainty at what this adventure would entail.

The past forty-eight hours had been about preparation. At Pops' instruction, Russell rolled up their sleeping bags and stuffed them into waterproof sacks, poured trail mix into plastic containers, took an inventory of supplies, and double-checked that they had batteries for their flashlights and ample rope to hang their food in a tree overnight.

"We can't forget the marshmallows," Pops said as he hunched over an overstuffed backpack while shoving a bright orange plastic tarp inside. "An absolute essential for evening campfire treats."

"Okay," Russell agreed, trying to imagine what a campfire in the darkened woods would be like. The marshmallows sounded like a good idea either way.

Judith seemed distracted since her return from the United Kingdom. Russell assumed her thoughts were focused on the job and the possibility of moving to London. She had set about cleaning the cabin obsessively for several days since her return, a clear indication that she was distracted and ruminating.

In any other set of circumstances, Russell would have been unnerved. But at Teapot Lake he was appeased by his surroundings and thrilled by the promise of continued exploration of this wonderland. In the comforting sheath of his newfound love for his grandfather, he found that he did not worry about things in the same way that he might have without him.

It took most of the morning to traverse the lake, during which time Pops and Russell did not exchange more than a few words. At the far side of Teapot Lake, Pops McCreary glided the canoe into a small inlet, where they floated until the gunwales scraped against a smooth rock. They steadied themselves and climbed out onto the rock.

Looking back toward the cabin, they could no longer see the far shore, where they had set out earlier that morning. They were officially in the wilderness, with no connection to the comforts of their home. An excited shiver went up Russell's back, cooling the glistening of sweat between his shoulder blades.

"Time to portage, Rusty," Pops announced.

Pops held the straps of Russell's backpack while the boy wriggled into them and stumbled, righting himself before slipping down the smooth rock face and into the water.

"We have a mile to hike, and then we'll have some grub. Are you up for the portage, or do you need to rest?"

Russell shook his head and followed his grandfather through an opening in the underbrush.

The air was still and humid. Mosquitoes pierced his exposed flesh, and he slapped at them as his footsteps crunched along a narrow path in the forest. His backpack was so heavy he felt as though he might trip and fall backward at any point during their hike. Pops' weathered canvas pack was twice the size of Russell's, and he was balancing the canoe on his shoulders as he steered them through the woods. To Russell, his grandfather's strength was godlike.

It was shortly past noon when they found themselves at the end of the portage trail. They were standing at the opening of what looked like a shallow river. A legion of tall reeds settled against the riverbanks, giving the watercourse the appearance of a walled canal. About thirty feet ahead, the stream twisted to the right. Russell was filled with a sense of mystery, wondering what secrets the river held around that bend.

"The river winds for about the next three miles and then opens up to Manitou Lake," Pops explained as if reading Russell's mind. "Once we get to Manitou, it's a short paddle to where we'll camp for the night."

"You've camped there before?"

"Many times, Rusty. I've camped at various points all over the lake. We'll set up on Hunter's Island on the south side. It's a great spot to watch the sunset."

They ate tuna sandwiches and trail mix with their backs pressed against the sun-warmed sides of the canoe. Once finished, they stretched and reloaded their packs, leaning them against the yoke. Russell assumed his position in the bow, and Pops adeptly pushed them back into the water and hopped into position at the stern.

The river turned constantly. It was so shallow they could clearly see the bottom where thousands of flattened reeds curled and shimmered like the flowing, golden hair of a mermaid living just below the water's surface.

They paddled and drifted languidly down the narrow river for the better part of the afternoon. When they arrived at the shores of Manitou Lake, Russell was surprised at its size. The breeze rippled the surface into waves that lapped against the front of the canoe and sprayed cool mist onto his cheeks.

"We're headed over there," Pops said as he pointed his paddle toward an island of steep rock with a cluster of pine trees at its top.

The stillness of the landscape once again struck Russell. A large white bird was perched on the end of a dead tree branch and turned its head slowly in their direction as they floated past. He noticed his grandfather's paddle go still as they passed by the statuesque observer. It was as if he didn't want their motion to alarm the bird. Russell felt a quiet comfort in the symbiosis of nature and the delicate balance of an ecosystem.

When they arrived at their campsite, they tied the canoe to a tree trunk and lugged their backpacks up the rock to the top of the island. Trees swayed in a steady warm breeze as they set about pitching their tent and gathering firewood. That afternoon would become one of the most pleasant and satisfying memories of Russell's early life, sharing this untamed, serene space, just him and his grandfather, arms and shoulders tired from paddling, miles from anyone or anything else in the world, and perfectly content in one another's company.

As dusk fell, Pops showed Russell how to start a fire. They cooked beans in a dented pot, and joked about the probable effects that their choice of dinner would have on their digestive systems, teasing each other about who would stink whom out of the tent first. Later, guided by the beam from their flashlight, they made their way down to the water's edge and listened to the tinny echoes of the pots tapping against water and rock as Pops washed their pans and metal plates.

Russell's eyes felt heavy as he sat at the fireside. Embers jumped from their campfire and glided momentarily on the soft night's breeze before flaming out above them. He yawned as his grandfather poked at the fire with a long, crooked branch. It was then that he noticed something shiny in his shirt pocket.

"What's that?" he said in a half-awake voice, pointing to his grandfather's chest.

"Mmmm . . ." Pops mumbled, reaching down, and pulling on a leather string that was tied around his neck. It was the first time Russell had seen it. "I was going to give you this later, but since you noticed it now, there's no sense in waiting."

He pulled the leather string over his head and held it out to Russell. A long, cylindrical metal object hung off the thin, leather necklace.

"What is it?"

"Something I want you to have, Rusty. It has quite a story behind it."

Russell took it and examined the object more closely. It was a coppery color and tapered to a point on one end. Now obscured and worn, what looked like words or symbols were etched in block script on the flat bottom of the cylinder. They were indistinguishable.

"Is it a bullet?" he asked.

"Close," said his grandfather. "It's the top part of a shell from an anti-aircraft gun. During the war, we had been trapped in a foxhole for over three days. It was fall of 1918, and we had been fighting in a place called Harbonniers in Northern France. I was an Army infantryman and had been in Europe for what seemed like forever. We fought back and forth with the Germans, winning some ground and then losing some. At one point, we had been forced to retreat and dig what we called foxholes while we waited for reinforcements and held back the Germans with mortar attacks. I can tell you, Rusty, sitting in that hole, just waiting for something to happen, almost drove me crazy. We had lost hundreds of men in what felt like an endless series of battles, and we were exhausted. Three of us hunkered down. We had watched so many of our fellow soldiers fall without being able to do anything to help them. Our spirits were almost broken."

Russell tried to imagine his grandfather, Pops McCreary, as a young man, crouched in a dirt hole in the middle of a battlefield. It seemed inconceivable.

"By the second day, we were getting desperate. We had been

conserving our rations but were running low. We were down to a package of peanuts that I had in my pocket and to dirty water that had to be collected from the bottom of our foxhole. It was October, cold, and it had rained for twenty-four hours straight. Once the rain stopped, we started a small fire beside the hole by carving pieces of wood down to the dry core. We boiled the water as best we could, but it was still full of grit and sand. Rusty, I have to admit that I had never been more afraid, and have never been since. By the third day, we had almost given up. We were becoming dehydrated. We were dirty and still cold and wet. I remember turning my head to the wall of the hole and crying. I could not see how we would get out of there."

To Russell, his grandfather possessed almost superhuman strength and fortitude of spirit. He could not picture him weeping.

"Just as it was becoming dark at the end of day, we heard explosions ahead of us where the Germans were stationed and the sound of tanks rolling from behind us. At first, I thought I was hallucinating. But it was real. Our tanks rumbled by us, and we jumped up and down and hugged each other in relief. We walked behind the tanks and began forming a larger group with the other members of our division who had also taken shelter. Our skin and eyes were as gray as the clouds and smoke in the sky above us. We began marching toward the town, stiff and sore in every joint, and, I must say that we certainly looked like a sorry lot. But we were all glad to be alive and moving again.

"We were walking on a path that seemed to be an old wagon trail of some sort. The path cut across an open field and led to the town. For a moment, the clouds and smoke parted above us, and a small slit of blue sky opened. A solid pillar of sunlight shone down, and I was nearly blinded by it. I immediately noticed something gleaming in front of me. The weather had been dull and gray for so long that it forced me to squint. I quickly moved out of our formation and bent down to pick up whatever it was. This was what I found."

Pops reached over and took the shell from Russell's hand. He held it to the firelight. Something brightened behind his eyes for a moment.

"I found out later that it was part of an anti-aircraft shell, a leftover from a previous battle. I turned it over and over and watched the sun glint off it. Then just as quickly, the clouds and smoke were again welded together, and the sun disappeared. Somehow, though, in that one moment of light, I was filled with a hope that I thought I would never feel again during that wretched war. I somehow knew I was going to be all right. We finished the march into Harbonniers, and I twirled the shell in my hand. I remember looking at it and repeating to myself, 'It's going to be all right, it's going to be all right.'"

For a long moment, Russell gazed into the fire in silence. After a while, Pops handed the shell back to him.

"To me, it was more than what most people would call a good luck charm," Pops said after a while. "It was a sign, a bright signal that life would once again emerge after the dark months of the war. I really want you to have it, Rusty."

Russell didn't know what to say. He wanted to respond that his grandfather should keep it. He wanted to thank him profusely, comprehending the significance of his grandfather giving him such a monumentally important object from his past. It was his talisman, and he wanted Russell to have it. Russell smiled and placed the shell in his pocket.

"I'll take good care of it," he said.

After this, Russell made a sleepy attempt to clean the campsite. Pops poured a pot of lake water over the fire, causing a hiss that permeated the dark woods around them.

The following morning, they canoed back to Teapot Lake and the cabin. Soon after they had dropped their backpacks heavily on the floor of the cabin, he noticed a transfiguration of the atmosphere. This summer of undisturbed isolation, within the cocoon of a new union with his grandfather, was about to come to an abrupt conclusion.

"How was your camping trip?" Judith asked, emerging from one of the back bedrooms, the floorboards creaking under her feet as she entered the main room. "Based on how incredibly dirty you both look, I'd have to say it was pretty good."

Russell smiled. He could feel the soot from the previous night's fire and the grime from two days of portaging and sweating caked to his skin.

Pops tussled the hair on the back of Russell's head with his palm. "Our Rusty is a real adventurer. He could've gone another week, I think."

Judith smiled tightly.

"I have some news, Russell," her voice becoming flat and serious. He immediately sensed that something unwelcome was coming. He had become attuned to the inflections and tempo of his mother's voice. Her intonation was intended to convey gravitas while, at the same time, came across as excessively excited and upbeat. Whatever her news, Russell steeled himself for it.

"Well, you know that I've been interviewing and had to leave over the past few days, right?"

"Yes," Russell affirmed timidly.

"They really liked me!" she beamed. Russell felt an unseen noose of supple velvet tightening. "They offered me a role right there, after I had finished the last interview. I couldn't believe it. The only hitch is that they want me to get started really, really soon." She scrunched her face up when she said this and then added what Russell was secretly dreading. "I'm afraid we're going to have to leave the cottage a bit earlier than expected."

A moment of uncomprehending silence hung between them.

"Why?" Russell asked, his voice hushed but agitated.

"Russell, this is outstanding for us," she said, trying to sound upbeat. Russell could tell she was concerned about his instinctive first reaction. "They want me over there to start working with one of the leading cardiac surgical teams in Europe. It's an opportunity I couldn't have imagined getting a few years ago. Unfortunately, it means that we have a lot to do in a few short weeks. We have to go back home, pack our furniture, and—"

"No!" It was the only response Russell could fathom. "I want to stay here with Pops. I don't want to go to London or the UK or wherever it is. Can't I at least stay for the rest of the summer?"

Judith stiffened. She had anticipated resistance, but not belligerence.

"There's no debate," she scolded. "Tonight, we need to pack our things. We'll head back to Toronto first thing in the morning."

Russell was poised to offer a rebuttal when she added, "I'm sorry, Russell. I know you've had a wonderful time here with your grandfather, and I know moving to a whole new country is a lot to digest. You simply don't have a choice in the matter unless you prefer to provide for yourself."

Russell winced. How strange it was when he considered how reticent he'd been to travel north to his grandfather's cabin at the beginning of the summer. Now, faced with being forced to abandon the haven of this magnificent summertime, he realized how attached he'd become to his surroundings and his grandfather.

He turned and pushed open the screen door. Frustrated, he walked heavily across the grass to the forest, plunging headfirst into the woods without purpose or direction. After ducking beneath branches and climbing a steep incline through the underbrush, he stopped, out of breath. He looked up at the swaying foliage moving lazily in the warm, trifling wind.

He stopped beside a giant boulder that seemed to have dropped randomly in the center of a thicket of underbrush. Without reason or forethought, he knelt beside the giant rock and began digging, shoveling handfuls of dirt as though he were a prospector on a frantic and crazed excavation in search of gold.

After he had burrowed a hole that was almost a foot deep, he reached into his pocket and extracted the shell that Pops had given him the night before. He could not bear the thought of keeping it with him and was overwrought with the irrational notions of a young boy. If he buried it here, he would have to come back very soon to retrieve it. He pushed the dirt back in the hole he'd made and then retraced his steps back to the cabin, wanting to cry but refusing to give in to the urge to do so.

Judith was in her bedroom at the back of the cabin. He could hear her already immersed in the project of packing belongings. The reality of suddenly having to depart hit him again and his spirits sank another couple of notches.

"Come over and have a seat with me, Rusty." His grandfather's voice met him as he walked into the main living area of the cabin. He was seated on the sofa in a far corner, his visage slightly shaded by the fading light of the day. "It was quite an adventure we just finished up, wasn't it? I haven't been on a solid canoe excursion like that one in a long time."

"Yeah," Russell said in a quiet voice, clearly dejected.

"You were a perfect partner. Couldn't imagine having as much fun with anyone else."

"Yeah," Russell repeated.

"Hey, come on over here, Rusty." Pops motioned for him to sit beside him on the sofa. Russell made his way over to his side and sat but couldn't bring himself to look at his grandfather. He stared straight ahead through the bay window. "I know you're upset about having to leave so quickly. I wish things had worked out so you could stay a bit longer, too."

His statement was met with a deep sigh.

"This is such a terrific thing for your mother. It's what she has worked for and sacrificed for over many, many years. I haven't seen her as relieved and truly happy as she has been since she shared the news," he said. "You know, a canoe trip is one kind of adventure.

Moving across the Atlantic and going to London is an even bigger one. The way you handled yourself on our camping trip, you're going to manage this next adventure like a pro."

Russell knew his grandfather was trying to cheer him up, but he just couldn't bring himself to be anything but disappointed.

"And we've done so much together here," Pops added. Then, with a wistful glance at the bay window Russell was staring through, he said, "Just think, in another year, maybe your mother will let you fly back to Canada, and we can do it again."

"Yeah," was all Russell could manage. "A year from now."

A long time passed with Russell and Pops sitting on the sofa, both looking through the window in silence. Then, without warning, Russell threw his arm around his grandfather and buried his face in his chest. A torrent of tears came as he sobbed into Pops' knitted, cotton sweater vest. Pops reached over and patted the back of Russell's head with his palm.

"I'm gonna miss you too, Rusty," he whispered. Russell thought he detected a crack in his grandfather's voice.

That night, as he lay in his bed for his last sleep at the cabin, Russell had heard the door groan gently and the shuffle of footsteps across the floor. As he fell asleep, a hand touched his shoulder. He felt the softest kiss on his forehead and heard a thick sigh before his grandfather left the room.

The following morning, Russell and his mother stuffed their belongings in the car and drove slowly down the gravel roadway. Pops left for a walk before they departed and did not come back to see them off. Russell understood Pops' need to avoid a formal farewell. It would be too hard for either one of them.

# 15

After the loss of their son, the demise of their marriage felt inevitable. And it was that inevitability that had propelled Russell into the affair with his boss—or at least that is what he had told himself. But in his heart, Russell knows this is not true. He was not forced to seek refuge outside of their marriage but, in doing so, he cut the final tether that sent his relationship with her rolling toward finality. He had risked not only Anna, but his career.

When he and Sarah Westroes found their connection tumbling into new dimensions, they should have both been stronger. The ethical gamble was something they both permitted, yielding to the surge of need that developed between them. They sat at the highest echelons of the Datatel organization chart, their accountability was set at the uppermost threshold. They were standard bearers. Yet, they had breached the most basic rules that prohibited illicit workplace fraternization. Their mutual love and attraction was graceful, yet an ill-advised tightrope walk.

There had always been an underlying attraction. The day Sarah had first arrived as the newly appointed CEO at Datatel and marched into his office, she was so pristinely put together that Russell had been immediately disarmed. She was remarkably beautiful; tall, confident, fine features, a strand of strawberry blond hair dropping languidly to the side of her face. As she introduced herself, Russell had found himself unexpectedly and somewhat awkwardly gazing into huge, hypnotic, blue eyes behind the tint of her thin glasses.

It was her genius that he found most irresistible. Sarah's was a feral intellect, untamed and devoid of angst or boundaries. This part of her being drew him with a magnetism so fierce it seemed to pull from the center of the earth. That undercurrent of desirability had always been a subterranean reality for Russell, but one that was easily suppressed. Even in the abstract, his marriage to Anna had been a sanctified thing. When it came to Sarah Westroes, he had maintained a structured scaffold of rational, professional respect, never allowing himself to even explore the concept of anything beyond.

Nonetheless, it happened.

In the months following Joshua's accident, he and Anna clung to one another, back-to-back, warding off ghosts. After the immediate and crushing aftermath of losing a child, Anna took a leave of absence from work. They drove together to the Florida Keys, where they stayed for several days and did little other than cry mournfully in each other's arms for what seemed like hours.

Eventually, when they returned to their daily lives and rituals, the softness between Russell and Anna hardened as they were forced to face the reality of a life without their son. Whereas, at first, they had been driven to one another as a source of understanding and comfort, over time, they repelled one another, as though each of them represented a constant reminder of what they had lost. The savory life they had enjoyed with their child transformed into an acid bitterness within only a few bites.

Anna began to focus every ounce of energy on her work, and they slowly began to spend less time together. When they did find themselves interacting, anger and rage emanated from her every pore. Intense grief had rearranged her emotions and how she processed her world.

Before the accident, Anna would let things move through her psychological filters until they settled and soaked. Only then would she typically respond or react. But over time, the wounds she could not heal grew wider and more porous until the automatic mechanisms that had previously regulated her reactions became inoperable.

Russell knew instinctively that Anna's rage was without a real target. She did not blame him for the accident. But she could not lash out at fate, could not scream and scratch at chance misfortune until it bled. So, he became the focal point of her wrath. Her uncontained fury spilled from the bottle that was her legacy, and her own father's fierceness came full circle. The more she attacked, the more vicious the verbal assaults became, the more Russell refused to engage and withdrew.

They both stood their ground stubbornly from their respective corners. Russell's mother had been Anna's mentor and surrogate parent for so long. She took the losses of both Dr. Judith and Joshua as an insult from the universe, an unpardonable injustice, and she coiled into a wild creature that crouched, ready to strike. Over the course of many months, Anna's antipathy toward the world swelled like an injured muscle, incapable of contracting and working in the usual manner and, instead, capable only of aching.

They were unable to discuss their fragile mental states and dissect the detritus of their crumbling union. While Anna survived through a hardening of her soul, Russell seemed to gravitate to the comfort of silence and introspection. It was as though Joshua's loss had given him a concussion that left the outside world muffled and distant. He would return from sleepwalking through the daytime hours at work by sitting alone in the evening, submerged in his grief.

They sold their house in Needham and moved to a leased condo downtown. Naively, Russell believed that a change of venue might facilitate the healing process and bring them back together as a couple. They both knew it would not; the flame of their marital union had danced its final flicker and was about to be extinguished. They should have known better.

"I think getting out of here and into a whole new lifestyle in the city will do us some good," he had expressed days before their move to the city center. "There won't be so many daily reminders of—"

"I know, I know what you're going to say," Anna interjected.

"Please don't. Just don't go there."

"Go where?" he retorted. "I'm simply talking about our new reality."

"It doesn't need to be vocalized."

"But—"

"I said please don't, Russell. You're stating the obvious, but hearing it just takes my breath away."

"Okay, okay. I was trying to convey that the change might be helpful."

Anna drew in a breath and held it before saying, "Nothing will be *helpful* enough. But, yes, that's why we made this decision to get out of the suburbs and change the scenery."

"Right. That's all I'm saying."

"Good. It's said now, and we can drop it and just get out of here this weekend and get into the condo."

These discussions would generally conclude with a long period of silence that often endured long past the time they closed down the day and retired to their bedroom.

On these nights, he often felt that there was no feeling lonelier than lying in the same bed beside someone with whom you shared a deep love and knowing it had been snuffed out, despairingly and permanently expired.

"I was thinking we should talk about how we can schedule more time together when we move," Russell blurted one night while they were lying in this state of suspended animation.

Anna had rolled over but was awake, looking at her smartphone. Russell had been pretending to read a book. He still liked the tactile feel of a printed book. On this night, he hadn't flipped a single page, but instead stared vacantly at the words. He was fixated on their upcoming move and the seemingly slim probability of him and Anna readjusting their lives in a way that could salvage their bond.

"I was almost asleep," she retorted. He knew this wasn't true as the light on her phone quickly diminished, "Is this really the best time to talk about it?"

"We're never together," he said, laying the still opened book on his lap and turning his palms to the ceiling. "When else are we supposed to talk about things?"

"Things. Right." She said cynically. "Things we need to talk about. Scheduling time in the new condo so we can be together."

"You don't have to shove it back in my face," Russell responded defensively. "I'm at least trying to make the effort to somehow improve things here."

"That's admirable, Russell. Congratulations for making the effort."

He added, "We're going to have to communicate at some point."

"Can we just please go to sleep? It's late." He noticed that she had not rolled back toward him and was talking to him while facing the bedroom wall. "We can talk about moving downtown and spending time together and getting it in our calendars, and all of that when we're rested. Later this week, maybe."

"We both know that will never happen," he snorted wryly. "You either avoid interacting with me or get angry. Neither is conducive to working things out."

He made invisible air quotes with the fingers of both hands that she could not see.

"Working things out!" Anna snapped. She now rolled over and sat up straight in one single motion. He could see that her blood pressure was rising to her cheeks. Her eyes shot invisible red flames toward him. "What are we supposed to work out, Russell? Huh?"

He stared back at her, knowing it was better not to attempt an answer.

"Whatever we do, it isn't going to bring him back!" Anna jabbed a finger in his direction. "So, what the fuck is the point? We can't solve the one problem that's killing us both. Work things out. Give me a break. Our son is dead, Russell. Just like that ... poof ... gone!"

Unable to restrain himself, Russell shot back. "I'm well aware of the situation, Anna. I'm talking about us and trying to be something that resembles a functioning couple."

"Sounds great . . . not now!" she yelled. Grabbing her phone off the bedside table, she swung out of the bed and left the room without another word.

He assumed she was going to sleep in their spare room. Neither of them had ventured into Joshua's room more than once or twice, so he doubted she was headed there.

Alone in the master bedroom Russell grunted in frustration; the futility of any attempts to converse cut fresh and raw. This grew to become the predominant dynamic of their partnership. He would try to talk; she would respond with increasing vitriol. Russell knew that he should attempt to give Anna more charity; some space and understanding. He found it difficult, however, to temper the incongruous feelings of contempt he was progressively directing toward her as these tempestuous exchanges between them piled on top of one another. Resentment had formed and taken shape in the substrate.

# 16

Elizabeth Alamotti had gotten news of the accident within days after Joshua died. She waited a week and called Russell with her condolences, suggesting that he postpone considering the Syncron role until some time had passed.

"I was actually preparing to call you right around the time it happened," he told her during that call. "And I was going to take the job. I just can't now. There's no point in waiting. There's no way I'll be any good for Syncron, and I'm sure not even in my current role at Datatel."

He was on a leave of absence for an undetermined amount of time. The team at Datatel had been sympathetic, and Sarah had told him to take months if needed. No one could relate to what he was experiencing. No colleague within his circle had lost a child. They were as compassionate as they could be without being able to relate.

"That's completely understandable, Russell," Alamotti had replied. "I know that the Syncron team really wants you. They were impressed enough with you that they basically said they'll wait as long as it takes."

"I appreciate that," Russell said. "I just can't even contemplate it right now."

"Then let's just keep it as an open item. We can revisit it later. If you had been planning to take the role, it means there is some part of you that saw a fit as well. There's no pressure or rush so why make a firm decision now?"

"Okay," he agreed.

"I'll call you in a few weeks."

Russell returned to work about two months after Joshua's funeral. Just as Anna worked increasingly long hours, Russell began to travel more often, ostensibly for work. He could have easily worked from Boston, but he instead elected to spend more time in Datatel's satellite offices. He hadn't been to Datatel's site in Mumbai, India in well over a year and decided to make the long flight and visit the company's development team there.

A week before he was scheduled to leave for Mumbai, Sarah learned of his planned trip. The CEO had decided to accompany him.

"I haven't made the trek over to our shop there in a while myself. I'm overdue," she mentioned. "I think I'll come along, and we can do a few all-employee, business updates together. It will be good for us to present together, demonstrate the cohesiveness of our senior team."

"Sure, that sounds like a plan."

"You could probably use the companionship," she added. "I've steered away from talking too much about Joshua and your state of mind since you came back to the office."

Russell tensed. It was a rarity that Sarah veered into the personal or expressed her perspectives on the individual circumstances of her employees or peers outside of the work environment.

She continued. "It's got to be hard, Russell. I can't imagine how you are picking yourself up every day. I'm impressed that you're even able to make the effort."

"Thank you," he had replied, voice cracking. "It's serving as a suitable distraction more than anything. There's no getting over what we've been through. I had to come back at some point."

"You don't need to be taking off halfway around the world on your own," Sarah continued. "It will be a chance for us to take a breath and catch up a bit."

He had already booked business-class tickets to Mumbai. Sarah said they would travel instead on the corporate jet, as this was a strictly business trip.

"I'm in meetings in New York with a few of the institutional investors," she had informed Russell before having her executive assistant schedule their flight. "We'll have to meet in New Jersey, and we'll fly out of the Morriston airport. If you book a flight up to Newark or JFK, I'll have the car pick you up and we can meet at the airport twenty minutes or so before we take off."

That same day, when he swiveled to one of the three large display monitors at his desk and prepared to book a flight to Newark, a pop-up window presented itself on the screen. It was from Elizabeth Alamotti.

*Probably to give me the news that they've moved on,* he surmised as he opened the email.

*How have you been doing?* Alamotti's message began. *I really wanted to give you some time, so I've waited before following up. Yesterday I got a call from David at Syncron. He was asking about you and wondered if we had been back in touch. I took it as a sign that I should connect with you again. They meant it when they said they would wait for you. The role is still yours if you are ready to consider it.*

Russell responded, *I'm just getting back into things. I don't think it's fair to keep them waiting on me. I can't honestly say I know if I'm ready to jump into the role in the short term. I'm sorry. I appreciate your patience and understanding, but I don't want to keep them waiting on me forever. I'm leaving for India in a few days as well, so I'm going to be out of pocket for about a week.*

Alamotti's return email came within minutes. *Don't apologize. Why don't we try and meet in person in the next couple of weeks when you are back? We can talk through it in a bit more detail. I promise I won't pressure you to take the job. I deal with a lot of different situations with executives weighing their options on offers such as this. I like to think I could help you sort through it a bit. I can come up to Boston any time.*

Russell agreed to reach out to Alamotti when he returned. A tingling of guilt followed him like a shadow, distorting his assessment of how to best manage her persistence. Sarah and Datatel had been incredibly accommodating. His intentions were a compass needle, caught between two magnets, exerting their pull in conflicting directions.

He received an instant message from Sarah's assistant with the itinerary for her New York trip. He decided to book a mid-morning flight to JFK to coincide with Sarah's last meeting, figuring they could link up there and have her limo take them to Morriston.

※

Three days later, he found himself in the Centurion lounge at JFK's Terminal 4, catching on up emails and putting the final touches on a PowerPoint slide deck for Sarah and him to deliver at the business update meetings they had planned in Mumbai.

A text message notification came up on his iPhone. It was Sarah.

*Slight change of plans*, it read. *Meeting finished early. Meet you at the airport. I'm starving. Can you find someplace for us to grab some lunch before we go to NJ?*

He left the lounge, found a wine bar with a decent menu, texted the location to Sarah and was picking at a charcuterie board he had ordered when she arrived.

He spotted her before she saw him as she was riding down the escalator. She wore her shoulder-length hair down and he watched it bounce as she stepped off the escalator and walked across the shining tiles. She was dressed in all black, with leather boots that extended to just below her kneecaps, a fitted skirt, tailored blazer, and ribbed turtleneck with a simple, silver necklace hanging at her neckline. As had happened occasionally in the past, he felt the inappropriateness at being so staggered by her exquisiteness. She was his boss. He caught himself staring at her when she pivoted and immediately met his gaze.

She waved enthusiastically and quickened her pace, giving him a quick embrace as he stood from his chair to greet her.

"Thank you so much for meeting me here," she said through her perfect, gleaming smile. "They had these crappy, nasty Danish things at the meeting. I'd be asleep by now from the sugar rush if I'd eaten one. I'm famished."

"No problem," he said. "I was just sitting upstairs tying off a few loose ends on the presentation."

"Oh, good. You're a lifesaver, Russell. I haven't even had time to look at the draft you sent."

"No worries," he assured her, "it's in good shape. I'll send it over to you on the flight with a few speaking points."

"I wish everyone was as on top of their shit, like you are," she said, tracing a long finger down the menu as she perused her lunch options. "Just one of the many reasons I love you."

It was a blithely delivered statement, Russell knew. Yet, something jumped in his lower stomach, a sharp awareness of sorts.

She ordered a salad with grilled salmon, and he continued to sample the charcuterie board while they briefly reviewed their itinerary for the next couple of days.

"I'm really glad we're doing this together," she offered, tucking an errant curl of hair from her temple behind her ear. "We haven't had much time to connect with everything that's happened, and I have to admit, I'm a drowning in chaos a little myself the past couple of months."

"Everything okay?"

"Yeah, yeah. Or at least it will be," she implied. "I've just been so busy. We're planning this investment road show to raise money for the next acquisition. And, to top it off, Derek and I haven't been seeing eye to eye on a few things. We haven't spent a lot of time together since the start of the year. He's been staying mostly at our place in San Diego, and I haven't made it out West much. Maybe intentionally."

Sarah had rarely confided in him in the past and spoke infrequently about her husband. Russell felt disquieted at her atypical candidness.

She continued. "Who knows, maybe these power couple unions are doomed from the beginning. Too many competing priorities."

"I hope you're able to work something out," Russell responded, uncertain what to say in the situation.

"It'll figure itself out, I'm guessing," she said, then pivoted back to work. "We have way too many great things ahead of us to focus on. The product launch is going well, once we expand the sales force and complete version 3.0 of the software-as-a-service offering, I'm driving for double-digit revenue growth this year."

"It's a really good time for the firm," Russell agreed. "Too bad it comes at a time when we're both facing personal struggles. I'd like to be able to enjoy the rewards of our efforts a bit more."

Sarah placed her fork on the side of her dish and brushed her lips with the edge of the napkin. She reached over and placed her hand on Russell's forearm and leaned forward. Her intense, sapphire eyes locked onto his.

"You're going to get to a place where you can enjoy things again, Russell. Trust me. It sounds like such a hackneyed attempt at support, but I want you to know that I'm here for you. We've always been guarded with each other when it comes to getting too close or delving into personal matters. This has been a tragedy you've suffered. If ever there was a time to crack open the fortress of our defenses, this is it. Right?"

Russell choked on his answer. "Yes, that would nice."

"You can use a friend, Russell," said Sarah, her eyes fixated on him. "To be honest, so could I."

After an hour, the conversation shifted to Anna. It was innocent enough. Sarah asked how his wife felt about him returning to his job, and Russell found himself continuing to reveal details about his state of mind. At one point, while sharing his frustration at Anna and her inconsolable ire, Russell looked intently into Sarah's eyes as if an answer to his dwindling marriage could be extracted from her. Then, as if recognizing that their exchange had gone on for over an hour and drifted into a zone of heightened personal significance, Sarah brought the conversation to a soft close.

"The car is outside waiting for us. Let's get rolling and on our way to Mumbai. Lots of time to talk further on a fifteen-hour flight."

Russell laughed and waved to their server for the bill.

The driver of the limo rolled the privacy window up. Russell opened his laptop again and resumed making finishing touches to the presentation. Sarah inserted her wireless ear buds and made a series of phone calls, threading a tapestry of information in brief updates to various key Datatel leadership and stakeholders, updating them on her investor appointments. From what Russell picked up in the periphery, she was gratified with her New York meetings.

When the limo glided to a stop, almost at the wingtip of a streamlined and imposing plane waiting for them on the tarmac, Russell glanced at Sarah. "You're well aware of how much I enjoy flying, right?"

"Ah, yes, my dear Russell," she said playfully. "I know you flew on a few trips with Cal back when we leased that Bombardier Learjet."

"All I remember was that I was just as jumpy in it as any other plane."

"But you have yet to travel with me overseas in this beauty," she said loudly as she stepped out of the back of the limo and came around to his side. The engines vibrated beside them. "This is a G650. It's going to make you a flying enthusiast by the time we get to India!"

"I highly doubt that." Russell shouted over the hum of the engines.

"You'll see." Sarah smiled and touched his elbow, steering him toward the boarding stairs.

Russell couldn't help but admire the elegance of the Gulfstream G650. Its polished fuselage glistened under the sunlight, displaying a quality of sophistication. He admitted to himself that the whole experience of pulling up to the impressive jet ignited his curiosity about the experience awaiting him.

Stepping into the cabin, he found himself enveloped in an atmosphere of opulence. The spacious interior was meticulously designed, with plush leather seats, multiple high-definition cabin monitors and a conference table in the rear section. Inside the aircraft, the piercing whine of the engines quieted to a barely perceptible whirr.

He settled into a seat across from Sarah. The pilot-in-command emerged from the cockpit and welcomed Sarah back before introducing himself to Russell. Moments later the co-pilot walked over and did the same. It seemed to him that it was only mere moments later that the jet gracefully took to the air, climbing at an incredible rate and effortlessly gliding through the clouds.

The display screen projected an image of their plane crossing over land and heading out over the Atlantic. As they settled into their cruising altitude, Russell found himself immersed in the pacifying quiet setting of the G650. The extraordinary experience of this flight would leave an indelible impression on his senses. And he noted that his stomach hadn't bottomed out once.

He and Sarah did a quick review of the talking notes he had provided for their meetings with the various teams in India, highlighting several key product enhancements that were planned for the next fiscal year. Not that Sarah really needed them; he had watched her present to audiences of thousands and she always managed to leave the crowd mesmerized with her incredible energy and intellect. When they finished the review, they both extended their seats to lay-flat and slept on and off overnight.

When the jet descended into Mumbai, the vast expanse of the city sprawled out below, a mass of concrete, steel, and chaos. The sparkling lights that adorned the urban landscape were not a romantic spectacle, but rather a testament to the unremitting energy that characterized the megacity. From the small cabin window, the glaring disparities of Mumbai were plain to Russell. Skyscrapers dominated the skyline, their richness standing in stark contrast to the makeshift shanties and crowded slums that speckled the city's periphery. The stark reality of the wealth divide was illuminated, with pockets of luxury and privilege juxtaposed against the harshest of conditions and penury endured by Mumbai's masses, the city straining against the swells of rapid urbanization.

Russell had been to the Mumbai office many times, however, it never ceased to serve as a stark reminder of the gritty reality of life in the developing country. It was a city that thrived on resilience and adaptability, where millions of people navigated the daily struggle for survival. Amidst disarray, complexities and contradictions, the city offered an unfiltered glimpse into the realities of modern India.

The day after they landed, Sarah and Russell immediately started a packed itinerary. They covered back-to-back divisional presentations, an all-employee general update, and several sessions with the top leadership group in the Mumbai office. They separated for other meetings when Russell had time allotted to spend directly with his product development and software engineering teams.

On their second evening, they were invited to dinner with the head of operations and most senior executive in India, Dinesh Jadhav. Dinesh was responsible for the full profit-and-loss portfolio of the sprawling and multipart Indian division and, as such, held a position of the highest esteem in Datatel's APAC Group and the firm overall. His accountability was massive, given the company's dependence on the India division for everything from product software engineering to cybersecurity infrastructure and its many specialized tech support call centers.

They shared a private car from the head office at the Bandra-Kurla Complex to a restaurant called Nariman, named after the neighborhood where the original bistro-style eatery had started, now located in the Colaba district. There, old-world colonial architecture butted up against modern-day, fashionable facades and building structures.

Dinesh exited the Mercedes Benz first, the impeccably attired driver jumping out and making a grandiose show of opening the door and bowing. He then ushered Sarah and Russell past a line of patrons toward an awaiting team of hosts at the restaurant's main door. Dinesh was well-known and treated like royalty in Mumbai as was the case in most of the major business hubs across the country.

The sounds and smells of the city presented themselves immediately to Russell as he left the comfort of the car's cool interior, stepping out into air that was plump and wilting with humidity. Blaring car horns from the perpetual traffic in the main thoroughfare were released in patterns that took the place of traffic signals as drivers announced their intended next direction; the whirring of hot winds, funneled between high-rise buildings, blowing discarded paper and plastic that scraped along concrete and dirt, and the unmistakable loamy aromas of tightly packed humanity mingled with spices and vehicle exhaust.

Their dinner consisted of immaculate food, served and eaten slowly at a pace that contrasted with the lurching vehicles outside the restaurant's windows, under power lines that sagged and crisscrossed over the traffic. Dinesh announced every dish as the fawning staff placed steaming dishes on the table—*panner tikka* and *biryanis* from the north, upscaled south Indian specialties of *dosas*, paired with local Maharashtrian cuisine of *puran poli* and *crab masala*.

As they settled into dinner, it became clear that Dinesh, holding court in his own fashion, was set on impressing Datatel's CEO, his short speeches annotated with the matching fluidity of his hands, fingers adorned with colorful rings and his wrist covered in gossamer gold bands.

"As an Indian national and especially as a senior business executive based in Mumbai, I often reflect on the incredible journey that my country has undertaken from the dark days of British colonialism to its emergence as such a prominent global player," he pontificated as the waiters replaced a basket of naan. "The era of British rule left scars on our nation's history, suppressing our inherent potential and exploiting our resources. We were subjects, not citizens. Yet, through self-determination, we emerged stronger, and India began to rewrite its narrative."

"Your country has certainly become a rising powerhouse," Sarah commented. Russell nodded in agreement.

On several occasions, he caught himself staring at her during dinner. Sarah had dressed for the occasion in a modern take on the traditional sari, in a chic, fitted, and intricately embellished crop top blouse along with a *pallu* that fell gracefully from her shoulder. "It's quite impressive."

Dinesh was clearly encouraged by her attentiveness and compliment. "The late 1990s was the turning point for India. I'm grateful to have been a part of it. Economic liberalization and globalization policies brought a shift in the business landscape. The Indian concept of *Jugaad*—a term used to describe our knack for finding innovative, low-cost solutions to problems—became a source of inspiration for businesses across the globe. The Indian workforce, known for its diligence, adaptability, and expertise in technology, started to attract international attention, reshaping the outsourcing and technology sectors."

"And something we certainly appreciate in your team at Datatel Mumbai," Russell said. "I can't imagine we would have the product successes we have had together without your team, Dinesh. They set a high bar for the rest of the company."

"Our company's growth mirrors India's journey, from a developing nation to a global business. I attribute a lot of this to our culture, Russell." Dinesh smiled broadly. "We admire diversity. This has contributed to our success, creating a rich pool of talent that thrives in a globalized world. The modern Indian identity is one of optimism and a commitment to creating a better future for all.

Whenever I look out of my office window at the city of Mumbai, I can't help but feel a sense of pride. I have experienced the evolution of this city into a financial and business hub. The skyline is adorned with skyscrapers, symbolizing the indomitable spirit of our people. The entrepreneurial spirit of Mumbai is alive."

"Cheers to that!" Sarah said and held her glass of red wine to Dinesh and then Russell in a toast.

"And hopefully you are enjoying the Bordeaux," Dinesh added. "One thing we haven't yet perfected in my country is the vintner's touch. I prefer French over Indian wine very much."

Polite laughter followed and the conversation shifted to work.

"So, where did you two get on the product launch discussions?" asked Sarah. "Are we ready for prime time?"

Dinesh nodded in the unique Indian manner, something Sarah referred to as the *pendulum wobble*, where the head neither affirms nor negates but sways within the realm of the possible. "It was a very good meeting Russell and I had today. We are almost ready for prime time. Almost."

Russell glanced at Sarah, knowing she would have little patience for "almost."

"We are on schedule," Russell intoned, quickly to reassure the CEO. "It'll be the usual push to the finish line, but we're in good shape."

※

After this initial evening outing with Dinesh, they met each night at the hotel bar, had a drink together and usually, a dinner that was much lighter than the extravaganza at Nariman on night one. The Datatel team fully embraced the Indian philosophy of *Atithi Devo Bhava* where guests to their country are considered the equivalent to God. Their tremendous sense of hospitality meant that Sarah and Russell were kept overfed during the workdays.

It was during one of these evening meetings that Sarah again broached the subject of her marriage.

She ordered her second vodka tonic from the waiter. "I'm gonna need a couple of these tonight."

"Yeah, I'm tired too. Long days," Russell said in reply.

"The full days of meetings are no problem. At this stage, I can do those in my sleep."

"Your energy and the pace you go at is impressive," Russell complimented, tapping her glass with his own.

"Thanks," Sarah said. "No, my current stresses are more on the home front. Remember when I mentioned my situation with Derek? It's getting clearer that we aren't going to be able to figure this out. Our text exchanges today were getting damn unpleasant."

"Sorry to hear that, Sarah."

"He's going on a three-month project, some bank financing for a construction conglomerate in China. He informed me out of the blue that he'll be going between Hong Kong and Beijing and seems to think I'm going to figure out a way to fit in three of four visits. He's giving me a major guilt trip, which seems to be his MO lately."

"That sounds like it would be nearly impossible. He won't come back to the US at all?," Russell asked.

"He could if he wanted to. It's predictable with Derek though. His career always comes before mine, he's never even contemplated sacrificing his time for us."

"I'm sure it's frustrating."

"Anyway, my apologies for unloading on you," she said. Her drink came, and she took a healthy sip before placing it down in front of her. Ripples of condensation trailed down her glass. "If I'd known how easy you are to talk with, these couple of years, I might have taken you on more of these trips and exposed the naked core of my being to you."

Russell laughed. It was true that their relationship had been expanding exponentially on this hastily planned international trip. And each evening, until the final night before their flight back to

North America, they continued this new ritual of meeting and casting open the vaults of their inner thoughts.

"I'm going to miss our nightly gossip dates," Sarah said on the eve of their departure. "I've started looking forward to them."

Russell took a moment to respond. "Me too."

"Maybe we'll have to find time to keep this newfound tradition when we are back home. At least occasionally," she mused.

After they had left each other and returned to their rooms, Russell lay awake, the realization emerging that his thoughts were continuously settling on Sarah. In those moments, his attention collapsed, and her image found its way through the labyrinthine corridors of his present mind. Every instinct admonished him, and he tried to convince himself their growing closeness was a silly, adolescent infatuation and that he was beyond succumbing to something so obvious. As much as he attempted to push it away, he could feel his pulse quickening each time he reflected on her and mentally relived their week together.

As the week progressed, he had also noticed a subtle specter of remorse surreptitiously weaving its tendrils into the fabric of his thoughts. Elizabeth Alamotti had sent him several emails during his India visit, reminding him of his promise to reconnect with her upon his return. The Synchron offer was still on the table. He felt more than just a twinge of guilt every time he thought about it. If he accepted the job, how would it look to have kept it concealed from Sarah with this recent openness they had come to share?

On the last night of their Mumbai trip, it had kept him in a state of sleeplessness. After several hours, he was overcome with the need to disclose his interactions with Elizabeth and his visits to interview with Synchron. He tapped his iPhone and texted Sarah, confirming if she was awake. She responded almost instantly. Russell dialed her number and laid bare the details of Synchron's perseverance in recruiting him.

Sarah heard him out in silence. When he was done, she stated unpretentiously, "You can't leave."

"I've only been considering it. I'm not sure the timing is right anyway."

"You can't leave," she repeated, "I rely on you."

"I think both you and Datatel would survive without me," said Russell modestly.

Sarah said nothing for a stultifying minute.

"I want you close to me Russell. This has been an amazing week. It's more than our work life together."

Until then, neither of them had uttered a word about the intimacy ripening between them.

"And anyway, you're my subordinate, right? So, I'm directing you to stay. You're staying with me."

And then, she disconnected the call. Russell stared at his phone, his emotional landscape a swirling mosaic of relief, joy, and confusion.

---

They landed back in Morriston on a Friday, mid-afternoon. At no point during the return flight did either of them address the substance of their late-night phone call.

"I think you told me you have a flight booked out of Newark back to Boston. Are you leaving tonight?" Sarah inquired.

"Tomorrow morning. I booked a room at the Hotel Saint-Tropez for tonight. We had a conference there once a few years ago and I've stayed there a few times since. It's a quaint little Relais & Châteaux, but sort of in the countryside. What's your plan?"

"Staying in our Manhattan condo for the weekend. I have to be in Dallas on Monday. It never slows. Hopefully, I can get past the jet lag in the next two days."

Russell nodded in agreement.

After a few moments, Sarah added, "You know, I've heard the Hotel Saint-Tropez has a great restaurant. Some Michelin star chef... I can't remember her name. I've never been. If you're up for it, we could have dinner."

Against the backdrop of her comments on their phone call the previous night, Russell intuitively understood the weight of this invitation.

By early evening, yielding to these relentless currents of attraction and intimacy, they found themselves in Russell's softly lit suite at the chateau hotel. A soft, classical track filled the room from the suite's sound system as the door closed behind them, the violin and piano tones greeting them like confessions of their desire.

Sarah sat lightly on a sweetheart thronet chair in the short hallway of the suite as Russell strode to the window and closed the blinds, his posture tense, his mind full of undeclared longings.

Russell increased the volume of the sound system slightly. "The music is beautiful."

"It is. It's Nuvole Bianche by Ludovico Einaudi. He's one of my favorite contemporary composers," Sarah informed him. "I'm somewhat of a classical music nerd."

"I'm impressed but somehow not surprised you could just identify the piece like that out of thin air. You have the most exceptional mind," Russell extoled.

He turned to look at her, his eyes filled with an intensity that made her breath catch. He walked toward her and extended his hand, a silent invitation. She hesitated for a moment, then placed her hand in his.

They moved to the center of the room, a grand chandelier above casting a wraithlike glow on them. Their bodies shifted in deliberate rhythm to the music, not dancing but moving together. Gently, Russell placed his hand on the small of her back, pulling her closer, their bodies almost touching. Sarah's face flushed, her senses heightened by their silent conversation of movement, each motion a word, each step an affirmation.

Her breath hitched as he touched her temple, his fingers lingering on her skin. It ignited the flame that she had been trying to suppress. She looked up at him, her eyes filled with a mix of apprehension and want. She raised her chin, their lips touching in a moment of raw hunger, breath merging.

The music faded and they broke apart, their eyes meeting in an implicit moment of understanding. Knowing this would change their relationship permanently, they stumbled to the bed, tossing the pillows to the floor, and grabbing desperately at each other.

They parted with a friendly, drawn-out embrace the following morning.

Russell understood the gravity of their actions. It was like driving across railway tracks with a train approaching, ignoring the flashing lights, knowing he should hit the brakes but unable to stop the inclination to press hard on the gas pedal with blind disregard for the perils. He returned to Boston, irresolute in how to regulate his relationships given the astonishing developments with Sarah in the milieu of his disintegrating marriage.

They continued to be close after he returned to Boston. Sarah and he arranged clandestine meetings at her home in Massachusetts and scheduled late-night video calls several times a week when she traveled. There were many opportunities for either of them to end the spinning dance they were performing. Neither of them did.

Weeks after their return from Mumbai, he found himself conjuring up reasons to be in New York where Sarah spent most of her weekends. He attempted to delude himself that their companionship had sprung from a combination of her sympathy for his loss and his need for distraction. In the hidden mirrors of his psyche, however, a truth stirred that could not be suppressed. It was an inconvenient and impractical affection that had brewed within him. He comprehended the futility of this byzantine emotional entanglement with Sarah while surrendering to the unruly nature of his heart, as it ventured into an alluring territory.

In that time, he met once more with Elizabeth Alamotti and let her know that he would remain in his role at Datatel. She was overtly disappointed but handled his news with the aplomb of a seasoned professional.

※

The levees that Russell had erected around his relationship with Anna finally broke that winter, their first without Joshua. Late in November, Anna informed Russell, through a terse and unaffectionate email message, that she had offered to take a series of twelve-hour shifts over the Christmas period.

Although he knew that this was simply an escape mechanism to avoid facing the season without their deceased son, he instantly resented her for it. With a scowl, he had typed a response from his iPhone and let her know that it was of little consequence since he planned to spend the holidays in New York. It was hasty email messages like this one that ultimately fastened them to a direction of finality. From his perspective, the words in those emails could have been likened to the sight and sound of a giant deadbolt slowly slid across a wooden door until it slipped into its cylinder with a defining and permanent snap.

When he was not with Sarah, he drifted through weightless days, fixating on his want to be with her, the intervening time between their meetings steeped in haziness.

Russell spent that Christmas Eve with Sarah. His mood could only be described as perplexing, a blend of colors mixed on a canvas of emotion that he had been painting over the past year. He felt the awful pang of missing Joshua on what would have been another Christmas holiday spent with him. Although he tried to dispel it, regret broke over him in waves, knowing he had abandoned Anna. And he sank into the comfort of Sarah's passion and welcoming warmth as he expelled other unpleasant thoughts.

They had an early meal in the city and walked in the cool air through the south end of Central Park. Light snow fell, and Russell removed his scarf and draped it over Sarah's shoulders. As he did, she stopped in her tracks and turned to him.

"You know that you are spending Christmas with your mistress," she said with a coy smile. "At least that's what I've labeled myself as."

Russell wrapped his arms around her waist and pulled her close. She held his gaze, and he was overcome with a desire to drink her in, to taste her skin, and hold her. Her hands touched his face, and their lips touched gently. He needed to feel her full spirit close and alive.

When Russell woke on Christmas morning, Sarah lay beside him breathing lightly and looking warm, naked, and stunning. He lay still until she stirred. She rolled over and nestled her chin into his neck.

"I wonder what it would be like to be like this all the time," she whispered in a deep, sleep-filled voice.

Sarah's speculating on them enduring as a couple tested the waters of his thoughts on their future, gripping him. How could they maintain a relationship as coworkers with her as the leader of the firm? Logically, he saw there would be another loss when the inevitable came to pass.

# 17

Signs begin to appear at the side of the road for the town of South River. Several decades ago, Russell and his mother had stopped at that small city. He feels strangely displaced, the span between the innocence of his childhood and now, exposing a root system of matted identity and faraway memory.

The past twenty kilometers have presented a view outside his windshield that confirms his transition from a more populated landscape to sprawling timberland. Rolling hills teeming with seemingly boundless and untamed greenery meet him. The vastness of it envelops him, leaving him acutely aware of his smallness in the grandness of nature.

The volume of traffic has tapered significantly. Vehicles with a canoe or kayak perched on its roof or one towing a recreational watercraft appear sporadically on the highway. However, it is now mostly freight trucks he encounters as he continues to cut a route north.

Scattered stratocumulus clouds hang fat in an otherwise unblemished blue sky. How peculiar it is to be here. His life has unfolded to be so urban. When he had spent his summer with Pops McCreary, he was convinced he would live in a rustic setting. As a teenager, he had on numerous occasions, left the UK, and embarked on camping trips, most often in Finland, the Nordic setting being like the Canadian geography. Now, in adulthood, his world has involved business travel to some of the busiest metropolises in the word and living in a major North American city. He wishes that his gradual detachment from these natural milieus hadn't come to pass.

His dashboard informs him he only has a quarter tank of fuel.

He hasn't passed a service station for a while, so he deviates from the highway and takes a bending off-ramp at the next sign for a gas station. After refueling, he parks the SUV on a gravel lot and hears the door chime as he enters a roadside café adjacent to the fuel pumps.

Seconds later, the smell of hot coffee fills his senses, and he decides he needs a cup, ordering it at the front counter and taking up a seat in a window booth. Out of habit, he takes his iPhone and checks for messages, but his inbox contains nothing other than several random spam messages. Toggling to the still open article Farouq had sent him, something brings him back to contemplate the consultant Sarah had engaged as a risk-management measure during the Jukes deal.

He swipes back from his email and starts typing a text message to Cal.

*Hey Cal. Quick question: Remember the consultant that had worked with Sarah on Jukes. The one she always called Jiminy?*

Cal responds within two minutes.

*Yeah. Why are you asking? Shouldn't you be focusing all your thoughts on the CEO offer?*

Russell smiles at the sarcastic jibe.

*No. Just read that article on her investigation. It hit me as odd. Any reason they aren't cooperating or supporting her?*

The spinning dots on the Instant Messaging app tell him Cal is writing a response. It arrives a moment later.

*Rumor is they are claiming it's all privileged. It was that law firm MN&C. I don't know. Can only figure they are trying to save themselves. They clearly missed a big turd of a ruse, probably want to protect their reputation. Those consulting services are growing and becoming more widely employed. It's a lucrative, expanding market for them, I'm sure.*

Russell responds. *MN&C, right. Thanks Cal. Did the Datatel legal team recommend them?*

Russell orders a refill as he awaits Cal's response.

*No. Remember it was some college friend of her husband's? He put them together and arranged the whole thing. Our team wasn't involved, other than paying the exorbitant damn bills! Gotta run now. Meeting in 2.*

*Appreciate it. TTYL.*

Russell sips his coffee and searches Google for MN&C in Boston. Under the About Us tab, he sees the familiar headshot of the partner who had worked directly with Sarah. Robert Pembroke. They had been introduced only once, and he had been at the Datatel headquarters infrequently, or so Russell assumed since he had not encountered Pembroke often during the acquisition project.

Something close to a theory has been cocooned within the chrysalis of Russell's thoughts, slowly metamorphosing but not yet ready to emerge as a fully developed hypothesis. But it is there, disquietingly just beyond comprehension. He fears that his affair with Sarah could potentially be revealed somehow in the course of the corporate investigation into her dealings. He recollects something she told him once when they were lying awake on the luxurious bed in her condo's spacious master bedroom.

"Even though Derek and I are heading toward a split, I need to make sure he doesn't get wind of us, at all," she had stated resolutely. "He can be very vindictive and conniving."

"Should we be concerned about it in terms of your safety?" asked Russell.

"No, no, nothing like that. Well, not in terms of him being violent or anything like that," she confirmed. "But I could see him putting some set of events in motion to bring us both down, humiliate us. I need to manage the next steps with him cautiously."

Needle pricks of suspicion punctuate his thoughts around Sarah's recent misfortunes as his imagination builds a tempest of possibilities. He scrolls down his contact list and locates the number for Sydney Abbasi.

Considered a luminary in the specialized field of cybersecurity and international digital financial crime, Sydney had served as Datatel's security chief for roughly four years before being enticed into a government career with the Cybersecurity & Infrastructure Security Agency. She had run an entire division at CISA with the arduous charge of coordinating activities with the NSA and, likely, many other opaque federal agencies. Born in Karachi, Pakistan, she immigrated with her family as a teenager to the United States. By her junior year, she had been tagged as both neuro divergent and a genius and found herself being offered a scholarship at MIT where she earned a PhD by the time she was twenty-two.

Several years earlier, she had left the government and started her own consulting firm while also taking on a part-time professorship at Virginia Tech. She now lived in Blacksburg, Virginia.

During her stint with Datatel, she had occupied an office directly across from Russell's. They had become instant friends, Russell appreciating her bombastic, unfiltered sense of humor, a complete contradiction to her image as one of the country's foremost intellects in the technology and security industry. They had traded emails over the past year but hadn't spoken often.

He presses her mobile number on his iPhone screen and waits for the familiar trilling artificial ring, expecting to get her voicemail.

"Mr. Russell, how are you?" Sydney answers. "I've thought about you so many times over the last months."

"Wow, I didn't think I would get you live," he says. "I know how busy you always are."

"Only a handful of people have this cell number. I was delighted to see your name show up on the display. How are you holding up?"

"You know what they say," replies Russell, "every day you just try to move forward."

"It is the only way to heal," she says, "gradually and thoughtfully."

"Thank you, Sydney. Or should I be calling you Dr. Abassi now that you are formally a professor?"

"Don't be such an idiot, Russell. You should *always* have called me Dr. Abassi."

"Ha!" Russell laughs. "I hate to call out of the blue after so long with a favor to ask, however, I wanted to see if you could help me with something. It may be nothing, but I can't get a notion out of my head these past few days."

"Happy to oblige if I can help," Sydney says cheerfully.

Russell explains the fundamentals of the premise he has been developing, as well as he possibly can. Sydney listens, murmuring occasionally to let him know she is following.

"So, do you still have access to certain technologies, like surveillance and monitoring systems?"

"I do, Russell. I'm still called up occasionally to assist, and there are some security clearances you keep for life once you have them. In the next five minutes, I could tell you everything you've typed into search engines this morning, who has tried to contact you by email or phone in the past week, exactly where you are in the world down to a meter and what color underwear you're wearing."

"That's comforting, Sydney, really. I'll save you the time. I'm in Canada taking a long overdue vacation up north."

"Sounds wonderful," Sydney says, "And . . . blue."

"Pardon?" Russell says.

"The underwear. But I was just guessing."

Russell laughs and looks around to check that it wasn't too loud. He is struck by how much he's missed Sydney's wit.

"You won't be at any risk looking into this, will you?" Russell finally asks. "If there is any chance it could cause you problems, I don't want you to even consider it."

"Not to boast, Russell, but I have a very wide berth when it comes to what I can access. There is no risk and I owe you one, anyway."

"How you possibly owe me anything?" he asks.

"I didn't make it to Joshua's ceremony. I was embroiled in a rather extreme crisis at the time and couldn't leave Virginia. I've felt so bad about it ever since."

"Please, Sydney, I understand," says Russell, consoling his former colleague.

"I had blocked some time in my day to prepare a lecture, and I'm less than motivated now so this will be a good excuse to procrastinate. It won't take more than a couple of hours. I'll let you know if I find a proverbial smoking gun."

Russell expresses his gratitude and collects his keys from the café table. He needs to start driving soon if he is going to have ample daylight remaining when he arrives at the cabin. The VW beeps in response to his automatic key and he slips behind the steering wheel and closes the door. Gazing down at his iPhone screen, he contemplates the next step. Deciding that if he ponders it too long, he will talk himself out of it, he goes to his text messages and finds the last one Sarah sent and replies.

He types, *Hello. Have you got some time?*

No response. He waits several minutes to see if a message appears, but none does. Russell starts the SUV, points it north and merges back into the sparse highway traffic. He drives through midday until hearing a notification on his iPhone and then checks in his rearview and sideview mirrors. There aren't any vehicles other than his own on this stretch, so he presses the screen on his iPhone and raises it above the steering wheel.

It's her.

Russell is too distracted and anxious to wait for the next exit to read her response, so he pulls over to park the vehicle. Pebbles are discharged from the rough shoulder with the spin of his tires, and they pepper the undercarriage noisily.

*Have you been living in a cave?* is the single line of text in Sarah's response.

The SUV idling, he types back, *No. But I am way up north in Canada. Why?*

*If you've had access to the news apps, you'd know I not only have time but might be doing time soon.*

Russell can't tell if she is being sarcastic or literal.

*I have been keeping up with your case.*

*And what's made you suddenly ignore the Datatel lawyers' edicts and contact the evil Sarah Westroes?* she probes.

*Just trying to connect a few dots. It may help you. Question. Did Derek ever learn about us?*

The answer is immediate. *Damn right, he did. In the end, I decided you were strong to tell Anna, not weak. I decided to be strong too. Even though I thought he would be furious.*

*And was he?*

*Nope. Calm as Buddha. Said he had deduced I was involved with someone all on his own.*

*It's complicated and I might be inventing things in my head. I have more questions. Need to talk live.* Russell writes.

*Meeting with my legal team until late. Can you call me tomorrow night, 7pm?*

*Yes.*

He exhales a pulsating discharge of air directed into the steering wheel. After shifting into drive gear, he checks his side mirror and eases back onto the unoccupied highway. This is the sunset stretch of his long journey to the cabin. His conscious mind triangulates on multiple sources of tension and anticipation, thrust into the overwhelming angsts of the octagon: his arrival at Teapot Lake and the culmination of all that has brought him back to its shores; the apprehension on how he will manage at the old cabin; the mystery of what Sydney might uncover regarding Sarah; the edginess that comes alongside reconnecting with Sarah.

Putting the VW into cruise control at eighty kilometers per hour, he attempts to self-regulate the tautness in his chest. He is looking forward to speaking with Sarah. He's not supposed to, in fact, he's probably encroaching on every recommendation he's been provided. And he unequivocally shouldn't be excited about it. Just reading her texts gave him a flutter of expectancy, the weight of uncertainty hanging like rain-sodden branches, strained by shouldering the dual blend of hopes and doubts.

As he glances in the rearview mirror, he catches his image and notices he is biting his lip. He wrestles with the growing distrust he has felt toward Sarah since the revelations of her suspected fraud. Reminiscing on Sarah still leaves him raw. That amorous interval prior to her downfall at Datatel presents itself as a wound. The affection he felt, still can't help but feel, for her is real. In the aftermath of all he has learned, all she is accused of, he can't help but hesitate to accept the veracity of her feelings for him.

Had she entered their affair to deflect attention from her secrets? Or had she manufactured the entire romance to garner his support and alignment in case her duplicitous actions were eventually uncovered? Clearly, she had lied about her marriage falling apart. How could a couple be heading toward ruin and concurrently sustain conspiracy and subterfuge? The fraud they are accused of together would have required exhaustive collaboration and commitment.

When Russell had been under his mentorship early in his career, Cal Morales had once pronounced to Russell that redemption comes only in straight truth. He had wholeheartedly believed that he and Sarah were legitimately in love. It is difficult to question her sincerity while still, admittedly, continuing to miss the intensity that came with being with her.

The affair had ended as abruptly as it had started. Several weeks after spending that Christmas holiday in New York with Sarah, on a frigid January night, irresolvable questioning, and guilt overwhelmed Russell.

He had driven out to Worcester County to attend a black-tie charity function. Morales, now serving on the board of Datatel, having handed the torch to Sarah, was a focused philanthropist of sorts. His sister's son, who was now a thirteen-year-old teenager, had been born with cystic fibrosis. For as many years, Morales gave prodigiously to the CF Foundation and contributed to fundraising events whenever he could. Recently, and because of the significant dollars that Datatel had contributed to the foundation over the years, he'd been asked to join the board of the National Cystic Fibrosis Foundation.

Given his frenetic and practically unmanageable schedule, he was forced to decline the invitation. However, he had asked Russell to represent him and join the board on his behalf. As a top member of the Datatel executive ranks, he was hardly able to refuse. Looking back, he also believed that Morales felt an overwhelming sense of sympathy for his situation, having watched him lose his son, he believed that Morales wanted to give him something that was personally important to him. It was Cal's way of offering his sympathy.

The CF board held its annual general meeting in January each year, and, coincidentally, this year, the meeting was being held in Worcester. The final evening included a gala dinner, followed the next morning by breakfast and closing remarks. Russell had dragged himself through the meetings, only partially paying attention to the recording of decisions and the review of the upcoming year's budget.

The intervening period since Christmas had been a whirlwind. Russell spent most of his days trying to focus on his responsibilities at work. He had continued to have regular contact with Sarah, but her travel schedule left them limited opportunities to meet. She had been to Boston overnight just once and they had spent the night together. Russell continued to struggle with the question of what came next.

His fallibility, both as a man and as a husband, left him breathless when he considered the stark impact his actions would have on others. He twisted in the knowledge that he had to face the truth and admit his affair to Anna. He thought often about the difficult upbringing Anna had endured, the solid foundation their relationship had been built on, and the bright promise of her stolen motherhood. His remorse was potent and overwhelming, and yet he felt immobilized, unable to bring himself to act.

By the last day of the CF annual meeting, Russell had decided to leave after the meal had been served at the gala. He could skip the closing remarks and breakfast the following day without being missed.

As dessert was being served, he had exited the conference center unobtrusively and quickly walked through the brisk night air to his parked SUV. He tuned the radio to a satellite station that broadcast the local traffic conditions in the city. Despite the late hour and having been delayed at the conference, Boston traffic was still congested. He wanted to avoid the backlogged routes, if possible.

In the countryside outside of Worcester, he was slowed by an accident in the opposite lane. Traffic had slackened to a crawl as emergency vehicles blocked all but the shoulders of the highway.

Instead of waiting for the traffic to clear, Russell pulled onto a side road. He turned left down a country lane and, a few miles later, made a right turn onto an unpaved street that, according to Google Maps, ran parallel to the main highway.

He turned on his high beams and grasped the steering wheel as his car drifted toward the middle of the uneven road. Suddenly, he heard a loud, popping sound from outside the car and, in what seemed to happen at the exact same moment, the car listed to the left and started to slide on the loose stones. He spun the steering wheel, and the vehicle heaved sideways in the opposite direction. He held his breath as everything played out in front of him as if in slow-motion video.

Russell had bought the SUV that he was driving a few years earlier. He'd researched the safety features and specifically looked for a large truck, naturally paranoid about driving in Boston traffic, at times in the snow, with a toddler. Recently, he had been thinking of trading it in, as the memories of Joshua kicking his legs in his car seat behind him were far too difficult to bear.

The SUV started to slow as it skidded toward the snowbank. Russell watched the white drifts approach and let out a deep, relieved breath as the car crunched against the snowbank and came to a stuttering halt.

The SUV's front right wheel had burrowed deep into the snow. He touched the gas and heard the wheel spinning hard against the gravel and ice. After a moment, he exhaled deeply, opened the driver-side door of the vehicle, and had to push it upward against gravity.

Bundled up in his coat, Russell stepped into the cold to survey the damage. It was clear that he would not be able to free the vehicle from its wedged position.

He tapped the screen of his smartphone several times but was unable to get a signal, so he started walking back toward the main roadway, cold air pressing against the exposed skin on his face. He had only driven a few miles down the country road, so he wasn't overtaken by any sense of panic, and he was confident he could make it to the road and flag down someone to help him.

It was the sound of his shoes crunching on the mix of gravel and snow that made Russell start recounting the events of the past four years. Grief was in control of his psyche. The degree of loss that he had experienced in recent years suddenly seemed astounding to him. The list included his mother's passing, the wretched tragedy that ended Joshua's budding existence, and now, the obvious devolution of his marriage. Russell's life had become a misplayed, off-pitch Aria, the predetermination of notes that were his destiny had become full of atonal music. He allowed the full force of these heartrending partings to pull on his awareness.

That grinding of his shoes on gravel propelled Russell back to the summer he had spent at Pops McCreary's cabin. It seemed to him that he had not walked an unpaved roadway like this once since those warm months in northern Canada. How had his life evolved from that childhood period of unbridled contentedness to the yawning and cavernous pool of desolation that he now swam in?

Russell felt so incredibly severed from that happy boy who had been satiated with the promise of the future. And he had, at the same time, become disconnected from the essence of life that had been imparted to him by his grandfather. It was like a kick to the stomach.

That once familiar sound dropped him to his knees.

He knelt in the darkness under a sky as alive with starlight as the night he'd sat beside a crackling fire with Pops on Manitou Lake so many decades before. Melting snow soaked his pant legs as he looked up into the night sky. He was shaking as much from the cold as from the agony of his stirring within.

The black dogs of self-reproach and depression that had stalked him for weeks in the shadows had finally attacked. Russell felt trampled and hopeless, unable to summon the desire to stand and fight.

Eventually, he managed to get to his feet and slowly made his way to the highway. The snow in front of him was ridged, scored with strange shapes he imagined told an accusatory story, carved in unique symbols. A trail of hieroglyphs in that snow that described his string of recent failings. He flagged down a transport truck driver and borrowed his mobile phone to call a tow truck. It was two in the morning when he finally opened the door to the condo in Boston. He was exhausted and, not surprisingly, he found that Anna was not at home. An email revealed that she was working a double shift at the hospital.

When she arrived home that morning around eight o'clock, Russell was waiting in the kitchen, sipping his third cup of coffee, and trying to wake himself up after only a few hours of fitful sleep.

He told Anna everything in as much detail as he could muster, revealing his duplicity and confessing to the affair with Sarah. He unloaded his guilty conscience on Anna, conveying his anguish over Joshua and the blame he shouldered for what had happened, and how he had withdrawn from and then betrayed her to assuage that guilt.

Anna's reaction surprised him. After months of witnessing her mercurial outbursts and wild tendency to lash out, he expected an enraged and visceral response from her. Instead, she simply broke down and cried softly.

Then, through red, tired eyes, Anna looked at Russell and said, "You know, I've concluded that the universe holds everything in such tight balance that you might as well not try to plan for anything. The pattern of our lives seems to be that every time we gain something, we are forced to lose something else."

Russell nodded and lowered his head. At that moment, he felt nothing but utter shame and regret. The space between them was as still and quiet as a tomb.

He tasted the salt of his own tears as they touched his lips.

"Is there any way to salvage us, Anna?" he asked in a quiet voice.

She looked at him and said simply, "Goodbye, Russell."

And with that, his marriage to the woman whom he'd adored profoundly for years and with whom he'd created the miracle of life abruptly ended. Suddenly, the relationship that Russell thought would last forever could now be added to the heap of losses defining his existence.

And the final injury was Sarah herself.

He had flown up to New York to speak with her in person on a quick stopover she had planned between trips. After imparting all the details about his recent mental health deterioration and his confession of their affair to Anna, he fell silent. They were seated in high-back chairs at the breakfast bar in her ultra-modern, immense condo, surrounded by sleek appliances sending corresponding notifications by Wi-Fi to Sarah's phone. Each time he'd stayed at her condo, Russell had marveled at the connectivity and state-of-the-art equipment Sarah had incorporated into her living space. It matched her demanding lifestyle, her home set up to maintain maximum efficiency.

"We should have talked about this before you took that step," she said sternly, not meeting his eyes.

"It just happened. I was overwhelmed and had to do it."

"Pretty weak of you."

"That's fair." Russell said, with a long exhale.

"And inconsiderate," she added. "There are two of us in this thing, right? And I have a lot to lose here."

"Maybe it's not ideal," replied Russell.

He had never seen Sarah enraged. Her no-nonsense, assertive, and often blunt manner didn't waiver and she conveyed her reactions effectively without ever having to raise her voice. He grasped easily that she was fuming under her composed bearing.

"It's far from ideal, Russell," she said, annunciating each word carefully. "Now that Anna knows, how long before everyone in our circle is made aware, hmmm? And what if she broadcasts it to the world in retribution?"

"She won't do that."

"I wish I shared your absolute confidence. You know we're both screwed if she does."

"I know, I know." Russell answered. "I'll talk to her."

"This sucks, you know? I mean really, it puts us in a pretty awful position."

Russell's signaled his affirmation. Then, to his astonishment, he saw the reddened lines in the whites of her eyes and tears forming. He had never seen Sarah express her emotions in this way.

"I'm sorry, Sarah."

"I'm in love with you, Russell," she said, her voice quivering. "I don't want this to end. And now it has to."

"Why? I don't get it. She doesn't want anything to do with me."

"I can't take the risk. I've built my career over decades. One word from her to the wrong person, whether out of spite or slip of the tongue, and I'm toast at Datatel and anywhere else, Russell. You know that. It's hard enough rising to the big chair as a woman. You get how many people would love to see me crash, right? Especially if they could peg me as some kind of homewrecker."

He didn't argue. He had tried to concoct some strategy for them to continue to be together. However, he knew the moment he told her that he'd admitted their relationship to Anna, Sarah would need to distance herself from him. She had too much responsibility, and her career was the core of her essence, an iridescent nucleus from which her entire self was issued.

He started to speak, "I wish there was some way we—"

"There isn't. It has to be over right now. I'd like you to leave. I have to start figuring out the placement of my feelings about us . . . for you. And sort out how I protect myself from—" Russell was crushed hearing the sadness in her voice. "I can't have you here, Russell, it will hurt too much."

Sarah stood from the chair and bridged the few strides it took to reach him. Inside that last, prolonged minute, they had clung to each other, rivulets of tears converging on their touching cheekbones, in a desperate embrace before he left her condo.

It's three o'clock in the afternoon when Russell pulls into South River, straining to see through the insect covered windshield. Unlike the small cities he has encountered so far on his northbound trip, the rural town appears to have defied the inexorable trek of progress. He notices an old-fashioned, family-owned grocery store with a wooden storefront and hand-painted murals adorning the sides of buildings with scenes of local wildlife.

There are some signs of modernity; a small solar farm glistens under the sun, climbing a slope behind South River's main street and, where most of the town's shops maintain their traditional facades, there is a new local library, made of contemporary glass walls, conspicuously situated in the city center.

He laughs at how ill-prepared he is for an extended stay in the cabin. Without much extra time, since arriving at Toronto's Pearson airport, he hasn't had a chance to plan out a list of supplies he will need.

Fortunately, he locates another sign of development, a mega-department store on the outskirts of the town and he starts hastily making a mental note of what he anticipates he'll need for the first couple of days. He fills a shopping cart with a sleeping bag, flashlight and batteries, a small propane burner for cooking, some tin pots and utensils and a utility knife. And he gathers bottled water, dried foods, and some prepared camping meals for staples.

There is still sufficient sunlight left in the day to make it to the cabin. He refuels at the mega-store gas station and presses hard on the squeegee to return the windshield to normal. Before turning over the engine and heading to his destination, he quickly checks his email.

*READ THIS ASAP.* The subject line of a message from Sydney Abissi is in bold caps..

He opens the email and reads the first paragraph: *That lawyer/consultant, Robert Pembrooke? He is all wrong. I can't believe what I've found in just a few hours, and I've only touched the tip of the digital iceberg (as us CISA veterans like to say).*

Sydney had even created a rough diagram using lines and connectors in PowerPoint to show the associations and relationships her examination has exposed. There are several other attachments showing redacted versions of offshore bank accounts, behind the scenes, veiled corporations, and arrangements between the parties.

It takes him over ten minutes to decipher the matrix of interconnections and dependencies that Sydney has charted. When he is finished, he forwards the emails with the attachments and texts to Sarah.

*You're not going to believe what I just sent you. Check your email!*

# 18

A thin vapor lifts from the lake by the immaculate, climbing sun. It drifts like the silent soul of a giant specter over mirror-like water before disappearing into the atmosphere. The distant tree line slowly transforms from a scaled, black serpent on the horizon, and a sparkling array of deep emerald pine trees take shape in the new light. On the land, the dew clings to rugged evergreen needles as it struggles to stay alive before evaporating or giving in to gravity's behest and dropping to the forest floor. A fresh scent emanates from the forest and breathes life into every living thing. And everything, everywhere is still. It feels as though time ceases for a thin moment, granting the day a momentary repose from its perpetual cycle. For Russell, it is a time of silent renewal.

He has been at the cabin for over a month. His eyes drink in the stunning sunrise before him. Every morning, apart from one, when an early rain shower cleansed the wide field and forest around it, this is his routine—a pensive, silent observation of the emergent sun. He has looked for Horatio's offspring, hoping to see a heron swooping out of the massive tree, but none has revealed itself as of this morning.

On the day he arrived at the cabin, after stopping in South River, Russell had felt anxiety rising within him knowing he was that much closer to the terminus of his travels. "Will the cabin even be livable?" he had questioned aloud to himself. The Google image he had searched showed that the structure was still in place but that was all he could be certain of.

As he pulled up to the property that late afternoon, he noted that the white fence had become tattered and was sagging badly. The hinges on the gate had long since oxidized and turned cadmium red. He opened the gate with a gentle push and observed the gravel road that leads to the cabin. It had been so incredibly long since he observed this sight and the fields on either side of it. It all looked smaller than he remembered.

The summer after Russell's mother and he left hurriedly to begin their new life in London, Pops McCreary had stayed at the lake until winter. They had exchanged one letter each that autumn. However, during the winter, he became ill and eventually had to leave his beloved lakeside cabin to receive full-time care. He died that winter, quickly and, according to Russell's mother, painlessly after suffering a stroke.

He was not surprised that Pops McCreary had passed soon after being forced to leave his refuge. He knows with certainty that never being permitted to return here would have led to his demise. This land, the cabin, and the wilderness around it held his grandfather's very soul.

The wheels of the rented SUV had spit gravel as he navigated the overgrown path. He drew in a breath when he first saw the water of Teapot Lake ahead of him after cresting a small incline.

And now, after twenty-nine days, he is firmly stationed here. The cabin is still standing. Russell is impressed by the building's fortitude, having endured the repeated onslaught of countless harsh seasons over the decades. The roof needs replacing, but fortunately has not entirely worn out.

The cabin itself is uneven and slumps toward the trees, its foundation has heaved under the invisible weight of neglect. To anyone else, the dilapidated state of the structure would be discouraging to behold. But to Russell, this weathered refuge has the same effect on his disposition as that of a warm, soft blanket wrapped around his shoulders.

The time has been cathartic, giving him this welcome interval to contemplate. It is almost impossible for him to link the events and influences that have led him back to this piece of land set deep in the woodlands of northern Ontario. But he knows it is necessary to be here, needed medicine that he must swallow to settle the stirrings and sentiments that haunt him.

As the sun continues to ascend, he departs from the lakeside and returns to the comforting, wood-infused smell of the cabin. He has no Wi-Fi connection here, but he pulls out his laptop anyway. On those occasions when he has needed to send or retrieve data, he has relied on the three-bar cellular signal his iPhone produces as a wireless hotspot.

This rudimentary process of connecting with the world had played out last night. He had spent over an hour crafting a draft email to Cal Morales turning down the CEO role. Now there was no need. The decision was made for him through an unpredicted and abrupt exoneration of Sarah and the accusations against her redirected. It also brought about a longed-for surge of release that seemed to merge with the pacifying forest insulating him.

He also decided to resign from Datatel. A clean slate. With no distractions and ample time to be alone and dwell upon the significance of his journey, he experienced incredible clarity of thought.

Awestruck at how rapidly things have reordered themselves, he followed Sarah's vindication unfolding in dramatic fashion across national media. They spoke frequently since their first text exchange weeks earlier.

At first, she couldn't stop expressing her gratitude.

"This all might have taken years to expose, if at all, if it weren't for your incredible powers of deduction," she said on one evening's call. "I suspected there was something amiss with Pembroke when MN&C wouldn't cooperate. I was handcuffed though. The lawyers wouldn't let me reach out to anyone. Tracking down Sydney was great thinking on your part."

Russell remained modest. "It's Sydney who is the real hero. She managed to fit the pieces together."

"I have a lot of people I'm indebted to, for sure. She is right up there with you at the top of the list."

The material Sydney Abissi had dug up ultimately shattered the public conjecture regarding Sarah's guilt. The cybersecurity guru had omitted the most private information she found. However, she had managed to convincingly connect a series of people and events through her hasty investigation of the legal consultant, Robert Pembroke, who turned out to be the nucleus of a series of nefarious ventures.

Russell shared with Sarah his original theory that the refusal of Pembroke to testify on her behalf, as the consultant who had been hired to protect her from liability in the Jukes acquisition, didn't pass the logic test. The fact that Derek Paulson had been linked to the hiring of MN&S and Pembroke seemed even more dubious. He surmised that Derek had influenced Pembroke to reject Sarah's requests for support, out of spite, after he had learned of their affair. Sarah had previously mentioned her former husband's vindictive temperament. It made sense that he would be compelled to add on to the personal damage she had sustained.

The truth turned out to be considerably more insidious.

Robert Pembroke and Derek Paulson were long-time college friends who discovered early in the friendship that they shared certain iniquitous inclinations. Over decades, they had created a global network of relationships and contacts, as well as their own web of international shell businesses and bank accounts. The pair had colluded in a string of financial crimes that intensified progressively over decades. And they had been smart, not publicly representing that they were acquainted at all and enveloping their connection in absolute concealment where their communications were always encrypted and using fictitious emails and cell phone accounts.

One of their more recent crimes included insider trading on information that Sarah had distributed in detail while MN&C and Pembroke were hired to provide her risk-mitigation services. When the Jukes deal was in its infancy, Derek stage-managed the process of getting Pembroke the contract with Datatel, and they used several offshore shells to place the purchase of shares long before the acquisition had closed.

Around the time that Tisdale Capital had launched its hostile takeover attempt of Datatel, Sarah and Derek's relationship started to crumble. When it became evident that they were likely headed toward a split, Derek became nervous. He had used Sarah's identity to set up over thirteen illegitimate corporations to further deflect attention from his and Pembroke's operations. This represented a substantial risk to his and Pembroke's illegal enterprise. If he and Sarah divorced, there would be an exhaustive asset audit which would reveal the many entities he had registered under her identity.

Derek and Pembroke orchestrated the downfall of Sarah Westroes. For months, while Sarah fought the Tisdale Capital proxy battle, they covered their tracks and removed Sarah from the records of their labyrinth of international corporations and financial vehicles. When Tisdale leveraged the press to vilify Sarah during the process, it gave Paulson an idea. They kept her credentials on one remaining set of contracts, the bank accounts and incorporation contracts they had used to accumulate large sums of Jukes stock. Subsequently, Pembroke anonymously transmitted details of those transactions to those journalists who had produced the most ravenous attacks on Sarah during the Tisdale takeover attempt. Their strategy was to ward off attention on their extensive, global corruption by ensuring Sarah became a criminal face associated with the crimes.

Russell had guessed correctly that Derek was somehow culpable in his wife's professional and legal woes. However, his theory that this intricate deception was borne from jealousy as a malicious corollary of her unfaithfulness was inaccurate. In fact, it was simple greed that had motivated Derek to take these actions.

When Sarah shared the material Russell had forwarded from Sydney Abissi with her legal team, they had immediately put it in the hands of the DOJ. The content had been detailed and compelling enough for them to suspend their investigation of Sarah and instead focus their attention on excavating the buried riddles of Pembroke and Paulson's extensive misdeeds.

Within a week, the most damning allegation was intentionally leaked to the press. It involved an offshore investment bank Derek had set up to launder money for a Chinese organization responsible for manufacturing and transporting illegal opioids. The article speculated that once the DEA got involved, both he and Pembroke, who had acted as the intermediary between the drug manufacturer and several transcontinental freight forwarding and shipping companies, would most likely be spending decades in maximum-security.

Sarah's exculpation came with equivalent promptness. Datatel moved to reinstate her swiftly, and the media shifted their collective narrative from an accusatory tenor to one of patronage and defense.

During one of their recent FaceTime conversations, Sarah had hypothesized about Datatel's motives in returning her to the CEO office with such speed. "My lawyers told me to expect their employment offer to include both a generous, six-figure signing bonus and some very precise indemnification clauses. The board may not want me back, but the price tag of the lawsuit I would level if they don't reinstate me has them shaking in their golf shoes, I'm sure."

"Either way, it's the right thing," Russell offered in support.

"Like the right thing is ever a consideration in these matters." Sarah parodied his words, her brow creasing visibly on his iPhone screen. "They are protecting their asses, simply and straightforwardly."

"At least you get to gloat a little bit. And there isn't a reporter or news anchor in the country that will put a bull's eye on you for years."

"You're either trying to be overly optimistic for my sake or you're being naive, Russell. They will spin up some drama around me again. I have no doubt whatsoever. Either way, I don't think I will ever stop thanking you for what you did."

Russell paused. "Hey, no credit is required. I did myself a huge favor as well."

"How's that?"

"I might have ended up in your job!" Sarah's laughter was light and cheerful.

"You would have made an excellent CEO. Speaking of which, what are your plans now?"

"I'm still thinking things through, to be honest," Russell admitted. "I'm ready to leave the company and maybe making a career change."

"I don't know if I could replace you, Russell. It would take a real star player to fill your shoes. Will you come back to Boston at some point?"

"Eventually, yes."

"If you don't come back here soon, I may have to come up to Canada and hide out with you. After I testify in Derek and Pembroke's trials, I imagine there are some shady characters they were involved with who I may want to avoid."

Russell contemplated this for a moment. "It's a good point. Can you get any sort of protection?"

"In yet another sign of their magnanimous generosity, Datatel has made it an employment condition that I have a full-time security detail."

"If that doesn't work out, you're welcome here. It's remote and close enough to off-the-grid that no one might track you down for eons."

"Don't tempt me," she replied with a playful and mildly coquettish tone.

It prompted Russell to contemplate the possibility of he and Sarah restarting and pursuing a legitimate relationship. The prospect of this has tempted his desires since they reestablished contact, however odd and unlikely. Irrespective, the fact that they have been conversing every couple of evenings as of late has to mean something.

In his resignation email, Russell explained to Cal that his recent awakening at the cabin has convinced him that he needs a wholesale change in all aspects of his life, including his career. In resigning, he offered to stay on for a period, once he returns to Boston, to help support Sarah as she resumes the CEO role.

At this point in time, he wants to approach his future with an openness to opportunities and a new sense of possibility. He is thinking of possibly launching another start-up venture. This idea, and the growing sense that he and Sarah could conceivably have a future, fills him with hopefulness.

The past is a bitter sea, gray and churning to the horizon, but for Russell, survival requires that he turn away from it, face land and venture into new and uncertain terrain. He feels a power in making this pivot and finally accepting freedom from the past, from guilt and fear, freedom to find more gravel roads that twist and turn in unknown directions.

The deck boards groan under his feet as he carefully crosses the worn configuration, being sure not to fall through any loose or rotten wooden slats. The door opens easily, and dust particles dance in the pillars of sunlight that stream through dirt-covered windows. He is greeted with the musty smell of damp wood.

The notion of remaining here for a prolonged stretch has settled comfortably in his thoughts. Within him lies a deep-rooted awareness that making a temporary home in his private cathedral up north might serve as a spiritual redemption of sorts. He would need to do some work to revive the dilapidated structure over the coming weeks, but the small cabin is in a decent enough state for him to remain living there.

Looking out the bay window, gray clouds are forming and rolling in, draping over the lake, and mellowing the brightness of the sun. The smell of impending rain lingers, earthy and metallic over the field. Soon, light rain introduces itself as a relentless drumbeat on the roof. It is a composed tempo that makes him feel alive.

Now that he has officially resigned, like pins in a lock slotting into position, he decides that this will be the day. Until this point, he delayed collecting what he has amusingly come to refer to as his buried treasure.

After washing his hands in the kitchen sink, he finds an old yellow rain slicker that hangs in the main closet. As he slaps dried and dirty powder off the plastic raincoat, he feels tears surge into the corners of his eyes, and he coughs. He gathers a similarly dust-infested pair of rubber boots in the same closet. It dawns on him that these are probably the same boots his grandfather wore on their expeditions many summers past. The boots are a bit loose but will do. He puts on the jacket, flips the hood over his scalp and walks out into the light rain, which is creating a hissing on the lake as it falls.

Hopping from the deck, he turns right and heads toward the woods, pushes aside the overgrown branches and rain-soaked leaves from his path and walks up an incline until he finds the massive boulder. The forest is quiet except for the sounds of rainwater trickling through the canopy.

He finds that he has to squeeze himself around a grouping of sturdy cinquefoil bushes to reach the base of the giant rock. He crouches and begins digging with his hands. The rain-moistened earth is cool to the touch. It doesn't take long before the tips of his fingers connect with the object that he has hiked up here to retrieve. He gently pushes the dirt aside, digging with his fingers and making circular motions with his palms, and pulls the anti-aircraft shell from its resting place.

The tiny muscles in his cheeks quiver as he smiles. It has been so long since he's produced a genuine smile.

Russell holds the shell he had buried here as a child and studies it carefully. As he takes in every detail, he is overwhelmed with hope. He will heal. He can choose to let his recent tragedies drag him into the undertow of depression, or he can take a sign of hope in something as simple as this century-old object in his palms that has crossed generations to heal the men who beheld it.

He is so far from London, far from Boston and all the places where his memories are contained. This distance, here in the forested northern land, is revitalizing.

He walks back down the hill toward the cabin and makes his way to the edge of Teapot Lake. The rain slows, and a glimmer of sunlight slips between the monstrous clouds. A haze begins to lift gently from the water. It is a still, flawless moment. He finds himself standing in the exact spot that he'd been drawn to when he first ventured alone from the cabin as an eight-year-old boy.

As if it were inscribed on the steel surface of Pops McCreary's treasured shell, a phrase suddenly comes to mind with great clarity. He can almost hear it whispered in the fragile breeze that keeps pace with his journey along the unpaved road. It is his grandfather's voice, repeating softly, *"It's going to be all right, Rusty, it's going to be all right."*

# Acknowledgments

I would like to thank Marly Rusoff and Mihai Radulescu for your friendship and dedication to the substance and art of storytelling and for introducing me to Kimberly Kafka whose editing and coaching has been instrumental in the development of my writing. To John and the entire team at Koehler Books.

www.ingramcontent.com/pod-product-compliance
Lightning Source LLC
LaVergne TN
LVHW041921070526
838199LV00051BA/2686